# PARADE OF DAYS

# PARADE OF DAYS

James A. Freeman

Copyright © 2004 by James A. Freeman.

| Library of Congress Number: | | 2004097361 |
|---|---|---|
| ISBN : | Hardcover | 1-4134-6663-X |
| | Softcover | 1-4134-6662-1 |

All rights reserved. No part of this book may be reproduced or transmitted in any form or by any means, electronic or mechanical, including photocopying, recording, or by any information storage and retrieval system, without permission in writing from the copyright owner.

This is a work of fiction. Names, characters, places and incidents either are the product of the author's imagination or are used fictitiously, and any resemblance to any actual persons, living or dead, events, or locales is entirely coincidental.

This book was printed in the United States of America.

**To order additional copies of this book, contact:**
Xlibris Corporation
1-888-795-4274
www.Xlibris.com
Orders@Xlibris.com

26059

# CONTENTS

Introduction and Acknowledgements ............................................. 9
Chapter 1 ........................................................................................ 15
Chapter 2: Eddie ............................................................................ 17
Chapter 3: Crime and Punishment ................................................ 22
Voices, Inner Chapter # 1: Lois Kenny ......................................... 28
Chapter 4: Margaret ....................................................................... 30
Chapter 5: Huckleberry Finn ......................................................... 37
Chapter 6: Eddie ............................................................................ 41
Chapter 7: Monday Night Football ............................................... 47
Voices, Inner Chapter Two: Eddie ................................................ 52
Chapter 8: The Brothers Karamazov ............................................. 55
Chapter 9 ........................................................................................ 60
Chapter 10 ...................................................................................... 65
Chapter 11 ...................................................................................... 70
Chapter 12: Snow Falling on Cedars ............................................. 76
Chapter 13 ...................................................................................... 83
Chapter 14: Cannery Row ............................................................. 89
Chapter 15: Pizza City ................................................................... 94
Chapter 16: The Way It Was ......................................................... 99
Chapter 17: The Grapes of Wrath ................................................. 104
Voices, Inner Chapter Three: Isn't Love What We've
    Been Making? ........................................................................... 109
Chapter 18: Descent into Madness ................................................ 111
Voices, Inner Chapter Four: Fooled Around and Fell in Love ..... 128
Chapter 19: Harry and the U-boat ................................................ 131
Chapter 20: Feeling Good, the New Mood Therapy .................... 135
Voices, Inner Chapter Five: Once in a Lifetime Love .................. 148
Chapter 21: Frozen Grandpa ......................................................... 152

Voices, Inner Chapter Six: Only Once in a Lifetime Love .......... 158
Chapter 22: "My Dinner with Andre" ...................................... 160
Chapter 23: Lois on the High Trapeze,
   a Fictional History of the Wallenda Family ........................ 181
Chapter 24: Searching for Debbie ............................................. 199
Chapter 25: The Great Wallendas, as told by Lois Kenny ......... 208
Voices, Inner Chapter Seven: Once in a Lifetime Love ............. 221
Chapter 26: Sex with a Stranger ................................................ 226
Voices, Inner Chapter Eight: Eddie ........................................... 237
Chapter 27: 9/11/'01 ................................................................ 239
Chapter 28: Losing You, The Boy Who Could Cry at Will ....... 243
Chapter 29: Long Term Care .................................................... 246
Chapter 30: The Free Man Who Fell from the Sky .................... 250
Voices, Inner Chapter Nine: Ann Lauren, Eddie's Ann ............. 254
Voices, Inner Chapter Ten: Dear Ann ....................................... 257
Chapter 31: Whole Life ............................................................ 259
Chapter 32: Final Obligation .................................................... 273
Voices, Inner Chapter Last: Lois ............................................... 275
Afterward ................................................................................. 277

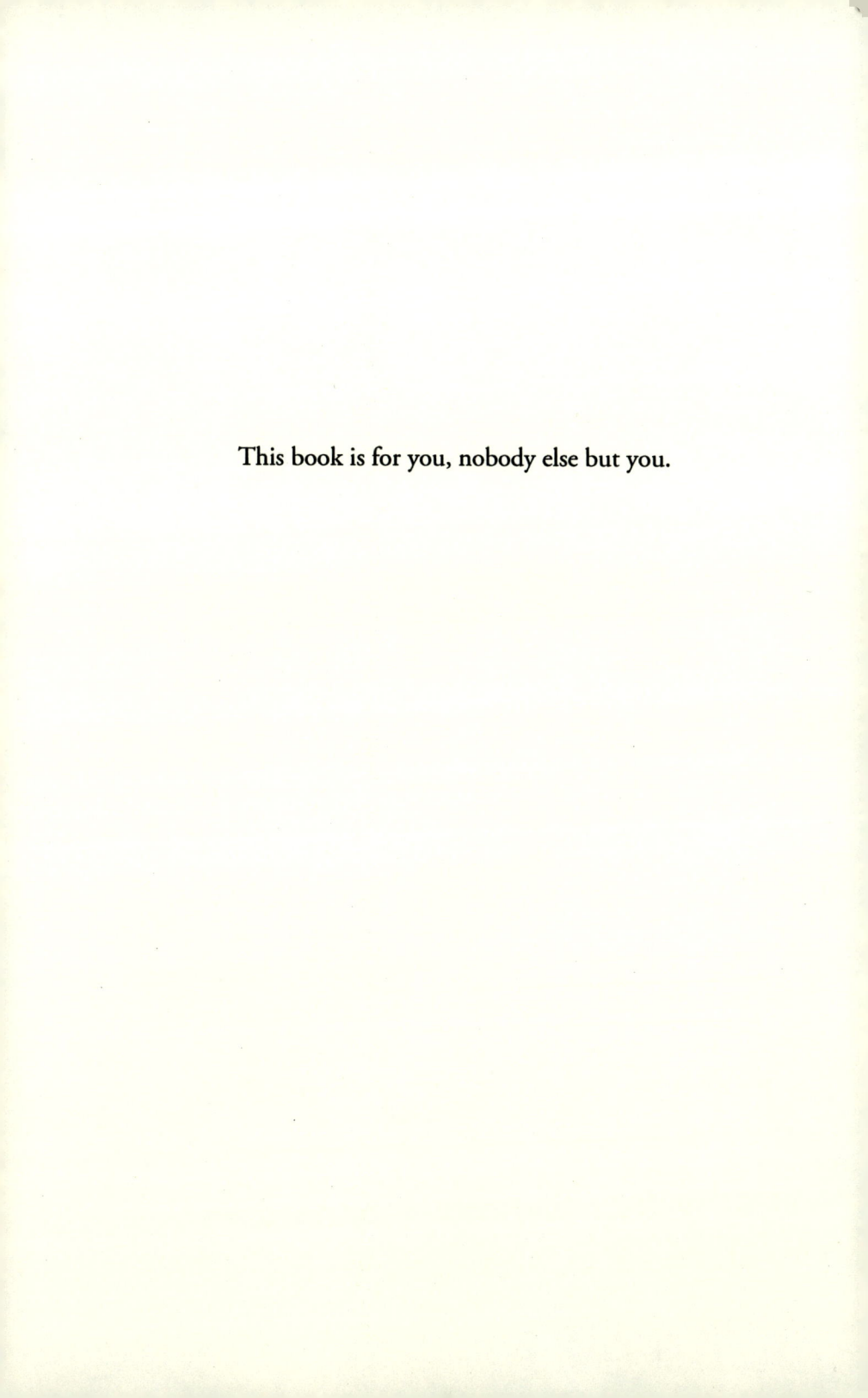

This book is for you, nobody else but you.

# Introduction and Acknowledgements

This book is a collection of interlocking stories that, like most novels, seeks to create an imaginary world. It is the author's hope that these common character stories cohere into a whole that is greater than the sum of its story parts. The true story chronicled briefly in the *afterward* is reprinted by permission of *The Bucks County Courier Times* newspaper. For a decade, the exploits of these two real people burned in the author's mind until they became a whole cast of fictionalized characters set on new adventures of the heart. The author hopes, also, that these fictional people will dance on this stage for the reader as they have danced so vividly in his imagination.

The author wishes to acknowledge the research of Gary Smith in his June, 1997 article "A Delicate Balance" in *Sports Illustrated* (Vol. 86, 23, 102). Smiths' excellent piece on the Ringling Brothers & Barnum & Bailey Circus aerialists is about the Guerrero family of trapeze artists, but it also offers a history of the famous Wallenda family from 50 years before. The author has adapted some of the Wallenda's performances fictively in Chapters 23 and 25 of *Parade of Days* through paraphrase. Likewise, in Chapter 20, there are paraphrases from Dr. David Burns' 1998 book *Feeling Good* used in fictional dialogue. The fictionalized conceit in Chapter 21 "Frozen Grandpa" comes loosely from the 1998 *Philadelphia Inquirer* newspaper article "Trying to avert possible thaw for frozen 'Grandpa'," an unattributed AP wire story. In Chapter 22, there are some real, non-copyrighted sayings adapted in dialogue from William Cole's anthology of egomaniac's quotations *I Am a Most Superior Person*. In "Voices" Inner Chapter 2, the character Eddie paraphrases William Least Heat Moon, author of *River Horse* and *Blue Highways*, on the fickle nature of change and human biology. The front cover is "Hale-Bopp Comet" over Shasta, CA by permission of Mary Barnard, Blue Skies Unlimited.

For any kindred spirit would-be writers, there are a million reasons not to write: the demands of work, spouses, kids, grandkids, and housework. There is only one legitimate reason *to* write: yourself. Sharing that self with others . . .

Onward and upward to where the magic plays . . .

This book is funded in part by a Cultural Incentive Grant from the Bucks County Community College Foundation. All first year royalties will go to the Ray Reilly Scholarship Fund to benefit an Act 101 student at Bucks County Community College.

# Blurb

Parade of Days sails at its own sweet will, with a quirky but compelling cast of characters—Big Eddie, Little Andre, and 87 year old Lois live secretly in the Bucks County Community College attic (PA) and conduct sessions of blue collar literary criticism, while down below long-time English teacher-turned head librarian Margaret ponders the disappearance of books, equipment, and left-over food. Shifts of point of view and time take us artfully back and forth through the characters' lives, and the Cowboys beat the Eagles 24-17. This half is masterful, good-natured story-telling—a book that is very hard to put down. But things get even better . . . Starting with the erotic relationship between Eddie and Ann and the death of Lois with 9/11 as backdrop and the whole sweeping turn toward the realm of the tragic, Parade picks up a terrible power—heightened by the Steinbeck-like earlier world of blitz-ball, absurdist humor—and even the literary discussion group romps. I think you are holding a masterwork in your hands-very, very powerful.

Bill Hotchkiss, author of Spirit Mountain and many others, Editor/Publisher of Castle
Peak Editions

"***Once*** for each. Just o*nce*, no more. And we too, just *once* to be."

—Rainer Maria Rilke

"Don't be too sure, Rilke."

—Lois Kenny

# Chapter 1

He heard them before he saw them, heard them ripping away at the wallboard. Soon a tear appeared, then widened, and the point of a shovel broke through. The brighter light from outside put its fists in his face, and he blinked, seeing shapes emerging below the hole in his wall.

A man in a uniform wielded the shovel which now bit into the hole, taking larger bites. After a few long minutes, the man climbed down, taking his shovel. Below, Eddie recognized the Bucks County Community College logo on the man's shirt, and, behind the security officer, he saw another policeman, this man in a Newtown Township, PA uniform. Off to the side, an elderly woman stood, a slightly sardonic smile on her face, her brownish hair looking like a helmet sitting askew on the top of her head, making Eddie think she had to be wearing a wig.

From behind him, big Eddie heard Andre, his partner, approach.

"What in Sam's hell?"

"I'm afraid the damn jig is up," Eddie said.

The hole was so large now that it had become a portal between the two groups, and Eddie only had to duck slightly in order to step through backwards onto the waiting ladder. He climbed down gingerly, then turned around. It was all he could do. He held out his hands expectantly, and the township police officer stepped forward to affix handcuffs on Eddie's wrists. The college security guard motioned for Andre to follow. Andre, much smaller than

Eddie, stepped backwards out into the light onto the ladder's top rung.

"It was the best of times; it was the worst of times," he said mockingly. At the bottom, Andre, too, was cuffed. "What, no Miranda rights garbage?" he asked the college guard sarcastically.

"Maybe when we're outside," the township officer said.

"Apologies to Dickens," Eddie mumbled. The bright fluorescent light stung his eyes.

"Apology accepted," the funny-looking woman chuckled and then nodded, her hair listing further off line on her head. She seemed to appreciate the reference.

Both hideaways sensed that this odd woman had somehow figured in finding them out, but it was Eddie who noticed the look of admiration in her knowing grey eyes. He straightened his stooped shoulders, stood up a little taller, inadvertently jingling his handcuff chain, and managed a smile.

The campus officer, half Eddie's girth, asked his counterpart, "shall we?" He picked up the shovel he had put down to cuff Andre.

"Yea, come on," the township cop urged. He looked at Andre and Eddie disgustedly. "You two are going to be charged for this nonsense."


Within minutes, the five of them were gone, leaving the gaping hole like a yelling mouth in the upstairs interior sheetrock at the community college library.

Inside the hidden space, unaware of her companion's capture, 87 year old Lois slept on her makeshift hammock made of mail bags.

# Chapter 2

## *Eddie*

Whenever my parents went out of town, they would write a goodbye letter to us children to be opened in the event of their deaths. If that weren't strange enough, Dad and Mom composed a new letter for each trip. I think that's where it came from.

I am afraid to fly. Oh, I know all about the statistics assuring us how safe air travel is compared to driving; I've heard all those comforting things that people say. But all it takes is one jetliner blown out of the sky, one plane that's lost its engines, one that slams into a mountainside, the television news and the papers amplifying the horror of it, the tragedy of all those poor peoples' lives, and whatever confidence I have been talked into hits the ground. There are the restless nights before the trip, tossing and turning, imagining the worst possible fiery death. Why is it that there's inevitably a crash within the days or weeks before it's your turn to fly so that the countdown becomes more intense as in the ticking of a terrorist's bomb? There's the last supper, then the too early drive to the airport, the long moments on the ground waiting, then taxiing out to the stacks of planes lined up to hurdle down the runway. And the headlong rush of takeoff to that climbing arc point where the pit of your stomach floats in no-man's-land, not on earth or yet of sky and when you look over at your child in the seat next to you, your wife next to her, your whole reason for living, and you realize this could end in seconds, minutes. And, please,

God, don't even say the word turbulence. None of it ends until you're on the ground again, ready to kiss the tarmac thank you. Then you can turn to worrying about the next time. When I had a job and a home and some money, I used to have to worry about flying. Not anymore.

I'm Eddie. Eddie Couch, and I've lost it all. Family, job, friends. Never mind how. What matters is the story. Everything that happened after; ending up without a home and what happened then.

Well, maybe a little bit about how. You see, I grew up Catholic and poor in northeast Philadelphia, grew up to meet Ellen, get married and start a family. Drove a truck first, then got on at a factory making grinding wheels. But all the time I wanted more, especially after the kids came, so I started taking night classes at the city community college. One at a time at first, building to two and three per term until the years passed, and I had an Associate's degree. I got loans, transferred to Temple University and eventually earned my Bachelor's degree. Everybody at home and work thought I was nuts at first, but eventually they came around. Ellen even threw a big bash for me upstairs at Dagwood's Pub when I got that B.A. Everybody came, my family, Jack, Jimmy, Frankie, Bobby, Patty and their crews. Then came the Master's degree. Before I knew it, I got hired on at Bucks County Community College, north of the city, teaching my beloved small business management.

Things were good for a while. Carolyn and little Eddie thrived while I commuted to the school in Newtown days and some nights and while Ellen worked for the I.R.S. office on Roosevelt Boulevard. We liked our row house neighborhood in the northeast. The kids went to Christ the King school, and I played softball there every Wednesday, although I'd gotten a bit fat. I loved the beginning of each semester at the community college: the fresh faced students right out of high school and the older ones, some of them returning to school with a vengeance like I had.

But then the bottom began to drop out. I got worn out by all the paperwork, by all the commuting and extra classes I taught to help make ends meet. I lost my confidence in the classroom, couldn't be the joyful dancing bear I'd been in class. After a couple of negative evaluations, the community college had to let me go. I started moping around the row house aimlessly. Fell into a dark pit of depression. When Ellen and I talked, the words sometimes cut like the blade of a knife, but the silences were worse. Instead of getting help, I let the dark pit cost me my wife and family, just as it had cost me my job. Almost all of us are only a few paychecks or a bad event or two away from homelessness. It happened to me. It can happen to you.

Things happen for a reason. I tell you all of this because everything that happened led me to Andre and Lois and the story.

Andre has an even deeper connection to Bucks County Community College. You see, the school is located on the former Tyler family estate next to what is now Tyler State Park. The wealthy Tylers lived in their Normandy revival mansion house with its 14 fireplaces and ran a full-blown enterprise with a dairy, farming, a rock quarry and all manner of business, until, eventually, Stella Tyler, the last of the blueblood family, gave the property to Temple University in the 1950's. Temple didn't want the land, what with it being so far from Philadelphia, and so ceded the property to Bucks County, PA. The county built the present day community college on the site in the 60's, incorporating the Tyler mansion as administrative offices and classrooms and using the Tyler's stone servants' cottages, located at the far end of the property, for college space as well.

It so happens that the Tylers had constructed a system of tunnels connecting the servants' quarters with the mansion some half a mile away. In winter, the servants could travel underground to the mansion to light the morning fires and do their morning duties without having to struggle through the snow. My friend Andre is the son of two of those Tyler family servants. When Stella Tyler gave the property away, Andre's elderly parents were homeless until an aunt and uncle in Lancaster County took them in. Andre and several of the other younger generation adults from the servants' cottages moved underground. They literally lived in the connection tunnels until the life of deliberate hiding grew tiresome, and food became harder and harder to come by. When the college opened in 1964, the last of the subterranean servants scattered like dividing mercury blobs out into Pennsylvania. Andre survived over 30 years in homeless shelters and on the steam grates of Center City Philadelphia, until 1999. That's when he returned home to Bucks County Community College and moved into the library ceiling's crawl space, where the pickings are much better than they'd been near the tunnels so many years before. That's when we met Lois, and the book discussion club began.

As sure as I'm Eddie Couch, Lois is an amazing woman. At 87, she's still spry enough to take care of herself while hiding out with us in our duct-filled space less than five feet high. Her mind is still as sharp as a new lawnmower blade, and she's read nearly everything a literate person can read in nearly one hundred years. She's Unitarian; I'm Catholic. I run about 270 pounds. She's maybe 130 soaking wet with long gray pigtails and clear brown eyes. I love her. She's the grandmother I never had.

Lois came to us in the way things often happen: by inevitable chance. She's from Machias, Maine originally but spent most of her life in Duxbury, Massachusetts. She was a pioneer of sorts, graduating from Vassar in 1931 when few women went to college. She married a kindly W.W. 1 veteran who went on to become the local superintendent of schools in Duxbury. Seven children came and grew up, and then her beloved husband passed on. Lois survived it, survived the passing of four of her kids, until the remaining three were elderly themselves and couldn't care for their Mom. Actually, she'd have been fine by herself if her money hadn't started to run out. Lois told me that the plan was for her to move in with her Vassar College roommate, who had a room in the nursing home at Pine Run, in Doylestown, PA. While Lois was on the train south from Boston, her college roommate died. In one of the days that followed in Pennsylvania, Lois wandered aimlessly to an Edward Muskie speech given at Bucks County Community College. She grew unaccountably restless and walked out of the auditorium, entering the college library minutes before its closure. Thumbing through books in the upstairs stacks, she ignored the loudspeaker closure announcements and then lingered, hidden in a remote alcove, until the main lights went out. It wasn't long before she heard what sounded for all the world like people moving around in the ceiling space above her.

# Chapter 3

## *Crime and Punishment*

Her softly wrinkled face was aglow in white from the automotive trouble light hooked to an extension cord. The three of them lay on separate chains of mail bags tied on each end to the rafters and suspended close to the floor joists like hammocks. Her long gray hair, out of its customary pigtails, fanned out behind her head and shoulders as she lay talking.

"It's obvious," Lois said, "Porfiry is just playing with Raskolnikov's mind. He knows Raskolnikov killed the pawnbroker and Lizavetta. He's just waiting for Raskolnikov to crack up."

Eddie and Andre shuffled through pages of their copies of Dostoevsky. It was almost time to get up for the night, to sneak downstairs to the bathrooms and refrigerators. For nearly two months, they had slept by day when the college library was open, rising at whatever hour they wished but talking and moving around only quietly until after 9 p.m. when the library closed. Lois' recent arrival had changed their whole dynamic, for the better. She'd talk about how simple all her long life had been but then come up with lines like "will gives birth to reason which in turn invents will as an idea." She was, Andre and Eddie had decided, an amazing woman. The only real problem was going so long without visiting the bathrooms. Makeshift chamber pots, three small purloined wastebaskets, took care of that. Another slight problem was that the library didn't always have multiple copies of the novels they discussed. They had gotten lucky with *Crime and Punishment*: three copies sitting side by side like familiar siblings in the 800 section.

Andre, a slight man compared with Eddie's bulk, climbed out of his hammock, stepping gingerly on the floor joists, leaving his copy of the novel on his bed. Even in the weak light, his full head of brown hair shone.

"Raskolnikov is terrified of this Svidrigylov fellow as well," Andre said. "As murderers go, Raskolnikov is a morally principled guy, I mean he commits his crime to test his superman theory, but Svid. is a hedonist plain and simple. A real creep." Andre fancied that he had learned a thing or two about human nature in his 52 years.

"Doesn't Raskolnikov see that there's no way he can escape?" Lois wondered. "That Porfiry is just waiting him out?"

Eddie smiled, then rolled his fireplug body, as thick as it was wide, out of bed.

"Sometimes what prevents us from discovering the truth is that we think we already know it." Eddie's 40 years had taught him a thing or two as well.

Though not very tall, Eddie had to duck to clear the heating ducts that ran overhead not more than five feet from their floor that was a daytime ceiling to the unsuspecting students and library staff below.

Lois, the discussion group's new grand dame, also moved to rise and shine, or at least to rise and shine as much as one can at 87 years old. She dressed herself, then began to braid her hair.

The routine was to walk carefully across the floor joists to a 2.5 foot-by-3.5 foot drywall panel that gave access to bathroom pipes running down to the library's large second floor bathroom. By popping the panel out, they could step carefully down onto the water tank of the commode below, then to its toilet lid or seat, if the lid were open, and on down to the ground and out the stall to roam freely on the second floor. The only other joining of the second floor with the ceiling crawl space above was at the opposite end of the building, where a raised section of vaulted ceiling rose to the roofline above the waste space, creating an airy area with a sealed window in the outside wall, but that joining had a solid sheetrock wall on the inside, which was their space's outside wall, and provided no access.

There were two refrigerators in the staff lounge areas, one on each floor, and they were almost always stocked with tuna sandwiches, frozen burritos, yogurt, apples and oranges, bottled drinks and the like, stored overnights by the staff to have in future days. Each lounge had a sink, microwave oven and other amenities. Once, Eddie had felt so guilty at pilfering the librarians' lunches that he'd left an apologetic note: "I'm only doing this because I have to." His sense of ethics led him to announce his presence in this way, but so far the group hadn't suffered for it.

Before Lois' arrival, Andre and Eddie had hauled a surprising amount of stuff up into their crawlspace. They had more than they needed. Their purloined gear included a radio, a fan, a crock pot, an overhead projector, a television and VCR, educational video tapes, flashlights, extension cords, and a revolving supply of books, always returned when they had been read and discussed.

This night the three of them visited the bathrooms, ate sparingly, and roamed the library's second and first floors freely for hours, being careful not to wander too close to the big glass entrance doors on the first floor, lest an occasional passing custodial worker see them. After being confined together for so long, they valued their independence and often walked through the stacks of books alone in the light from the few subdued after-hours safety lamps. Andre settled in at the current issue magazine section, leafing through copies of *National Geographic* and *Popular Mechanics*, while Lois, dressed in comfortable blue slacks, an old white top and her beloved though tattered Reebok sneakers, looked through a history of maritime New England. Eddie had chugged up the stairs to the second floor, hanging on to the railing for support and propulsion, and he checked for multiple copies of a novel they might discuss.

Later, after they had climbed back home, carrying up books in the middle of the night that was their day, they came together again to talk, sitting on their homemade hammocks.

Andre ran his hand through his hair; his eyes tracked Eddie's and Lois'. She looked back at Andre with what was becoming a familiar smile, her face wrinkling even more but softly at the effort that was no effort, and Andre remembered hearing somewhere that smiling requires the use of fewer muscles than frowning demands. Eddie looked back too, his wonderfully expressive face and head somehow too small for his body below were it not for the light that danced in his brown eyes, drawing everyone in to the conspiracy of his irrepressibly positive attitude. Eddie lay back on his hammock heavily, put one short hairless leg over the other to rest. He almost always wore shorts.

"I've got a sad story that needs a moral," Andre said. "I've been trying to figure out what to conclude from it for years." His voice seemed full of regret.

"Fire away," Eddie answered, "Babe and I will do our best."

Lois smiled inside at his new term of endearment.

Andre began the telling.

"I had a woman friend in her fifties. She had a son who was 29.

"Her son had become a magician, and he got a job performing regularly at a summer camp. The young man met a couple of boys who palled around together at the camp. One boy always carried around his little green blanket, and the other kids, you know how kids can be, teased the boy mercilessly."

Lois nodded her understanding.

"Well," Andre said, "the 29 year old offered to keep the blanket for the kid. You know, he was just being kind, trying to stop the teasing. And the kid gave the blanket to my friend's son."

Eddie sat up in his hammock. "Yes," he said.

"After that summer, the 29 year old gassed himself in his garage," Andre said flatly. The suicide happened on a Tuesday, but the magician wasn't discovered until days later when his Mom came back from a trip to Europe. She was the one who found him."

"Jesus, God," Lois said.

"You see, the 29 year old had been accused of pedophilia by the summer camp little boy's family."

Andre swallowed hard. "There was a message on the 29 year old's answering machine by the time his Mom, my friend, came home. It was from the young man's lawyer. He said, 'Call me immediately; I've got good news for you.'"

Eddie leaned forward. "Damn. Too late."

"At the time, all my friend could think was 'I hope the bastards who did this to him are satisfied.' Such a waste," Andre said, "a damn shame.

"The years passed, and the Mom healed as much as anybody who's lost a child can," Andre continued. "Then one day there was a phone call. It was the two pals from the summer camp. They'd grown up to be students at the University of Pennsylvania, and they wanted to talk about years before."

"My friend invited them to dinner," Andre said. The two young men showed up as planned, and they came as a couple, if you know what I mean.

"Somewhere during the course of the evening, the boy who'd been teased so much mentioned his green blanket from all those years before," Andre said, clearly pained by what had happened.

He looked to Lois, who was taking all this in stoically, and then to Eddie, his best friend. The outside world had once again come into the ceiling crawlspace at the community college library.

"My friend's mother got up from the dinner table and went away for a moment to an upstairs bedroom closet," Andre said. "When she came back, she had the little green blanket clutched to her. The two college students got up and moved to her, and, by the time they had their arms around her for comforting, all three of them were crying."

There was silence above the rafters and nothing but silence below. Nobody broke the quiet until Andre ran his hand through his hair again and asked "What the hell could it all possibly mean?"

Lois instinctively knew what he was asking. Andre was asking the question behind most questions, the one that hides there in the background yet is always there.

She stood up slowly, painstakingly stepping on the floor joists in her Reeboks until she stood white haired and slightly stooped over in front of Andre's hammock.

"Life can be so good," she countered. "Life can be the biggest blessing of all," she said softly. "Now that I am near the end, I know that most of all. Don't you think I struggle with what it all means every moment?" Lois wondered aloud.

She leaned over and kissed Andre on the cheek, and he'd never felt so soft a touch of human lips across his skin.

# Voices, Inner Chapter # 1

## *Lois Kenny*

This is the beginning of the end... It's a story my grandmother told me when she was an old lady, past 90 I think, and I was a little girl sitting on her lap, being read to on a rocker on our porch. One day, she closed the book she'd been reading from, her strident voice rising, falling and then just going silent. I heard her breathing next to me, imagined I could even hear the sound of her heart beating there among the sounds of breeze song and bird language.

"Look, Lois," she said. "There's a cardinal. So pretty."

Mom and Dad's feeder always drew birds, especially in winter. That year, they'd hung suet dipped in peanut butter and then in seed.

"So red," I'd said. Or something similar.

"Your Mom and Dad have told you all about baby Jesus and his manger," grandma said, the question in her clouded pools of brown eyes. "They told you childs all about the Star of Bethlehem and the wise men and the manger, right?"

"Yes Grammy," I said obediently, still watching the bird while we rocked on Christmas morning.

Grandma was up to mischief, though I didn't know it then. "Well, a long time before that," she said, "back in ancient times the old people would see a star they called the morning star. It shimmered in the late night sky just before dawn, if there weren't too many clouds, and when the sun came up the light washed the morning star away."

I knew. "I've seen in sometimes in the winter when we walk to school before the sunrise."

"Yes, child. But do you know about the evening star?"

"Which one?" I asked, watching the bird eat, rocking, seeing its red splash above snow.

"Those ancient ones called the brightest star in the night sky the evening star," Grammy said.

"So there were two?"

"Yes, Lois, there were two stars. Two bright stars shining brighter than all the rest." Grandma looked down at me with a little bit of the devil in her eyes. "Two bright stars shining in ancient times until somebody stayed up all night to watch the evening star track across the sky and become the morning star right before the sun."

We sat rocking for a long time. We watched the cardinal fly away.

—Lois Kenny

# Chapter 4

## *Margaret*

Margaret Dorris knew that they talked about her on campus. She knew, in fact, that she was something of an icon at Bucks County Community College. She didn't care. She'd grown up Quaker, gone on from Quaker schools to the University of Pennsylvania, and she had more important causes to attend to than the state of her reputation at the college. Stopping the spread of nuclear power plants for one thing. Furthering the peace movement. Stopping fetal alcohol syndrome. Curbing suburban sprawl in the counties around Philadelphia. Yes, there were more important things to worry about. More important things to do.

She worked steadily at alphabetically filing the new students' library identification cards. Her hands never tired as she put the laminated cards into long cardboard boxes so they'd be in good order as students came in to pick them up. A head librarian ordinarily wouldn't be doing such a menial task, but two of the work study students were out sick; hence, they were short-staffed for such an important day early in the semester. She hadn't always been a librarian. For years, she'd taught English Composition and Literature in the English Department and had the reputation of a brilliant although eccentric professor. As she got older and more eccentric, however, began doing such things as holding office hours from four to seven in the evening, the administration launched an attempt to get her to retire. It nearly worked too. Margaret was seventy then, and her student evaluations weren't what they once were. But she was a fighter who did her homework, and she found that the Federal law regarding compulsory retirement had changed to her benefit. She got the faculty union grievance chair Bain Bloomfield to represent her, and, after months of haggling, a deal was struck: she would take over the library to replace the departing director Mark Hadley, and she would be allowed to teach English part-time whenever she wished and park free in any of the college's approved lots.

Directing the library suited her. Her Master's Degrees from the University of Pennsylvania and Drexel were in English and in Library Science, and, with the exception of some perplexing thefts, she was proud to be in charge of 140,000 volumes, not to mention all the microfilm, microfiche, CD-ROM programs and the high-tech, computerized card catalogue. She was popular with her small but able library staff. Margaret accepted the stories that still swirled across campus, told by the faculty, office staff and administrators alike. She was a woman who lived for the moment, such as in working behind the circulation desk, filling up these cardboard boxes with all these plastic cards. Besides, half the people telling stories about her told them with a kind of fond admiration.

Academic Dean Crane remembered being invited for dinner one Thanksgiving at Margaret and her live-in boyfriend Harry's house. When Dean Crane arrived, she found the half-eaten turkey carcass already on the dining room table, one of Margaret's many cats standing inside the bird's ribcage, eating away.

Margaret had been banned from parking on campus once, the result of far too many parking infractions and tickets from a campus security staff that didn't look upon her so fondly. For a whole semester, she'd parked across from campus on the other side of Swamp Road, the school's main access. She'd walked across the busy road and across the long campus, built on a slight bluff overlooking Tyler Park. The hike was pretty but tedious and so Margaret finally decided to pay her multi-hundred dollar fine in bags of pennies. They still snicker about that one in the Bookkeeping Office on the second floor of Tyler Hall. Rumor had it that the Dean sent Margaret back a memo telling her that, among the thousands of pennies, were two rare ones. Pennies from heaven worth hundreds of dollars apiece, the Dean claimed, perhaps giving the college the last laugh.

Legendary is the tale of the time Margaret flashed. She had been teaching Hemingway's "Big, Two-Hearted River," circling around the orange podium in her classroom, when she looked down to see a huge run in her pantyhose. Stopping her lecture on the role of the burnt grasshoppers in the story, Margaret marched out of the class, down the hall, down the familiar flight of steps and into the English Department office. Smiling at the head secretary Jane, Margaret picked up a stapler from the front desk and then, in full view of God and the three or four teachers and assorted students milling around the department's front room mail slots, she hiked her woolen skirt up to waist level, exposing her pantyhose and cotton underwear, and, pulling the hose away from her skin, she proceeded to staple the ripped section of pantyhose with a long run of staples. It didn't work very well.

Damn the stories, she thought as she worked. There were more pressing things. An alarming amount of her equipment was disappearing: a television and VCR, an overhead projector, and all kinds of smaller items. Officer Harrack of Security had told her it was most likely the work of her own employees or perhaps visiting workers had taken the things. Was it possible that someone on her own staff was ripping the school off?

A couple of students stopped in front of her at the circulation desk. Margaret gave them their cards, glancing at the pictures of their faces as she handed them over. So young. So much to learn. She liked being around the fresh faces, the infectious energy of the young. Beside her, Cathy Tan checked out books to the students who brought them up. After one group left, clicking through the exit turnstile one by one with their backpacks, Cathy looked over to her boss.

"So much non-fiction," she said. "So many books tied directly to an assignment they're doing. Would they read on their own if they didn't have to?"

"No more or less than we did," Margaret answered. "And it's not all non-fiction. Look at all the Stephen King that passes through."

"How could I have forgotten Stephen King?" Cathy wondered, turning back to her work.

The two women fell into their silent reveries of comfortable routine.

Well, there was that one story, Margaret thought. It held more than a grain of truth. She was going to a nuclear power protest down in Washington D.C., and she wanted to make a splash. The only catch was that she had a night class that evening, posing a partial time conflict. The protest march ended at three, she knew, and, allowing for the three and one half to four hour drive, she'd be hard pressed to teach her Composition class in Pennsylvania at seven p.m. She'd enlisted young Michael Shakarchi, the department's new darling teacher, as a substitute, assuring him that she'd be back to take over her class by seven thirty or eight p.m. Margaret Dorris had drawn up her usual elaborate notes to get Michael through the first portion of the class.

She and Harry had decided to make an effigy for the roof of her beat-up sedan. The wanted a skeleton with burned up clothes, someone who'd clearly been irradiated in some nuclear accident. The two of them had never officially married, though she and Harry had lived together for decades, and this was another secret that everybody knew. You can rehearse a wedding, but not a marriage, they both knew. Anyway, they set about making the effigy, and like almost everything Margaret did, it was gloriously done. Tied to the roof of her big Chevy, his grasping skeleton arms holding the ropes tied to her front bumper and his skeleton legs in rags splayed out and tied by ropes to the back bumper, the nuked man clearly made the point.

Somehow, he hung on at 70 miles an hour all the way to Washington, D.C. as Margaret drove alone. He was still hanging in there, positively glowing, even though one of his ropes had worked loose and one leg was flopping around, when Margaret pulled off Swamp Road onto the campus at nine thirty five in a driving rain. She hurried to the ten minute parking zone behind Penn Hall. As she pulled in, she smashed nose first into the metal "Ten Minute Only" parking sign, causing the irradiated effigy to flip forward when his remaining leg rope broke. The dummy's back now blocked her view out the windshield, but Margaret didn't care. She had some teaching to do. She hurried to room 226.

Michael Shakarchi had just dismissed the class after one final flick of his mop of black hair when Margaret burst in, drenched, her wig even more askew than normal but her new panty hose intact.

"Hold it!" she hollered. "We've still got some things about next week to discuss!"

No matter what happens, there is always someone who knew it would. Count Margaret's Tuesday night composition students among them. By ten fifteen, when everybody fully understood the role of the burnt grasshoppers as symbols of the war Nick Adams had been through in Hemingway's famous story, class was officially over.

Michael Sharkarchi had been busily taking notes he thought he might be able to use in his eight a.m. Lit. Class the next morning. He was shocked when on the way out the building together Margaret asked him whether he might be interested in driving into Newtown for a friendly drink or two. After he declined, citing his early morning class and the late hour, Michael was even more surprised to walk by Margaret's hulking sedan impaled over what had been a sign, its radiator hissing softly in the slackening rain, a glow-in-the-dark skeleton in tie-dyed rags pitched forward on its neck and back and legs over the car's windshield and hood. It was enough to start him questioning his view of tenure, though for all the wrong reasons.

Margaret Dorris was 71 years old when she took over the Bucks County Community College Library, and she liked to daydream while she worked, but most of the time she had all the fire and tenacity of an inspired 30 year old. Somewhere in the "Ps" among the identification cards going into the long, cardboard boxes, she began to daydream.

> The Maine woods in autumn are the country's most beautiful. I don't care what anybody says. Dawn in autumn is my favorite time, at sunup, when the first light has a blue-silver look to it. I can't say it exactly, but it's like you're looking through the clearest, cleanest pool of water in the world. First light in other places is not the same. The first time I saw my Harry, he was chopping wood for a farmer just outside Thomaston. He had his shirt off already and the sweat ran down his glistening chest as he swung the axe over and over through the sunrise and long after. Knew right there he was the one for me, and that he has been all these years. When our David was born and grew to be a man, I could surely see how he wanted to leave Pennsylvania to build his home in Maine, to grow trees and raise his family there. When we lost our David to pneumonia that winter, after the fiery colors of the turning leaves and the onset of the hard frosts, his wife Cathy and I sorted out David's things. We came across a little brown bottle filled with murky liquid in his desk drawer. Floating inside was what looked for all the world to be half a human finger. Already griefstricken, Cathy and I had no idea what to do. It was out of the realm of possibility that our David could have cut off or saved someone's finger. I finally talked Harry into emptying the bottle, dumping the dark liquid down the kitchen sink, one of the secrets of a life revealed. What came out was a little ginseng root. Sometimes when we so want things to make sense or truths to be momentously revealed, especially when life has wounded you and sent you seeking for answers as to why, the answers we get are trivial, or else are further mysteries themselves.

"It's so bizarre how the mind works," Margaret said to Cathy, who had moved close to her to pass some books over the circulation desk to a student waiting on the other side of the security alarm machine.

"I'm just happy when mine works at all," Cathy Tan grinned. She looked up at her boss, a few inches taller. "Have you heard the latest?"

"Let me guess," Margaret answered as Cathy went on.

"Three more videotapes are missing. I'm trying to keep tabs on all these thefts: security is helping."

"You're a good librarian," Margaret praised, smiling down at her. "Besides, diplomacy is being able to look up to someone who is shorter than you."

Cathy moved back to her earlier station. "Pretty funny, boss."

"I'll do better next time," Margaret answered, then tried to straighten her wig unobtrusively. "The best thing you can give someone is another chance."

# Chapter 5

## *Huckleberry Finn*

"It is so ridiculous," Lois said, "all this misguided fuss about Samuel Clemens being a racist. "I lived through that time when black and white were separate and when even good white people used the word nigger, and I'm telling you that all Samuel Clemens wanted to do was be realistic and true to that time."

She had been braiding her hair, a process Andre and Eddie loved to watch, but now Lois was through, and her voice rose higher as she jumped into the conversation.

The group had been up for a couple of hours, reading, talking, waiting for the library downstairs to close so they could roam free. Talking about *Huck Finn*.

Eddie sat on a wooden pallet over the floor joists, just a few feet from his hammock. Ordinarily, the TV and VCR sat on the pallet, extension cords trailing behind, but Eddie had tried something new, moving the whole mess aside, first offering Lois the wooden seat and then taking it himself when she declined. He wore his typical shorts with a colored tee shirt, extra large: his stubby neck and head that seemed a little too small for his body did nothing to change the fact that he was a warm and imposing man.

"Babe, Mark Twain wanted to be more than realistic. He wanted to make a point. Twain hated racism and uses Huck to make his point that racism is wrong. We all know that Huck loves Jim, don't we?"

Lois and Andre both answered, "Yes."

"Well, even Huck, who loves Jim, has internalized a lot of the prejudice around him," Eddie went on. "Five will get you ten that I can show you a dozen places in here where Huck, despite his best intentions, thinks of nigger Jim as a second class citizen."

Eddie held up his copy of Twain's masterpiece. "Sometimes Huck can't even believe that he's growing to appreciate Jim as a full fledged human being as they float down the river together."

Andre swung gently back and forth in his suspended hammock, nodded his head in agreement, sending a lock of hair down over his forehead.

"You might be right," he said. "Huck is constantly thinking things like 'I can't believe I am helping a runaway nigger to get free.'"

Lois moved to stretch her legs. "I can buy that Samuel Clemens ingrains some of the prejudice he hates in Huck's character to make a point, but I still say he mainly wanted to be realistic: to hold up a mirror to society, show us how ugly we can be."

"We're really talking about the same thing, Babe," Eddie said. "We're on the same page. Twain wanted us to look closely at ourselves and then to change when we don't like what we see."

Eddie still held his copy of the novel dramatically in the air. "Huck learns that Jim is honest, completely trustworthy, unselfish and loyal and that those things don't square with all the clichés about niggers he's been taught. Huck grows . . ."

"But he still makes fun of Jim's superstitions," Lois interrupted. "Huck ridicules Jim's hairball and all of that."

"It's what you said before," Andre added. "Huck is learning to overcome all the negativity he's been taught, but he's not yet a complete package; some of the bias and stigma comes leaking through."

Lois smiled, brightened their whole crawlspace as far as the two men were concerned. "Amen! And speaking of changing people, think about this. If you want to understand how hard it is to change someone else, think about how you've tried to change yourself."

"You go girl," Eddie joked.

Andre couldn't resist. "We should try to be smarter than other people-we just can't tell them so."

Eddie grinned maniacally and set down his book. "Here's what I've learned. There's no such thing as 'one size fits all,' 'never needs ironing,' 'making up for lost time,' and 'tastes just like chicken.'"

"Case closed," Lois said, and then she walked carefully over to the relocated television and VCR to put on a tape about whales. The bright screen drew their eyes as they set about killing some of what would become their lost time.

Later, when the tape ended and Michael Jackson had finished singing about killer whales, Lois told them a story. *Huck Finn* still weighed on her mind.

"Back in Duxbury, Mass., when I was a young woman, a curious little race scandal occurred," Lois began.

> *My Charles, gone forever. All my children long grown up and gone or moved away. There's no one left back home who remembers my name as anything other than Mrs. Kenny, the oldest person in town.*

"A young white lady moved down to Duxbury from Boston. The rumor was that she was pregnant and that there was no father in the picture. She sure looked like she was showing when we'd see her in the grocery store or at Tura's Pharmacy downtown.

"The months passed, and, eventually, she had a little mulatto boy. Of course, tongues wagged all over town. You know how small towns are, and this was the 1930's."

> *The time kept passing us by in a relentless parade of days until first Richard and then Mary and then my husband Charles were gone.*

"One day the mother says that Billy Prescott, our local auto mechanic and one of the few black men in town, is the father. She brought her little half black and half white son to Billy's house and said 'You're the Daddy—you've got to raise your son.' Then she handed Billie her boy, and Billie took him, no questions asked."

Lois cleared her throat. "The mother went back to Boston. For two years, Billie Prescott raised that baby as if he were his own, all the while ignoring the whispers that always accompanied him around Duxbury town.

"Billy raised that boy into a toddler, fed him, loved him, took him to work during the day at Benny's garage and sang to the boy at night. Even named him William."

*Where have the years gone?*

"Sounds like real compassion, Babe," Eddie said. "Maybe real love."

Lois continued the telling. "After two years, two whole years, the young woman came back down from Boston. Seems she wanted her son back. She finally came clean that Billy Prescott wasn't the father at all but rather it was the man she was still living with up in Boston. She hadn't even known our Billy except as someone she'd seen in Benny's garage.

"Our Billy Prescott gave up William, no questions asked, although it surely must have broken his heart because he was never the same afterwards. The mother took the boy back up to Boston, and we never saw either of them again," Lois said softly. "We learned more than a little something about prejudice and clichés. How many people would have done what Billy did?" she wondered aloud.

*My babies gone.*

"Not very damn many," Andre answered.

Below them, loudspeakers announced the closing of the library. Soon, it would be time to venture downstairs, but Lois couldn't wait.

"So it goes," Lois said. She moved off gingerly into the shadows, walking on the floor joists and ducking below the ductwork, carrying her chamber pot wastebasket.

Eddie and Andre looked the other way.

# Chapter 6

## *Eddie*

As I said, anyone can end up homeless, but there are other pains. As human beings, we quite naturally want to comfort others who have been hurt. Lois and Andre certainly have that instinct and act on it. Even I, Eddie Couch, am sometimes touched by grace. There's a lot of time to think up here, and just yesterday I went thinking about anything positive I've done for others, for the world. It took me quite a while, but in the end I came up with this.

Ellen's and my old friends, the Killian family, Jackie, Jimmy, Frankie, Bobby and Patty, had the greatest parents whom everyone called simply Mom and Pop. We were all thick as thieves; saw each other at least every weekend at each other's houses or at some church function at Christ the King. We all kept track of each other's families, went to all the kids' birthday parties, knew what they were up to in sports and school. We were family for years, related and not. But the center of it all was always Mom and Pop's house, a row home behind the Academy Plaza Shopping Center, five doors away from Patty and Andy's house. Most Saturdays, everyone would congregate at Mom and Pop's for sandwiches, beer, gossip and jokes, maybe a college football game on TV. Pop was a gruff old guy, six foot two and 100% Irish and had a heart of gold. Mom was barely over five feet and 100 pounds dripping wet: she could handle all of Pop's gruff manner with ease, disarm it with softness, or shoot back funny verbal barbs when the situation warranted it. They quite obviously were made for each other. They loved each other. A love with warts that is the most real kind.

Mom fell sick first. Had a stroke one Sunday while visiting over at Patty's. Her left leg and arm just went numb. After four months at the rehabilitation hospital, Mom came home, and Patty and Andy cared for her, making meals and doing diapers, carrying her in the transfer chair to the car or just outside. Also, she'd had a growth on her neck for years that she'd ignored, and it became cancerous, spread through her body. She had chemo and radiation and heat therapy at Thomas Jefferson Hospital downtown, but all the treatments failed. Mom died on Easter Monday, after two and one half years of struggle, two and one half years after she'd retired from the paper bag company.

Pop got lost in the shuffle. He'd been complaining about pains in his stomach, and, sure enough, when the family finally could get him checked out, they learned he had colon cancer. A bowel resection operation followed, then months of chemo. Patty and her Andy did most of the care giving. Pop died in January, less than a year after Mom. The cemetery ground was frozen; ice storms prevented a lot of people from getting to his viewing. I still miss them both so much.

I loved them, and I saw the pain that the family had been through. I had to do something. That's how I, Eddie Couch, did one of the best things in my life. I put together the first annual Mom and Pop Killian golf outing with a buffet dinner and open bar upstairs at Dagwood's Pub to follow.

It's been three years now, and every year we raise several thousand dollars for the Sunshine Foundation, a group that grants wishes and pays for trips for terminally ill children. We've grown to over 80 guys on the public course at Bensalem every October. It's a mix of good golfers and total screw-ups, like Patty's Andy who just has a good time. Local companies like the grinding wheel place sponsor holes: things like longest drive, best ball and so on. So far, God's given us a good day each October. I love the smell of the mown grass and driving the golf cart and seeing the smiling faces of all these guys I've brought together in the name of Mom and Pop.

Later, at Dagwood's, the crowd grows to about 100 people, counting spouses and grown kids, and there's a raffle for a basket of cheer and all kinds of goofy prizes for things like lowest and highest golf score. Catholics love raffles. Last year, one of the prizes was a green Astroturf hat that looked like a golf hole with a flag sprouting from the center of the green and a plastic golf ball tethered to the base of the pole. Big Jackie won the hat and wore it out on the dance floor when he did the Macarena and the Electric Slide. Aunt Fran, she's Pop Killian's brother's widow, brought little tissue paper parasol umbrellas by the dozen and passed them out when the D.J. put on the music for the Mummer's strut. People drink too much and sometimes tell each other too much of the truth, but all in all everybody remembers why we're there. I think Mom and Pop would have liked it. Sometimes I think they're up there, beaming their approval by having God send us a sunny day every year. So that's one good thing that I do, and, if I can get out of here anytime soon, I'll keep planning the outing every year.

*I'll take a sandwich, sure Mom. Cheese steak sounds fine. Thank you so much. How was Seaside Heights last weekend? That's good. Did you get to hang out with Pop at Jack & Bill's, or were you too busy handing out dollars to the kids and walking them up and down the boardwalk? What's that you say, Pop? Sure, the Heights has changed. It's not like it was when Jackie, Jimmy, Patty, Frankie and Bobby were kids, for sure, but now they've all got kids, your grandkids, who want to go, and the rides and games are still a thrill for them. I hear you, Pop, I'd rather go to Atlantic City too, but Seaside is tradition. You ought to know Pop: you started the whole thing. Yup. You're right, Mom, change is a constant. Sandwich smells terrific. Thank you so much for everything. I love you, Mom. I miss you most of all. Miss you most of all. I miss Pop telling us how to do everything and always demanding to know how much things cost. I want to go back to what we had. Want our Saturdays back.*

We got out last night! It was the most amazing thing. Andre and Lois and I had had enough confinement, so we decided to take a risk. After the library closed, we snuck down to the main floor, and from there it was easy to push through the breakaway door bars to get out the front entrance. Lois made sure we braced the double doors open just a bit, so as not to make it look too obvious that the doors were ajar should any passing security officer happen by before we returned. Thank God no alarms went off. We were able to do the same thing with the library's back doors. Andre thinks the recent budget cuts are what saved us. There are a lot fewer security patrols making their way around at night.

Outside behind the red brick library's rear facade, the three of us felt like little kids on the first day of summer vacation as we breathed in the sweet, night air. A halo of light fell down on the pathway between us and Penn Hall, cast by the path's lone light pole.

"Lead on, McDuff," Lois joked. In the weak light, she looked far younger than her 87 years. "I've got my walking shoes on," she cajoled.

"Are we sure this is a good idea?" Andre wanted to know.

"Time's a wasting," I remember I said. We'd just set off for a walk toward the Hick's Art Building when I remembered that I still had my office key from all those months and years before.

"Let's see if we can get into Penn's basement. See my old stomping grounds."

The automatic doors in front of Penn Hall were locked for the night, as were the side and back doors.

"I didn't break out of the library to crawl around again in some building," Lois said. She started off toward the art building and the campus totem pole.

There was a crescent moon peeking through heavy clouds, so we could see enough to walk all right. We held hands and moved pretty quickly past the infirmary with its weird rocking sculpture on the left, then red brick Founder's Hall on the right, and the red brick Student Union building again on the left.

"I sure hope this is a good idea," Andre said as we walked, but to be outside was so intoxicating, to be breathing fresh air so welcome that I almost didn't care about the risk.

It began to rain lightly as we got to the carved totem pole. We stood under it for a moment, looking up at the pole looming some 75 feet straight up, dark animal faces carved its whole length, and to the darkening sky above.

"Whoever carved this was doing more than a project," Lois said. "This is a labor of love." Her long gray hair, tied back in braids, glistened in the wet.

I heard the sound of a car coming, then saw its headlights stabbing at the parking lot in front of the Admissions and Records Building, directly in front of our totem pole. "It's a squad car. We've got to get the hell out of here."

"Come on," Andre said. "I know a way."

We moved quickly around the parking lot, avoiding the lights, skirting past Hick's Art Building, until we came to the first of the three stone servant's cottages on our right. Andre tried the lock on the front door just for chance. It was locked tight. He led us around to the side of the little building where two metal storm doors outside led to the basement.

"Praise the Lord," he said as he swung one of the heavy doors open and over on its side with a bang. "We used to be able to get into one of the tunnels from down here."

"Tunnels?" Lois asked as we stepped down the concrete steps into the dark.

"Don't ask, Babe."

Andre led the way by memory. I couldn't see a thing, but I felt Lois take my hand as we stood in darkness on the basement floor, and I squeezed her hand reassuringly. I heard Andre try a door latch, then heard metal rattling.

"Damn," he swore. "They've got the entrance barred off. We're screwed."

I heard Lois' measured breathing next to me. "We'll just have to retrace our steps back home."

Andre laughed a little. "Guess we've had enough fun."

"You know what?" Lois asked, then answered her own rhetorical question. "Fun is like life insurance—the older you get the more it costs."

"Ba-da-boom," I teased. "Let's get the heck out of here."

Outside the cottage basement, the rain had quit. It took us only minutes to sneak back past the art building and the totem pole. We saw no sign of the security patrol car, so the three of us walked rather boldly past Founder's Hall in the wash of the emerging moonlight. The clouds above had separated.

I looked behind us, above the shadows of Penn Hall. That moon was a toenail on a dark carpet sky. It was the last thing I saw before we reentered the back door of the library, still thankfully blocked open. Sometimes the magic works. The entrance double door still had one side wedged ajar as well. The magic had worked twice.

Before long, our bathroom panel access was down, and Andre, his clothes still damp, climbed on the toilet tank and up through the small opening while Lois and I stood in the stall waiting. Lois' turn was next. I gave her fanny a little polite boost as she went through the opening. She was obviously beyond modesty among friends. You see, counting the golf outing and the fund raiser for Mom and Pop and helping Lois up, there's two good things I've done. The good Lord willing, there'll be more. I thought about that as I climbed through the entrance, then turned around, reaching down to grasp the access panel and then pulling it tightly sealed into inconspicuous place. We moved in semi-darkness again, stepping on floor joists, until we got to our living area and Andre turned on the lights.

# Chapter 7

## *Monday Night Football*

Frank Killian and Tony and Stephen Di Javon were grilling hamburgers and hot dogs, and the food smelled pretty darn good. The beer wasn't bad either. Their grill sat behind Frankie's mini van in a city-owned parking lot outside Veteran's Stadium amid a sea of cars, trucks and buses and a thousand other smoking grills. Among the crowds of tailgaters, an occasional football flew in some semblance of a spiral from one pair of hands to another or to the ground. Car radios and portable stereos put out an impossibly complex blend of songs mixed with talk from the Philadelphia all sports station that many of the tailgaters had on. The stadium loomed beyond the many parking lots, an old circle of concrete monstrosity built in the 60's like so many football stadiums, ready to swallow up some 60,000 people within a couple of hours. Eagles vs. Cowboys. Monday night. The biggest game of the year.

Frankie took a big swallow of his fourth Coors Light. "Ain't this great?" he asked the Di Javon brothers. They all had season tickets and had been sitting together in the 800 section of Veteran's Stadium for years. He bit into a juicy hamburger, grilled just right, and savored both the taste and the anticipation of the game. The best times are the times right before something good is going to happen, he thought.

"Play some catch?" Tony asked. He was compactly built, handsome, and well-muscled, with long black hair.

Stephen and Frankie both put their beers and food down and jogged down the asphalt between the two nearest rows of cars. Tony's throw, strong and accurate, sailed over Frankie's head into Stephen's outstretched hands.

"Touchdown," Stephen said, and then flipped the ball to Frankie, who lobbed it back to Tony. They made a throwing triangle of Frankie to Tony, Tony to Stephen, Stephen to Tony, Tony to Frankie and on until they got thirsty again and returned to the van. They had Patty Killian's husband Andy Ferazua with them and Tony's ex-girlfriend Lynn: neither were regular season ticket holders and neither Andy nor Lynn really knew the drill, so the three friends didn't want to stay away too long.

Next to them, a group with a pickup truck had set up a huge Eagles green and white canopy tent on poles, and among the many people milling underneath was a guy with his bare chest painted green and with his hair dyed green as well. At regular intervals, he kept yelling "Party!" A keg of beer sat in an ice-filled metal tub at the center of the throng.

Stephen Di Javon, a disabled auto mechanic who treated pain with Sambuca, yelled back "Party!" He was surprised to see Andy and Lynn underneath the tent, mixing with the fans.

"What a set up," he admired. "Outrageous."

His brother Tony agreed. "They really did it up right."

Frankie Killian wore a well-kept beard and always had his light brown hair, now accented with gray at the temples, cut stylishly. He'd been making stone grinding wheels for years, had a good family, a wife Kirby and two good kids, one boy of eight and a girl of eleven whom he loved dearly, but he enjoyed the company of his friends and all the Eagles' home games.

"Say Stevie," he said, "what say we clear the rest of the food off our grill and go over to check on our two lost puppies?"

"Lost, my ass," Stephen said. "They look pretty found."

Tony chuckled. "Let's go over," he smiled.

There were still nearly two hours until game time. Philadelphia might have more than its share of urban decay, but anyone in the Delaware Valley can tell you that most people around Philly are sports nuts and that football is the preferred sport. Southeastern Pennsylvanians love their Eggels with a passion bordering on fanaticism. Frankie even had a theory that the worse the living conditions in a given city the more rabid the fans became: rooting for the home team became an escape. But he wasn't thinking about such things as they shut down their grill.

The three old friends moved under the party tent. As soon as they got to the tent, a big guy in a number 32 Ricky Watters jersey came up to them with three plastic cups.

"Help yourself," he said, pointing to the keg.

"Don't mind if we do," Stephen replied.

"Yo, Frankie," Andy called out, holding up his beer cup. "It's your favorite, Coors Light." Lynn was busy talking to the guy with the green chest about the Dallas offensive line.

Frank said, "Great minds think alike."

Bodies bumped against each other as folks made their way back and forth to the keg and to talk to each other in realigning knots of people. Nearly everyone had on Eagles' green. Station 610 WIP blared talk of the game via loudspeakers in the party tent.

"We're going to crush those stinking losers and avenge last year's playoff loss," radio host Angelo Cataldi barked.

"Only if we can contain Emmett Smith," Tony Bruno, his co-host warned.

"And now a word from our sponsors."

Stephen and Tony took up the cause, talking about how they saw the game unfolding. "It will be a war," Tony said. "I don't care what the Cowboys' record is so far this year. They're the defending Super Bowl champions."

"When they get Michael Irvin back from drug suspension, watch out," Stephen agreed.

Frankie made his way over to his brother-in-law, Andy, who wore an Eagles cap on his blonde head but also wore a contrasting 49'ers shirt out of deference to northern California, where he originated. He'd landed at job teaching English at Bucks County Community College, had moved all the way across country some years before, and had met and married Frankie's sister Patty, who was a secretary at the school. The two guys had been through caring for Mom and Pop Killian together and with that common bond just naturally got along.

"Yo, Teach," Frank said, "shall we go rescue Lynn?"

"Nah, she seems to be having a good time."

"Are you going to Vermont again with us this winter?" Frankie wanted to know.

Every March, a group of the guys went skiing together at Killington, VT, a combination of male bonding, skiing, drinking and escape. Stephen, Tony and Frank were the ring leaders who organized all the details of the trip. Timed it to coincide with "Jack Daniels Week." The previous year, ten of them had set a record of a $400 bar tab at happy hour at The Wobbly Barn. They'd serenaded Amy, the bartender, with "Amy/ I'm in love with you/ I could stay for a while/ maybe longer if I do" when the band played the right song. They even sounded pretty good.

"Sure I'm in," Andy Ferazua said. "I live for the day." He moved aside for a couple of Eagles' fans headed out from under the green and white tent.

"We need you," Frankie said. "You're the only sane one among us. Besides, you saved Tommy Rovin from turning gay."

The previous year, the happy hour band at The Wobbly Barn had been a duo: two seemingly gay guys named Shawn and Jeremy who'd played the infamous "Amy" song. Long after closing out happy hour, returning to the rented house for showers and dinner and then going back to the Wobbly for more beers until about one a.m. when almost everybody went home again, Frankie and Andy discovered that young Tommy Rovin, on his first trip with the guys, was nowhere to be found. Andy volunteered to drive back to the bar, and, sure enough, when he got there, he spied Tommy sitting at the bar, pie-eyed drunk, with Jeremy's arm around him and several shot glasses in front of them on the bar.

"Come on," Andy had said, rousting young Tommy, extricating him from Jeremy's arm and getting him up from the bar. "You've had enough. You're going home with me." Tommy left peacefully, and the legend of Andy's rescue of Tommy had grown.

Andy pushed his Eagles cap back on his head. He took a swig of Coors. "I wouldn't miss it."

"Good," Frank said. "Money's due to Stephen by Thanksgiving. We'll make it the best trip ever."

Andy said, "If we don't, it'll be our own damn fault."

Frankie drank some more beer. "So what's your prediction for the game?"

"Eagles 17, Cowboys 14. Irving Fryer catches a touchdown pass, Watters runs another one in, and a late field goal wins it. Emmett Smith gets held in check."

"We'll take it," Frank said.

Stephen and Tony came over, beers in hand. The tent tailgaters had really gotten louder, and WIP blasted "Eagles, Eagles, go Eagles," so they had to talk loudly to be heard over the din. Off to the side, Frank saw Lynn still chatting up the green haired fan.

"I've got some good news I've been meaning to tell you," Tony said over the crowd. "You know I got laid off over at the pipe fitter's hall, right?

Well, last week I got on with a roofer in Bucks County. I'm hoping for some jobs up there soon."

Stephen nodded to his brother. "I know what you're going through."

"It's tough out there," Andy said. "Reality sucks sometimes."

"Reality is for people who can't handle science fiction," Frankie said, and they all laughed.

"You're becoming quite the philosopher," Tony kidded. He pushed a thick strand of black hair back behind his ear. "I just want a job."

Lynn rejoined the guys, saying "back the same day," and the pre game party progressed on.

Final score: Eagles 17, Cowboys 24.

# Voices, Inner Chapter Two

## *Eddie*

Once, before I hurt my back and before I needed the cane, before the diabetes set in and my life changed, I lay on the ground on my back on the dirt on the little island in the middle of our cul-de-sac street in northeast Philly. I could do things like that in those days. Anyway I lay there one spring day and watched the cirrus clouds scud overhead, seeing them as warnings of some approaching system, as ships of vapor that would dissipate before they ever sailed over the Atlantic Ocean. The sky was clear above me; there was no summertime haze to block my view and make me cough. I didn't give a damn what my row house neighbors might think, seeing me lay on our common dirt and dog poop island from through their replacement windows. It was a fine spring day in my corner of the world. Sap was rising. I thought about how near and far I was from where my life had begun. Lying on the cool earth, I thought about how distant I was from that man who had passed for me only a few years before, the ambitious guy who came from honest dirt, went back to school, became a community college professor. Could that other man, that man that was me who still had his wife Ellen and his kids Eddie and Carolyn, could that guy lie down next to me, watching the Philadelphia sky drift overhead? If that other guy could visit me, would he want to know what I knew now that I'd lost everything? Would he want to feel what I'd experienced since he was me? If we could lie side by side, would he regard me jealously, just like I do with astronauts who've just returned from a space shuttle ride? It was a silly idea, I decided. There would always have to be a difference between us: I went on living a new life, a life of some suffering and some redemption, while he stayed back. He may have set the voyage of my newer life in motion, but he could not take the journey with me. Just as I, who lay on the dirt watching clouds, could not know that I'd meet new friends like Lois, Andre, Margaret and Harry, this other, older Eddie, though younger in years, could never see the outcome of his preparations for me, unless somehow, on some other side of time, we could meet our past selves and all those we might have been, all in the same room at once, or floating on the same island cul-de-sac. One of my HMO doctors once told me that our physical components change completely on a seven year cycle; the very biology of our minds continually passes our memories along to the new brain cells of a stranger, he said. The same with the cells of all our organs, our very beings. Who we were is only a ghost chimera of a fellow traveler of the organic person we once were. Change *is* a constant, he said when he handed me a prescription and disappeared into another waiting room. As for me, this Eddie Couch, lying on the moist soil, what might I learn from that earlier Eddie who'd set me into motion? What the hell could I inherit from all those others I once was? The nineteen year old trying to seduce Ellen so long ago, the middle-aged man who wanted to teach business while making his first million, the husband who couldn't hold his marriage together and who fell from grace, the son who heard his father calling one night 'God just let me die in my own home,' the shy geek whose heart pounded when Ellen finally did kiss him back, the kid who wet his bed until he as 12? What a state of the union I might deliver to all the other ones who were me. What reminders and futures they could show me. First kisses, sex and deaths. The fierce and beautiful green cliffs of the Napali coast of Kauai dropping down to black sand beaches and blue Pacific just at sunset. The Walt Whitman

Bridge lit up at night. These other me's could retrace weak lines and boundaries on the traveling map of my journey here to northeast Philly. They could show me where it was that I took roads other than what they intended, let me know here and now whether they approved of those transgressions, whether my choices were foolish or wise. The travel book writer William Least Heat Moon says that he is reborn almost hourly, that he is not one person start to finish, because forgetfulness and imperfect and incomplete memory force him to always be reborn. Biology seconds the motion. Alzheimer's patients are all of us enhanced, although for a different cause. The philosopher Santanya says, I who cannot fully remember my past must proceed on in time without it. Sort of . . .

When a shadow that turned out to be my neighbor Mr. Googe loomed over me, blocking the sky, I startled, not really knowing where I was for fractions of a second. "A pigeon crapped on your shirt," he said.

"A rat with wings."

"It's my lucky day," I told him. Already, I was trying to think of some reasonable explanation for my behavior.

Damn, I remember thinking, how quickly other lives can suck us in.

—Eddie Couch

# Chapter 8

## *The Brothers Karamazov*

Dr. Zchivago was just over, and the hideaway's television screen went to blue, casting a bluish wash all over their living area. The ice palace was what Lois remembered most.

"That house was so beautiful," she said. "It's a shame they only had such a short time to find their love there."

Andre sat back down on his hammock with a sigh. He had been pacing on the small floored area where he and Eddie had laid a piece of plywood across the floor joists. He'd been up and down throughout the whole film. Twice Lois had urged him to sit still.

"I'll let you in on a secret," he said. "That whole film was shot in Spain. Warm weather for the whole thing.

"The ice palace was painted white. They made icicles out of plaster of Paris for inside the house, and they spray painted them too. Outside the palace, they lay sheets of cotton for snow fields and painted over them as well."

Eddie belly-laughed from his mail bag hammock. Instead of his customary shorts, he wore blue jeans with the pant legs rolled up into cuffs and a red San Francisco 49'ers sweatshirt. The air in their attic crawlspace had turned decidedly cooler despite the warm air running through their ductwork when the library heat cycled on. Andre, too, had on an Eagle's sweatshirt, and Lois had her sweater on over her long-sleeved white top.

"I'm disillusioned," Eddie chuckled. "So many things aren't what they seem." The smile that spread across his darker-skinned face, that transformed his thin lips into a crescent inviting you to smile along, never failed to make Lois feel warm inside.

"Come on, you guys, we're supposed to be talking about the *Brothers Karamazov* this evening . . ."

"Well, at least we're already talking Russia," Andre interrupted.

"You mean Spain," Eddie chided.

"I like Alyosha the best," Lois plowed ahead. "He's questing after something, after faith and God. All that studying he's doing with Father Zossima is part of his quest." She pointed at Andre, as if to keep him on track, then reached down into her sweater pocket to find her reading glasses. With them on, she looked like everyone's grandmother, a dignified lady with pointed glasses, pigtail braids, and a softly wrinkled face, creased but not destroyed by decades. She looked down at her book.

"There's all this tension and rivalry between the brothers. Ivan is always trying to shake Alyosha's faith, and Dimitry is a real hedonist. What do you guys think?"

"The guy we're supposed to like the least is the father, Fyodor. He's always drunk and complaining," Eddie said. "That's what I think, babe." He sat on his bed with his legs crossed, jiggling one foot on his ankle.

Andre jumped in. "It's interesting that Dostoevsky gave his most negative character his own first name. What do you make of that?"

Eddie questioned, "A little self-judgment? A way of working out his bad side vicariously on paper?"

"Maybe all of the above," Lois said. "Karamazov, the family name, means dark woods in Russian."

"Leave it to Lois to cut through hundreds of pages to the core," Eddie said approvingly.

Andre cleared his throat dramatically. "My favorite part is the 'Grand Inquisitor' scene, when Ivan tells Alyosha the story of the meeting of Jesus and the Inquisitor, who wants to burn Jesus at the stake for raising mankind's hopes. It's Ivan trying to break Alyosha's faith again, to lure him away from Father Zossima's pull.

"You remember, the Inquisitor has just burned 500 supposed heretics during the time of the Spanish Inquisitions, and Dostoevsky has Jesus come back. The Inquisitor jails Jesus for raising mankind's expectations too high. He accuses Jesus of not setting a reasonable standard when he refused to take the three temptations. The Inquisitor says that men want to be fed, not freed."

Lois nodded, "All the while, in telling his story, Ivan is trying to shake up Alyosha's belief. Remember, the Inquisitor demands that Christ answer for why God gives man freedom rather than ruling over him with the Inquisitor's kind of absolute authority."

"That's right, babe," Eddie said. "And Jesus' only answer is to kiss the Inquisitor on the lips."

"That's the question," Andre added. "What is the kiss? Is it a kiss of forgiveness for the Inquisitor's sin? Is it unconditional love for all people, even a scumbag like the Inquisitor? What is it?"

Lois rose off her hammock and walked to where Andre sat. She bent over, her book in hand, and kissed Andre's cheek.

"Touché, babe. There's your answer," Eddie said.

Lois looked approvingly at her two men. "In the book, the Inquisitor opens the cell door and lets Jesus walk away. Dostoevsky says that Christ's kiss burned on the Inquisitor's lips. That's all we need to know."

> *Charles and I paddling in his canoe on Ross' pond in summer. Next month he's leaving for Europe and the war. The one they call the war to end all wars. Sun dapples the water all around us, and our paddles make circles when they touch the water. Behind our canoe the gentle wake grows wider into an ever increasing V. We have this time together here, and he is with me, not in some foreign land. The sun lights up his brown hair and is all around him and behind him, making him a partial silhouette. His outline is moving toward me, leaning in. I lean to meet his face in the middle of our canoe, to meet his lips that kiss my lips, my cheeks, my eyes just softly touching, warm and inviting. Will you marry me, forever and always? Oh, yes, Charles,*

*yes, we have this time together, forever and always. Now, right here. Before World War I. And after, when you come wounded from the Battle of Verdun but still alive. After we have our first son and the other children come like presents under our biological Christmas tree. We have this time, this place. Here and now. This sunlight, this canoe, this water rippling, the taste of our lips. No one can take it away. But it was so long ago . . .*

"I've got an idea," Eddie said, and Lois came out of her reverie. "Yes?"

"Waddya say we put away Dostoevsky and go exploring? This library has a big auditorium, right?" Eddie said.

"Yea, so?" Andre wanted to know.

"I think I know how to get over the stage area, where the scaffolding and projection lights are. You know, that area of far wall where the sheetrock doesn't quite go all the way to the roofline," Eddie said, gesturing off to the shadows to the right of their access to the downstairs bathroom. "That's the way. You can hear the sound when there's some event going on down there."

"We've heard it," Andre said.

"Well are you with me?" Eddie demanded in his best booming voice, almost impossible to ignore.

Andre wanted answers. "How do we get over the wall?"

"I'll boost you."

"That counts me out," Lois said. "I think I'll stay here and read some more."

"Think of it," Eddie giggled. "Free tickets to any shows held in the auditorium."

"Yeah, above stage seats," Andre added, looking over sardonically at Lois who met his sideways glance and smiled.

Eddie was on his way. "Let's go."

"Back shortly," Andre said.

Eddie, all nearly 300 pounds of him, kidded Andre. "Who gets to do the boosting and who the climbing?"

"I think it best if you boost," slender Andre said as the two men walked off carefully, leaving Lois to her turgid Russian literature. "Besides, I have always depended on the kindness of strangers."

"O.K., Blanche Dubois, you climb."

> *One sun dappled afternoon turned into 60 years. That's the way life is. Time can compress and expand to fit the inner life. The only constant is chance. And maybe God driving it all. I can hardly believe I've made it this far, lived on through so many bends and twists in time. First we lost our first born son Rick to brain cancer. It nearly killed Charles and me. But we went on, lived on, tried to shorten that time. Then it was our daughter Elizabeth to a diabetic heart attack. When they're babies, you swaddle them in blankets and love, try to keep them safe. When they're children you try to shepherd them safely to the teenage years and then to survive those years until they fly more or less on their own. But you can't prepare for what you can't know. Can't be with them always. It was Elizabeth, and Charles and I had to live on, walk on. He had the greatest laugh I could never ignore, having to laugh along too, sometimes until the tears streamed down our faces. I'd ask him whether he'd like strawberry or vanilla ice cream, and he had habit of saying "both!" These are the things I remember as my memory fades. Then Charles was gone. The heart that gave so much broke down. I wanted to die, but life is strong within us. Eventually, I went on. You will too, Alyosha, you too will journey on. I grew elderly. Lost Robert and then Sarah too. Time and the losses marched on. But life was strong within me, as it is in you, Eddie, my babe, and in you Andre. It is what brought me time traveling through all these years to you and to our library home. Life is strong within us. That's what I know.*

# Chapter 9

Margaret Dorris had been working in her windowless back office since lunch break, so she hadn't seen the Bucks County sky begin to darken in the south toward Philadelphia nor had she seen the zigzag lines of lightening spiking far off in the west. But later in the afternoon, when Margaret came out to help at the reference desk, she could hear the low rumble of thunder in the distance.

A middle-aged man stopped at the "Ask Me" sign by reference to ask about *Who's Who in America*.

"That one stays in the library," Margaret said. "It's in the mid 900's, 956 F. Want to look something up and then get home before it rains?"

The man began to roll up his sleeve. "Going to be more than rain," he said authoritatively. He showed Margaret his old wounds that had left his arm crimped and pitted with long bands of scar tissue. "Shrapnel from 'Nam."

He looked at his bare arm for a long moment as if the wounds still surprised him, then pushed his sleeve back down. "When a storm is coming, I feel it early on. Right now this arm tells me a good one's on the way." The weatherman walked away.

When Margaret came off the reference desk at three o' clock, the library seemed almost empty. Most of the students had hurried away, leaving piles of books on the library's long study tables. Some hurried through checkout at the circulation desk, their eyes on the darkening sky outside the library's tall southern facing windows.

Some of her staff wished they could leave too. Cathy Tan had two pre-school aged children at home with the babysitter—one who couldn't sleep when the wind came up and another who panicked at the sound of thunder. One of the assistant librarians said her five-year-old still had nightmares about flash floods after the previous summer's heavy rains and floods in Yardley and New Hope.

Margaret Dorris had long gotten used to the idea that southeastern Pennsylvania got big, Great Lakes storm systems, Nor'easters from the south, and even an occasional tornado. But idea and reality are not always the same. By the time she closed up at five o'clock that Sunday, the sky was closing in, dropping down ominous and gray over the college and Newtown.

Margaret decided to go straight home to Harry even though she needed to stop at Guinardi's supermarket. She could skip the groceries, could always come back later, but passing up the Mobil station in town would be riskier because her battered Chevy was empty, the gas gauge needle resting squarely over the big red E. While she filled the tank, a bolt of lightening cracked close enough that the downy hair on her arms stood up.

Once home, Margaret took off her coat and hung it up in the hall closet, then found Harry in the kitchen, gathering a flashlight and some candles in case they lost power.

"TV just put out a severe thunderstorm warning. They spotted a funnel cloud east of Harrisburg," Harry warned.

Just then the lights dimmed for an instant, followed by a sharp crack of thunder, causing Margaret to flinch.

"Close one," Harry said.

"Too close."

Harry took up Margaret's hand, felt the bones under her cool skin.

"There's nothing better than the familiar touch of the long married," Margaret said.

"Or the long unmarried," Harry smiled.

Outside, the air was so still that nothing moved, so heavy that even dust and pollen held to the ground. No leaves stirred. No wind whispered. The sky around Newtown was dark green, dark and growing darker, an odd shade of green, light trapped in a dark green bottle.

Bucks County Community College looked abandoned. No students or faculty walked its concrete paths. None of the blue and white security police cars could be seen driving the linked roads that connected Hicks and Founders and Penn Halls with the Tyler Mansion. The totem pole over by Hicks Hall, carved by past art students as a special project, pointed dramatically at the green sky, its animal faces glowering in the dark. The "Perpetual Motion" sculpture over by the Infirmary, a upside down white metal V hinged at the V point to another right side up white metal V, also someone's art project, began rocking its top V in the rising wind.

Inside their library hideaway, Eddie and Andre and Lois had their radio and television tuned to the weather. Outside, the wind increased. Quick gusts of wind lifted the branches of maple trees and sent miniature dust devils scooting across the campus parking lots. The wind grew so strong that the three hideaways heard it creaking the library roof above their heads. A cottontail rabbit hopped into the middle of the playground behind Hobby House, the college's daycare center. It cowered there in the grass until hail began to pelt down, and then the rabbit ran under some brush along the fence line for cover, as bigger hailstones, the size of ripe grapes, began to fall.

The hail bounced in grass all over campus and ricocheted off pavement, pellets springing up, colliding, spinning cross flat surfaces, a dance of ice balls. The television Eddie and his group watched went out along with their radio and lights, leaving them in darkness.

Margaret Dorris watched out her window. Stones pelted the daffodils in Harry's flower bed, ripping off the petals, bending over the stalks. The roof of their house clattered, the sounds disconnected and staccato. When they heard glass shatter, she and Harry locked eyes. Then the lights went out.

Suddenly, just as suddenly as it had begun, the hail quit, and it was quiet again.

"Thank God," Lois whispered.

"Yes," Andre said in the darkness.

Nearby, Margaret and Harry went outside in front of their house. A siren began to wail in Newtown. Margaret wanted it to be a fire or police horn, but, although she'd never heard one before, she knew what it was—a tornado warning coming from the high school a few blocks away. The hair on her arms rose again. "Shit," she said, but the returning wind blew her voice away.

Dark clouds blistered the sky, fermenting, exploding into weird, fierce shapes, clouds moving so low and fast that Margaret almost believed she could touch them. From somewhere above them, she and Harry thought they could hear the sound of breathing, the sound of ancient and powerful breathing. Junk was beginning to sail around their yard. Their outside garbage can flew away; their tree limbs waved madly.

"We'd better get back in."

Harry saw it first. Coiling, spiraling, dipping down like a giant gnarled ginseng root or finger reaching for the earth ... The air filled up with a roaring noise and got hotter and began swirling, stinging their skin with minute particles. Something small stung Margaret in the cheek, something hard and small that skipped across their yard away in the wind.

"Shit," Margaret said again.

"We'd better get back in."

The traffic sign on the street in front of their house vibrated madly in the wind.

"Shit. It's headed right at the college."

"Maggie, we have to go back in," Harry repeated, this time more forcefully.


In the library crawlspace, Lois and her two men couldn't see much in the light from the one candle Eddie had lit, but they could hear and feel it all. Grit and tiny pieces of blown in attic insulation swirled around them, stung their eyes. The air, suddenly punishing and humid, began to rush out of the crawlspace, sucking out the flame from Eddie's candle, extracting dust and little pieces of duct wrap, anything small enough to be drawn out between the tiny gaps in their walls, snatching daddy longlegs spiders from their webs and flattening them against the interior walls. A sound like a freight train roared above near them, and then a tremendous crash from outside shook the walls and sent a tremor rippling across their floor. A small and ragged section of their roof ripped away, sending weak dust-flecked light bathing on the disordered attic. And then the train was gone.

"Is everybody O.K.?" Lois asked, astonishment in her voice.

"We're here," Andre said, already thinking about what problems a hole in the roof posed for them.


"Jesus, God," Margaret exclaimed from behind her front window. "Harry, it passed right over the college. Jesus, God."

## Chapter 10

His years as a pipe fitter had gotten Tony used to hard work, often under less than ideal conditions, so working temporarily as a roofer's assistant was no big adjustment. Within days of the big Eagles game, he'd been called for a couple of small jobs in a posh suburban development called Knob Hill that bordered Newtown. The work was easy enough: using a nail gun to nail down roof shingle tabs in neat lines on two different suburban roofs. Those jobs complete, Tony Di Javon had a few days off. When a big storm blew over his northeast Philadelphia neighborhood, Tony suspected there'd be more work on the way.

He wasn't surprised when the phone in his apartment rang way before dawn. Tony rolled over reluctantly, saw that the red digital numbers on his alarm clock read 5:03.

"Hello?"

"We've got a job up at the community college in Newtown," his new boss said. "Can you be there by 7:00?"

"Sure, I guess so," Tony said, still half asleep. He got out of bed, wearing only his boxer shorts, his chest covered with dark, curly hair.

"It's up off Route 413, take Swamp Road one mile north and watch for the signs. We're repairing the roof on the library," his boss said.

"I'll be there," Tony said, then hung up the phone. He wandered to the bathroom, turned on the light, peed. Tony hit the shower and then got dressed.

Full sunlight shone through his truck window onto the dashboard as Tony parked his truck in the visitor's lot at Bucks County Community College. He had no trouble finding the library, a late sixties institutional red brick building at the center of the pretty campus. Tony saw one of the work trucks parked at a corner of the building. His new company already had extension ladders up past the second floor to the roof, and Tony saw his boss scurrying around on the ground giving instructions to one of Tony's new co-workers.

His boss, a pasty faced man of about fifty, motioned Tony over.

"They had a friggin' tornado right here in Bucks County. Imagine that. There's only one damaged section up there, so we should be out of here in a couple of hours," he said. "I want you and Terry to carry up some new sheathing and nail it in. I'll be back to take care of the finish shingles." With that, the owner of Blaylock Roofing headed off toward the parking lots.

Tony went to the truck and put on a tool belt, then gathered up his sheathing materials. "Yo, Terry," he called, "support the ladder for me as I go up?"

He felt each step upward on the ladder, rung by rung, in his instep arches despite the work boots he wore, a feeling that was becoming familiar in recent weeks. Tony breathed deeply as he reached his stopping point two rungs below the top of the two-pointed ladder leaning on the southwest corner of the library's slightly pitched roof.

He put his armload of wooden sheathing down on the edge of the roof, then pushed the small wood sheets a little further up from the edge where they'd be safer. Tony looked around at the sweeping view below him. This really is a pretty campus, he thought. He saw Penn and Founder's Halls next to the library, more unexceptional red brick structures, but, beyond the portable classrooms and parking lots south of the main buildings, large cornfields opened up expansively, the cornstalks only recently beginning to turn brown, and beyond the cornfields into Tyler Park Tony saw dense green tree cover. Neshaminy Creek curved gently through the middle of the park, its water appearing a lighter shade of green. From his high perch, Tony saw the little dam crossing the creek and, near it, some outbuildings, one with stacks of canoes outside on racks. Above the dam, where the water deepened, a couple paddled their rented canoe, their paddles leaving small Vs behind in the water with each dip, their canoe leaving a larger V as it glided forward. A big flock of Canadian geese flew over the library, honking to each other, and Tony turned his attention back to the job at hand.

He brushed some hair out of his eyes with one gloved hand, then reached to his side and pulled the hammer and a bag of nails out of his tool belt. Tony set them carefully on the roof. Falling tools were no good, he knew.

"Terry, can you bring up one more load of sheathing? That should do it. The hole is not too bad up here," he called down. That said, he climbed fully onto the roof and began to work, scraping old broken shingle tabs away from the edge of the hole, then beginning to nail wooden sheets over the nearest edge of the opening.

Terry climbed up behind him, unloaded more sheathing and nails.

"Got it covered up here?"

"Made in the shade," Tony said, "but you could bring up more of the red shingles. I'll get them ready for when Mr. Blaylock gets back."

Tony worked for a while, the sun warming his face and hands. By the time Terry returned with additional shingles, Tony had the hole half repaired. From time to time, he looked down into the attic area, seeing only some ductwork in the shadows and floor boarding below.

He liked the work, welcomed it even. He'd been the second youngest of seven kids in a south Philadelphia Italian family, and one thing he'd known from an early age on was the value of hard work. Tony was the spitting image of his father, handsome and dark with shining eyes. For forty years, his Dad had run a vegetable booth in the Italian Market. As a young woman, his mother was often compared to Sophia Loren, and even now that decades of cleaning other people's houses had worn her out, she was still a commanding woman, her long black hair now mostly gone to distinguished silver. Say what you want about the decline and fall of Philadelphia as a once great city. There are still hundreds of thousands of good, hard working people living there.

Tony Di Javon sang as he pounded nails in the sun. It was his three-year-old nephew's favorite song: "Do you want to swing on a star?/ Carry moonbeams home in a jar?/ To be better off than you are?/ Do you wanna be a duck?/ A duck is an animal that lives in the zoo . . ." My God, he thought, I'm becoming a blithering idiot. It was a long way from Veteran's Stadium Eagles' game parties to weeknight visits with his favorite nephew at his sister Connie's row home in Mt. Airy. Tony had grown to enjoy both.

Something in his heart told him that he would not be alone much longer, that a woman who would be good for him was headed unalterably toward his life. Tony smiled broadly at the prospect. Someone to share his bed. Someone to share his life. He might do as well as his parents had. Worse things could happen. His repair was nearly finished. Only a two foot section of roof still needed to be covered over and sealed.

Something in Tony's heart told him he was not alone. That there were other people nearby. Someone other than Terry down on the ground and the many students wandering the walkway paths below. He sensed that there was someone near. Tony set his hammer down on the rooftop. He pulled himself over the new plywood he'd put down, staring through the opening into the shadows below. A big heating duct running near the roofline obscured much of the view down.

He heard them before he saw anything. When he held his own breath, Tony could faintly hear someone else's measured breathing coming from below. Or was it more than one person?

Now he thought he heard two people breathing. A lone Canadian goose flew over the library, honking every few seconds. The bird call interrupted what he thought he heard. Tony couldn't be sure.

Tony Di Javon made his move. He crawled further forward over the roof sheathing repair, then rolled over on his back. Using his abdomen and legs for counterbalance, he hung his torso and his head upside down into the remaining opening. In the moments that it took for his eyes to adjust, a vision coalesced. Tony saw two upside down men, one squat and massive, the other lean and startled looking, standing off in the edge of where the roof light fell.

The big one said "Damn!" He pushed the upside down other one back further in the dark.

Holy shit, Tony thought. What in the holy hell? I'm going to have to report this.

Lois Kenny was otherwise occupied by using her chamber pot off in a far corner of the library attic.

# Chapter 11

Lois soon grew unaccountably tired of living alone. Her loved family had come and gone before her, and Eddie and Andre, her adoptive family, were most likely in jail. The muted conversations of students and staff below her during business hours made her all the more lonesome now that she had taken to awakening during the day. She looked at the two empty mailbag hammocks, at their blank television and all their other assorted paraphernalia. Lois was surprised that no one had come to investigate their hideaway in the nearly two days she'd been alone: she knew it would be only a matter of time before the authorities were back. She almost welcomed the idea of her discovery. At least there would be other people to talk with . . . other souls to bump up against. She fantasized being arrested and being placed in the same cell as Andre and Eddie so that they could continue talking about their beloved books. Toward the end, the simple joys take on an added resonance, she thought. We should all plant some trees we'll never sit under.

She pulled her blue slacks higher up her legs, seeing the thin blue lines of veins running like so many roads across the tops of her thighs. She finished dressing, then laced up her Reeboks.

*Charles is next to me in the car driving us home from the hospital. Richard, our first born, is on my lap in his blue receiving blanket. The pain had torn through me so quickly I had no time to get my body ready for it. It twisted inside me, pulling at my center, taking me to the edge of what I could stand, and at the edge I gave myself to it, holding nothing back. It took me, wrapped itself around me with such strength, such force that it cut off my breath and it began to move, the pain inside me, taking something from me as it pushed itself deeper, some part of me tearing away as it pushed lower, and there was life to my pain as it stretched and twisted, straining against me, using my resistance to make its way. And then it was free, the release too sudden, too final. I'm holding our son in my lap, going home to our house in Massachusetts, going home to a new life. Can it have been over seventy years?*

Lois stood up as best she could, stretched to her straightest bent over height of five foot six. High time to give myself up, she thought. She stepped deliberately on a floor joist and then another, like walking on railroad ties as she had as a child, now heading for the access panel to the downstairs bathroom. Suddenly, she missed a step, stepped too heavily where there was no railroad tie. The world gave way.

Students studying below heard a terrific crash that jostled the stacks of books nearby, knocking a couple of books down. A white shower of acoustical ceiling panel dust drifted down to the floor. Some of the young people ran to the spot where the crumpled body of an old woman lay splayed out on the carpeting, pieces of ceiling panel and broken metal support brackets littering her clothes. She had long white pigtail braids, porcelain face skin now flushed red in spots, and she was wearing tennis shoes, a fallen angel sprinkled with white angel's dust. They thought she was dead until one of them saw her gnarled fingers curling and releasing.

An older woman wearing a nametag pushed through the knot of students circled around the woman on the floor. She stood, open mouthed, her hair askew, just as the fallen woman came to consciousness and sat up, deliberately wiping chunks of debris off her shoulders and her blouse. When the woman in pigtails stood up and steadied herself, looking pretty good for someone who just fallen through the ceiling, the woman with the nametag stepped forward and put out her hand.

"I'm Margaret Dorris, head librarian at Bucks County Community College."

Lois shook her hand, then went back to brushing herself off.

"I am Lois, Lois Kenny," she said. "Pleased to meet you. I suspect we have some things to talk about."

"Follow me, please," Margaret said rather sternly.

The two women walked off, Margaret in the lead and Lois following a couple of steps behind, leaving the startled group of students to stare at the hole in roof and to dissect what had just happened.

"This way."

They went past the circulation desk, where Cathy Tan waved sheepishly to Margaret, toward the microfilm viewers on the front wall of the library and the entrance to two instructional classrooms. The far right hand door led to the Director's office.

"Come on in," Margaret said. She was pleased by the prospect of talking with someone older than herself. Margaret turned the light on, then straightened her skirt before sitting down behind her desk. She motioned for Lois to sit in the chair in front. Lois sat down gracefully, flecks of debris still peppering her hair and braids.

"Nice of you to drop in on us," Margaret deadpanned, just the faintest trace of a smile beginning to play at her lips.

Lois wasn't quite sure what to make of this unusual woman's manner. She knew she was in trouble. That much was clear. Beyond that, Lois sensed that as usual of late she had nothing left to lose.

"I didn't have any other invitations to the ball," she said. "There haven't been any gentleman callers around for a while . . ."

"Speaking of gentlemen," Margaret interrupted, "we arrested two thieves just the other day. You wouldn't know anything about that, would you? And about thousands of dollars of missing library equipment?" She laid her hands flat on the desk. As on her own hands, Lois noticed the age spots marking the other woman's skin.

"To be honest, Eddie and Andre aren't . . ."

"Is there any other way than being honest?" Margaret interrupted again.

"Andre and Eddie aren't thieves. They are just two guys who had nowhere else to go," Lois went on.

"So you know them I gather?"

Lois looked straight back, right into Margaret's eyes. "Of course I know them: I lived with them for weeks. They're my friends."

Margaret scratched her wig. "And now you want to be Clarence Darrow on their behalf?"

"They're my friends," Lois repeated. She shifted uncomfortably on her chair.

"Are you all right?"

"I do believe so. Just a little sore, that's all. I'm just not so young any more."

"I hear you sister," Margaret said, this time breaking into a smile. "What do you suggest that I do with you?"

"Give me a job in the library?" Lois offered.

"No can do."

"Adopt me?"

"I've already got a family."

"Well then," Lois said, "look how limited your options are." She too smiled. The two formidable women obviously had a grudging respect building for each other.

"Listen, Lois," Margaret said. "You could stay with my Harry and me for a few days until we sort things out. What would you think of that?"

Lois crossed her legs, looked for a window in the office, some way to see out and, finding none, set her hands palm down on the blue material covering her thighs.

"Where are Eddie and Andre now?"

"They're in the Newtown jail," Margaret said. "A roofer we had doing some repair work saw them and let us know. Apparently, he missed seeing you. They're being charged with all sorts of things."

"Such as?"

"Such as breaking and entering. Grand theft for another thing. You didn't help steal any of our equipment, did you?"

It wasn't stealing, Lois thought. "The guys had everything set up before I joined them. They only took what they needed to get by . . ."

"Somebody even left us a note," Margaret interrupted, "but we couldn't figure out who was taking everything. There were some pretty peeved librarians when their leftover food wasn't waiting for them the next day." She shot Lois a disapproving look. "Taking people's things isn't nice."

Lois sat up straighter in the office chair. "We felt badly about it, but we really didn't have any choice."

Ever tenacious, Margaret bore right in. "I've got a million questions for you, Lois, for instance how did you get up in the roof in the first place and how did you hook up with the two guys, but behind all my questions is another one. Namely, what am I going to do with you?"

Lois took her hands off her legs, folded them in her lap. Her brown eyes fixed on Margaret's gaze. "I think I should be with Andre and Eddie. They are my family now."

"Are you sure, Lois?" Margaret said kindly. Sure I'm the Library Director, she thought, but that doesn't mean I can't have a heart. This graceful elderly woman who sat before her now with floor dust and pieces of debris on her shoulders had fallen almost literally into her lap. Margaret felt a growing responsibility and bond. "You're more than welcome to stay with me."

"I don't want to be treated any differently than the guys."

"Suit yourself," Margaret said. She picked up her phone and dialed.

"I'm calling Security."

At the second ring, she hung up the phone.

"Please don't make me do this," Margaret pleaded. She looked directly into Lois' eyes, seeing the life behind them. "Come stay with Harry and me."

Lois acknowledged the genuine intent of the gesture. "Could I visit my two men?"

"Absolutely. We could bring them books and try to work this whole thing out somehow," Margaret said. "What's the sense of putting you in jail?"

Maybe I could do more to get them out from the outside, Lois thought. She stood up straight to her full five foot six height and offered her hand across the desk.

"You've got yourself a deal."

Margaret stood up from behind her desk, took the other woman's hand, and felt the warmth there.

They stood for a while, two women of 87 and 71 years of age, hand in hand.

# Chapter 12

## *Snow Falling on Cedars*

Margaret Dorris was enjoying her new role as facilitator of the discussion group. She only wished that Lois and Eddie and Andre would let her have more say in picking the novels to talk about. But this book pleased her. They've got a good one, she thought, and they picked it on their own.

"Lois and I can only visit for an hour," she said, "so we'd better get started."

Eddie had other ideas. "Can we talk about getting out of here before we get too deep into fantasyland?" He sat in his blue prison uniform on a cot on the opposite side of the cell from Andre who sat next to Lois on his cot, wearing the same type of uniform. Andre ran his fingers through his thick brown hair.

"Yea, when do we get out of here?"

Margaret paced in the middle of the cell. "Right now, you don't have anywhere else to go."

"They could stay with us too," Harry, who stood near Margaret and who had come along for the visit, said.

"There's still the matter of the charges," Margaret reminded him.

"Charges you're a part of," Andre reminded her.

"He's got you on a technicality Maggie," Harry said, his ruddy face showing a smile.

"As I was about to say," Lois harrumphed, "we are going to talk about *Snow Falling on Cedars*. Who wants to start the bidding?"

Eddie took his copy of the Guterson book out from under his pillow. "It's a beautiful book, wonderfully written," she said. "So artfully told."

"It's amazing it got on the best seller list," Andre said, "it's too good."

"The way the snowstorm blends in is beautifully done," Lois added from her seat on Andre's cot.

Andre said, "Sometimes good taste wins out. You never know."

Eddie couldn't shake the fact that he and Andre stood facing such serious charges, brought on behalf of the college by Newtown Township. His heart wasn't yet fully into talking about David Guterson's book. He hated his prison style clothing, longing instead for his own shorts or sweats, and he couldn't sleep worth a damn on the narrow jail cell cot. He just didn't fit.

"Say Mrs. Dorris," he said. "It's not as if your library won't get back all the things we borrowed. There's really no harm done, is there?"

Andre chimed in, "You could charge us rental fees on the video tapes we borrowed."

"Or overdue fines on any of the books we still had after we got found out!" Lois warmed to the task.

"And what's with all this reverse sexism in charging the men but treating me with kid gloves?" she added.

Harry looked bewildered by the questions. "One at a time," he said. "Give Maggie a chance to answer."

Margaret wore a dark business suit that contrasted with the silver of her newest wig. "Most of this is out of my hands. Newtown is pressing the charges now, even though the college is the injured party—because that's where the school is located. We'll just have to see how it all works out."

"Of course Maggie will do what she can," Harry added.

"May we?" Margaret asked Eddie. She gestured at his cot.

"Certainly," Eddie answered. He got up laboriously and moved to the end of his cot, making room for Margaret and Harry to sit down.

"Can we get back to *Snow Falling*?" Margaret wondered.

"It's a fine book," Eddie said. "A murder mystery that's so much more. David Guterson paints the island setting so well, and his characters are as real as your next door neighbor." Eddie looked over at Margaret and Harry, smiled at his cot mates. "Who is your favorite character?"

Before they could answer, Andre jumped in. "Hatsue is a great character: she's so real."

"I haven't read it," Harry said, "but Maggie tells me that the Ishmael character is a troubled dude but easy to empathize with."

"I'll buy that," Lois agreed. "but Kabuo Miyamoto is the character that interests me most. Here's this innocent Japanese man who's fought for this country in World War II, and now he's the victim of prejudice again as he stands trial for supposedly killing Carl Heine. Nearly everybody on San Pedro Island figures he's guilty because he's Japanese and because he doesn't offer explanations about how Carl drowned." Her voice rose to a higher pitch.

Andre looked over at her determined profile, saw dignity in her wrinkles and in her white locks. Like Eddie, he had grown to love Lois like a family member.

"Not everybody who is accused of something is guilty, that's for sure," Margaret said. "Even if they are guilty in a technical sense, sometimes there are overwhelmingly good reasons why they've done what they've done."

Harry reached over and held Margaret's hand, as if to console her.

> *Saturday night and I'm on my first date to the Junior Prom with Billy Vohlers. We're in his parent's car after the dance at George School and he wants to park at the lookout spot above the Schuylkill River in Fairmont Park. We're there, and everything is O.K. for awhile. We just talk and enjoy the nighttime view. There are cars parked nearby us.*

*Everyone has their headlights out. Billy moved toward me from the driver's seat. His mouth pressed hard against mine and his hands were on me, groping at my private places. Stop it Billy, please stop it. Stop now. But he wouldn't stop. He kept after me. Said come on Margaret. Come on, you know you want to. I tried the door handle, but he pulled my hand away. Climbed on top of me on my seat. He tore my blouse. Stop it Billy, please stop it now. He undid his belt and pants. You know you want to. No, I don't. Leave me alone. He tried to pull my skirt up, and I fought him. My brother. My brother Scott. He said he and his girlfriend Jane often came to the overlook after dances. Scott! Scott! Help me. Billy's pressing me back against the seat. Please stop. No. No. No. Help me Scott! I'm screaming. Big brother help me. Someone's at my door now, pounding at the window. It's Scott, thank God. Oh God, he sees what's going on. He's ripping the door open, pulling Billy off of me. They're fighting. God, they're fighting. Scott's face is red fury, and he's hitting Billy over and over on his head. They're outside the car while I'm pulling my clothes back into place, and my brother is pounding Billy into a bloody pulp. Oh God, Scott, thank you, but that's enough. That's enough. You're killing him. I jumped out of the car on unsteady feet, tried to pull my brother off. But he had Billy by the throat and wouldn't let go. Stop, Scott. You're killing him! But he wouldn't let go, and Billy's face was turning blue. Jesus, God, Scott, you've got to stop. Billy's eyes rolled back in his head, and all our lives changed forever. My brother defended me and ended up convicted of murder. I wanted to tell, but it was another time when rape stigmatized the victim even more than today, and Scott absolutely refused to let me say what really happened. Some lovers take poison for the other. My brother went to jail for me.*

Margaret held onto Harry's hand. Each knew what the other was thinking, though the rest of the group had no idea. The discussion went on, although, as usual, it strayed fairly quickly from the book to its readers.

"Kabu Miyamoto faces his accusers with so much dignity. He knows he's innocent," Lois said, "and that knowledge protects him from all the stones thrown his way."

Andre nodded. "You're right. There's a justness in knowing you are right no matter what anybody else thinks. There's an inner strength and an acceptance in Kabu that's missing in Ishmael. You've got that inner strength too, Lois. It's part of who you are."

Lois smiled at her friend. "Why, thank you, Andre."

"He's pretty smooth, isn't he babe?" Eddie asked.

"Not as smooth as you," Andre said.

"What is this, some kind of mutual admiration society?" Margaret teased.

"We like each other, if that's what you mean," Andre answered. "We get along pretty well."

"I'd say you must if you were able to coexist in such close quarters for that long," Harry added.

"But it was not always light," Andre said, pointing down to the floor. "There's darkness in us too. You can't come from dirt without dirt following you in your shoes."

Lois' face looked troubled: the lines in her forehead deepened. Her nostrils flared. Clearly, she wanted to move on.

"Sometimes we'd play a game to pass the time," Lois said. "We'd play 'try to be profound.' You just say whatever thing you can think of that sounds the most profound. The others help you or try to top what you've come up with." She looked across the small cell to where Harry and Margaret sat next to her beloved Eddie.

"Can we try it now?" Margaret asked. She sat up straighter on Eddie's cot, warming to the task.

"If you're willing to start the bidding," Lois said.

"How about some advice to cowboys: always speak your mind, but ride a fast horse."

"Not bad," Eddie said. "How's about this cowboy advice? Don't ever squat naked with your spurs on."

Andre stood up, laughing, his mood lightening, and moved to the center of the cell, as if to serve as ringmaster.

"If there's artificial intelligence, then there must be artificial stupidity," he added.

"Amen," Margaret said. "How about this? One nice thing about egomaniacs is that they don't talk about other people." Next to her, Harry's chest convulsed with laughter held in.

"Some people's ambition is never disturbed by reality," he chimed in.

"That's what happened to the prosecutor trying Kabu in *Snow Falling*," Margaret said, "reality disturbed his proof that Kabu murdered Carl Heine." How's that for tying things to the book, she thought to herself.

Andre, still standing, pointed to Eddie, as if to direct the game and say you're next. Eddie's body dwarfed Margaret and Harry next to him: the span of his blue uniform equaled the width of both of them.

"I've got some political definitions," he said, a wicked grin spreading across his face. "A conservative is someone who believes nothing should be done for the first time."

"You go, son," Lois teased.

Eddie nodded toward his friend. "A liberal is someone with his mind open at both ends."

"Ain't that the truth," Andre agreed. "Think about this. In 1492, Columbus had no idea where he was going; he had a mutinous crew, and he depended entirely on borrowed money." Andre surveyed the cell for effect, looking at each seated person's eyes for attention. "Today, he'd be running for office!"

"Baa, da boom," Eddie said.

Harry couldn't resist. "Nothing in the world is so perfect that someone, somewhere won't hate it."

"Why so optimistic?" Lois wondered. "We should all try to be the kind of person our dog thinks we are," she said. "That's a good guide."

"I like it, babe," Eddie said. "Touché."

"Did you ever notice," Margaret asked, "that we're usually our most tolerant when it's our own mistakes we're forgiving?"

"Wow," Harry said.

"I'm sitting down after that one," Andre said, and he did.

"Listen," Margaret added, changing her whole tone. "We don't have a whole lot longer this visit. Don't you think we should talk about ways to get Andre and Eddie out of here?"

"Here, here," Lois said. "We need a plan."


No one talked about the darkness in Andre, Eddie, Margaret, Harry, and, to a lesser extent, Lois that day, nor for many days to come, but a plan did come to light. The plan.

# Chapter 13

It's amazing really. The things Margaret Dorris can do when she puts her full effort to the task. There I was, Eddie Couch, with my two friends, two of the three of us in jail and the other in some peril under the law, and old Margaret just made it all go away, as if none of our illegal activities had ever happened. Not only that. She upped the ante. She got us a National Endowment for the Humanities grant to lead book discussions at a Bucks County library. Imagine that! Andre and I were released just the other day, and, along with Lois, we're staying with Harry and Margaret for awhile. It's amazing the way it's all fallen into place. Margaret called every official with clout in Bucks County, the way Harry told it, and she called in the few favors she had left to call in after years of rather radical or at least unintimidated behavior. She put her titanic will up against those at the college who wanted to prosecute us and against the township police who were doing the same. Her will won. I suspect, privately, that nobody dared to get on Margaret's bad side, that the powers-that-be caved in for no more elaborate reason than that. Whatever the reason, I sure am grateful. It's nice to be cared for by somebody who is not family or friends, like the Killians or Andre and Lois. You expect your friends and family to care. But not a stranger.

*It's Saturday night and Dad's just home from the bar and all tuned up. And suddenly everything's my fault. "You never listen," he's saying. "You stupid son of a bitch. Come here right now and listen to me. That's right. I said stand in front of me right this damned second. Who the hell do you think you are, kid? I said stand right here. Wipe that smirk off your face. You smart ass."* And then he's hitting me around my head with closed fists, pounding me, and I can't hit back. Won't hit back. I won't do what he does. I taste blood in my mouth. My ears are ringing with pain. He won't stop, the son of a bitch. *"Don't just stand there,"* he's saying. *"Fight back."* How do you fight back against your father? How do you fight back against something that makes no sense? My ears ring, my face burns, he's hitting me, and it happened all the time. Until I moved out. Some things you never forget.

When a stranger goes to bat for you, it feels pretty good. When life surprises you that way, it gives you a reason to go on. And believe you me, there have been times when I've been looking for a reason to go on. It was a new start for Andre and me, especially, but in a sense a new start for Lois too, as much as an 87 year old can have a fresh start. Often, it's all about starting over. It's scary but exciting too, all these remakings of ourselves. Our private selves revealed over and over, changing with the birdcall sounds of the dawns and the darks.

So we began anew. The first thing that happened was that we all had to learn to live together. Our first morning together, Lois was up before everyone else, and, when I got to Margaret and Harry's kitchen, she'd already cooked a big high cholesterol breakfast for everybody. Bacon, eggs, sausage, the whole bit. What smelled like Dunkin Donuts coffee. Soon, Andre padded out wearing a long green Eagles nightshirt over his blue jeans, and Harry and Margaret followed a few moments later. It was the first time I'd seen Margaret without her wig: her real hair was a close cropped dark brown peppered with gray, and she had on a red flannel nightgown.

"Morning everybody," she said cheerily. "I see Lois has been busy. Did you find everything you needed, dear?"

"No problem," Lois said. She had long ago taken care of her toiletry and had already braided her long hair.

"Looks like our hearts might be getting clogged," Harry observed.

Lois, as always, said what she felt. "Hey, you two bought the stuff. It was all in your fridge. Don't blame the messenger for fatty food news."

"That's right, Harry," Margaret said. "Anyway, it's good to break from routine once in a while."

Andre sat down at the kitchen table. "Sounds good to me."

"Smells good to me," I added. "Thank you, chef babe."

We all sat down at Margaret and Harry's big pine kitchen table and ate a leisurely high calorie breakfast, making the kind of small talk that people make when they're really just getting to know each other, polite conversation interspersed with awkward silence.

"I've got a line on a job for you Andre," Harry said. "It's a delivery job for a place in northeast Philly. Pizza City. If you want it, the job could be a good complement to the library gig since that's only part time. Pizza City provides the truck."

"You sound like you're selling this job pretty hard. Do you get a cut, Harry?" I asked.

"I'll take it," Andre said. "Never lick a gift pizza delivery job in the mouth."

"Praise the lord and pass the sausage," Lois said. She got up from the table and began to clear the dishes.

"Come on Harry. Get your butt out of that chair and give her a hand," Margaret said. "It's the late nineties, remember?"

"Your wish is my command Maggie," Harry said, rising to help. He brought plates and cups to the sink until the table was nearly cleared, leaving only the coffee cups and spoons that the others were still using as they sat and talked. He joined Lois at the sink, finally, rolled up his sleeves, and began to help her wash dishes. Harry washed and Lois dried. As he handed her the wet dishes from the plastic tub in the sink, Harry noticed Lois' hands. They were hands of character, he thought, wrinkled hands with dark age spots and skin worn thin on the backs, to be sure, but they were strong hands. She took the wet dishes from him with a firm grasp, dried them efficiently with her towel.

"Come on and sit with us you two," Andre called after a while.

"Yes, come sit down," I agreed. "You two are putting us to shame."

Our two helpers finished the dishes, then rejoined us at the table. Harry pulled Lois' chair out for her with a flourish, and, after she sat down gracefully, he pushed her chair in close to the table.

"Mochas gracias," she said smiling. Lois looked to Margaret. "So where's our first library gig?"

"They're all going to be at the Wrightstown Library. What would you folks think of using Steinbeck's *The Grapes of Wrath* for a first book to talk about?" Margaret looked around the table for a response.

"You can't get a much better author than John Steinbeck," I said. "But what about doing *Cannery Row*? That one gets overlooked."

Andre slapped his open palms on the table in approval. "Yeah, *Cannery Row* would be perfect!"

"Mack and the boys it is," Lois agreed.

"To Steinbeck," Margaret said, raising her coffee cup in a toast.

We raised our cups too. "To John Steinbeck." Everyone but Harry joined the toast. I thought I heard him mutter, "Steinbeck sucks" under his breath.

Shortly after, we all got up from Margaret and Harry's table, and, after putting the last cups and spoons in the sink, we more or less went our separate ways to different places in Margaret's house. Lois and Margaret went to the living room to talk, while Andre went back to the spare bedroom he and I were sharing temporarily. Harry and I went outside to chop some firewood as Margaret had asked.

Outside their house, Harry showed me their woodpile. A big stack of firewood lay next to the garage almost touching its side wall. Rounds of clean yellow Douglas fir, solid and sawed but not split, waited for our axes. Harry went around to the front of the garage, raised the door, and, a moment later, emerged with a splitting maul and a small hand axe.

"Here ya go, Eddie," he said, handing me the heavy maul. "You're younger than I."

I held the maul in front of me and inspected it. Its blade was tapered like an axe but weighted like a sledgehammer. The whole thing, handle and all, looked well-used but still serviceable. I tested the heft of the handle as I moved to the jumbled pile of fir rounds.

"I might need some help, Harry. I haven't done this since Boy Scout camp over twenty years ago."

"Just like riding a bike," Harry said, laughing sardonically.

I shifted a wood round with the toe of my boot. I addressed the log, then choked up on the handle of the maul, and swung it in an overhead motion. The blade came down in the center of the bright, clean log, and there was a satisfying dry popping thud. The log fell neatly in two halves, split by the edge and the weight of the maul.

"That's the way to do it Eddie!" Harry said encouragingly.

"Not bad for a fat man," I said and then tipped one of the newly split half-rounds up on end and snapped the maul down into it as if I'd been doing nothing else for years. The wood parted as neatly as if it had been cut by a laser.

"Look at the grain on that," Harry admired. The straight grain of the newly exposed wood was soft white gold.

I tipped the other half-round on end and split it, then kicked the new fireplace length to one side with my toe. I was positioning the next full round when I sensed someone come up behind us. Harry turned around first.

"What's up, Maggie? Come to check up on us?"

Margaret had one of her wigs on, a new silver colored one, and she wore blue jeans and a sweater covered up by a pretty heavy coat she'd left unzipped.

"What the hell are you doing letting Eddie do all the work?" she asked Harry. Her gray eyes blazed with more than her usual intensity.

"I need the exercise," I said quickly.

"Yes, sweetheart, and I plan to help," Harry added.

"See that you do," she said, then turned back toward the house.

I adjusted a new log with my toe, then stepped back and addressed it, swinging the maul in a full overhead arc, enjoying the flex and seldom-used muscles of my body. A split opened in the log, but large slivers of wood still held, joining the two halves. I grimaced, irritated with myself. I bent over, turned up the two halves of the second log, and split each with a single, relatively easy stroke. I moved on to the next log, kicked it upright, and cracked it with two blows. I fell into a measured workman's rhythm, focusing on the physical task and letting everything else slide away save for an occasional exchange with Harry while he waited for his turn to spell me. It felt good to be outdoors, to be out of confinement in the library, and to be free.

# Chapter 14

## *Cannery Row*

Lois stood at the lectern in the small library dressed in a neat purple business suit borrowed from Margaret Dorris for the occasion.

"For me, the best scene in the whole book is the scene where Mac and the boys are sitting on a bench with their backs to the street. Maybe it's Labor Day or the Fourth of July, but, whatever it is, there's a big parade planned for Monterey, and the bands and marchers and floats start to parade down the main drag along Cannery Row. Not one of the gang even turns around to see. Not Mac. Not any of the boys. The whole damn parade goes by with all that hoopla, and the boys just sit on their bench with their backs to the street, making the same shorthand small talk as if nothing, as if no pageantry and pomp and circumstance, were passing just a few feet behind them. It's great. The whole scene shows how caught up in our own world view we all can be. How we have our own separate reality." She stepped out from behind the podium, moving amazingly spryly for her years. "What are some of your favorite parts?" She asked. A long, tense silence stretched on.

Finally, a gray-bearded man stood up from his folding metal chair among the semi-circle of a half-dozen other chairs and the occupants in the small audience who sat in them facing front. He wore a brown flannel shirt, and his expression showed that he was nervous about being there. "I've got one," he said with the voice timbre of a youngster. "I've got a favorite."

"It's the plot event of catching the frogs. You know, when Mac and the boys are desperate for ways to make money. They approach Doc, and he tells Mac that he'll pay a fair price by the dozen for all the frogs they can bring him at his lab."

Lois smiled. Behind her, Eddie, Andre and Margaret sat in their metal chairs, listening. "Do go on," she encouraged.

The distinguished looking older man continued, his voice growing stronger. "Mac knows about this pond that's loaded with frogs, but the catch is that the pond is on private property. As you'll no doubt recall, the boys, with Mac as ringleader, hatch a plan. They borrow a Model T truck from the local Chinese grocery man on the promise that he'll get a fair share of the frogs too, and the gang sets off at night with flashlights and nets and buckets to sneak up on the pond under cover of darkness."

Lois moved back to her folding chair, sat down, then crossed her legs, nodding her head approvingly. "Everything goes off without a hitch," she agreed. "Well, almost everything. The bottom line is that the poor frogs never knew what hit them."

"Yes," the bearded man said, "the boys wade into the shallow pond in a line with their nets and sweep across the water, netting hundreds and hundreds of frogs by the time they've reached the opposite side. It's a veritable massacre, and their buckets get overloaded with manic frogs..."

"There you are," Margaret joined in. "The Model T is one overloaded frog taxi as Mac and the gang make their way back to town. It's quite a haul in frogs and frog dollars."

Someone else in the small audience in the library stood up, a teenaged girl with a long brown ponytail who was dressed in military fatigue pants and a green top. She stood decisively and spoke in a high, reedy voice.

"I felt badly for the frogs. For the ones the boys had taken away from the pond and for the frogs left behind. They all must have missed their friends and family. I mean I know they're only frogs and all, but family and friends are family and friends. Nobody looks at it from the frog's point of view."

Rather suddenly, Lois got up again, moved in a brisk purple blur to the lectern.

"What a sensitive thing to notice, young lady," she said. "Not many people would think about the frogs being lonely. I'm not sure that's what Steinbeck intended for us to think about, but so what? Your idea is a good example of how open-ended strong literature can be, of how many different views of the same events there can be."

The young lady sat down, nodded her head in acknowledgment toward Lois.

Lois decided to take a chance.

"In the spirit of multiple interpretations of literature, let me tell you a little bit about loneliness. I'm no expert, no more than you folks, except that I've lived a lot longer than most of you and a little longer than one of you in front of me and one of you behind me." She looked at the man in the beard who had spoken earlier, and then Lois turned back around to the audience in front.

"As I say, I'm no expert, but I know a little bit about loneliness. That sounds strange coming from someone who had as many kids as I did, who had such a big family, but, in some ways, the more you've had, the more you stand to lose.

"It's a terribly difficult thing for a parent to outlive her child, worse still to outlive several of your kids, to outlive your friends, all your neighbors and people you knew. You begin to wonder why you've been chosen to persevere. I've read that it's called survivor's guilt, but, whatever you call it, someone as old as I am, who has been as blessed as I have been with a long life and good health, someone like me can't help wondering why they've been so lucky when so many people they love have been taken away. It just doesn't make sense sometimes."

The people sitting in the small semi-circle in front of Lois listened intently. The older man in the beard leaned forward in his metal chair, waiting for her to go on, to tell it all the way through.

Lois smoothed a crease out of her borrowed purple pant suit. She stood almost perfectly upright, her posture like a much younger person's.

"On the one hand, there's the desire to live on and on, to go on as long and as well as you can. There's that strong life force driving you on. But when so many of your loved ones are gone, it's hard. Sometimes you feel like quitting, just going to sleep and not waking up. That love of life stays in you, though, even when you're old, even then it can flicker and burn to full flame and keep you going. It's amazing really, how, just when you think there's no reason to go on, something pushes you forward."

Lois sensed someone rising behind her. Before she could turn around, Margaret stood by her shoulder.

"I know exactly what you mean," she said. "When I was younger, I dated a fellow all the way through college. We were engaged and looked forward to living our lives together. Like just about all young lovers, we thought we were forever. But fate intervened. My beau was killed in a car accident. The other driver didn't even stop."

Margaret paused to swallow hard. She looked around to the others behind her for support.

"So at twenty one I started out all over again from what I thought was ground zero. Anyway," Margaret said, "I know what Lois and this fine young lady mean about loneliness. I know whereof they speak."

Lois reached over to touch Margaret's shoulder. The two women exchanged a knowing glance.

"We've all struggled with loneliness in our lives," Andre said from behind them. It's one thing that makes us all the same."

"Amen," Eddie said. He reached over to where Andre was seated next to him and patted his friend on the back.

"I don't think we're far off track," Lois said. "Part of **Cannery Row** is about loneliness. Doc's lonely. Mac is too despite having the boys as his friends."

*Charles is off to war. Not married even six months yet and he's gone off to Europe to help end all wars. A letter came last month with some pictures my Charles took. He'd been in the battle of Verdun and survived somehow. He writes about the bodies falling everywhere, about stopping the fighting sometimes to drag the bodies off the field so the fighting could go on. I had to turn my head away from the pictures the first time I looked. But when I looked again, I couldn't take my eyes off the dark shapes of bodies on the snowy ground. Another letter came today. Charles has been shot, but is alive and writing me. A sniper's bullet hit him in the head but it was a grazing blow and he had his helmet on. He's in the hospital with a concussion, but when he's better they're going to send him home. Home! He's coming home. Home to the rest of our lives.*

# Chapter 15

## *Pizza City*

Andre started the truck's engine. It came to life quickly, then settled into a steady idle beat. He looked in the left side mirror outside the truck. Andre was surprised to see his own reflection looking back. Not so bad for fifty two, for a man who'd spent a good deal of his life homeless, he thought: his hair was still thick, his eyes clear, the set in his jaw line strong. More importantly, Andre saw past his reflection that the way was clear. He put the truck in drive and pulled away from the neon lit glass front face of the Pizza City store with its red Pizza City lettering. Behind him, in the bed of the Pizza City pickup, a stainless steel oven stood bolted upright. A propane tank and burner kept the pizzas hot while he made his deliveries. His route was all over northeast Philadelphia, neighborhood after neighborhood of brick row homes and the pizza ordering owners who inhabited them. This night, his deliveries were mostly near the regional airport in the Morrell Park and Cromwell Heights area. He drove out of the Academy Plaza Shopping Center and turned right on Liberty Bell Drive, then made another right onto Cromwell Street. Andre was a nearly lifelong Bucks Countian, but he'd learned this new area well in his first two weeks driving.

He turned left off of Cromwell onto a little cul de sac named Woburn Place, watching the address numbers for 10202. He found the right row—house, pulled into the driveway, and put the truck in park, leaving the engine running. Andre got out of the cab, stretched out his legs and walked to the oven in the back of the pickup truck. He swung the chrome burner door open and pulled two boxed pies off the rack. The boxes were quite warm in his hands. He bounded up the concrete steps to the front door, found the doorbell, then rang it. Immediately, two dogs started barking on the other side of the screened and wooden doors.

Oh boy, he thought. I could get chewed up on this one. Most of the time, dogs and deliveries were bad news. The barking quieted and first the heavier door swung open. An attractive woman who looked to be about in her mid-forties opened the screened door. He noticed her face was a pleasant oval shape, and she had blue eyes with nearly flawless skin. Her hair was cut pretty short and was light brown with traces of red. She held back two dogs, a yellow Labrador who strained against her grip on its collar and a seemingly better behaved shepherd mix that didn't pull against the lady's grasp on its collar.

"It's $14.95 for the two pies," Andre said.

The lady relaxed her grip on the shepherd, reached over to take her handbag off her opposite side shoulder. "I'm Pat Killian," she said warmly. "You wouldn't happen to be Andre, would you?"

He was stunned. Andre handed her the two pizza boxes while she fiddled with her purse. "I sure am," he said. "How did you know that?"

"My whole family are friends with your pal Eddie Couch," she said. "He called when you got this job. Said you'd be working in the neighborhood and to try to say hi sometime. "We've been ordering from Pizza City every few days for the last two weeks, but, until now, it's always been a different driver. So, I'm pleased to meet you." She reached out her hand, no small task while holding back a dog and holding two pizzas.

Eddie shook her hand. It was soft and warm to the touch.

"Can't you come in for a minute to meet the rest of the family?"

He considered. "I suppose I could, just for a little while," he said. "Let me shut off the truck."

She gave him $30 and a certain look that clearly told him he was expected to keep the change.

Andre went out to the truck's cab, shut off the engine, then bounded back up the stairs. Pat Killian was waiting to let him in. She held the door open.

Inside and up a couple of carpeted steps, the Killian row home opened to a big living room. The front wall was mirrored except on the left where an open staircase led upward. A big television sat dead center on the floor in front of the mirrors. On the street side of the living room sat a sofa, and there was another matching green one to the right. Perched on that sofa, a good sized blonde man smiled, then got up and extended his hand.

"I'm Andy, Andy Ferazua," he said. "Pat kept her maiden name. Can we get you anything to drink?"

Pat Killian took the pizzas out to the kitchen. Andy motioned for Andre to sit beside him.

"No thanks. I can't stay long," Andre answered.

"How long have you known our Eddie?" Andy asked. "When we were losing Pat's parents, Eddie was there for us. He was more than a good friend. He was a rock. That man would not only give you the shirt off his back but his back as well and his shoes too if you wanted them."

Pat came back into the room, and, seeing that Andre was still standing, said "Sure you won't sit down with us?"

"Can't stay long mam. I'm working for the man. Got to deliver the dough to make the dough, if you know what I mean."

A broad smile spread across Andy's face. "I like that."

"What's not to like?" Andre kidded.

Pat Killian sat next to her husband.

Andre could sense the genuine affection there.

There was a knock at the door.

Before Andy got up to answer it, Andre said "I can get it if you don't mind."

"Thanks," Pat said as Andre moved to the door.

He was surprised to see a priest standing outside the Killian's screen door.

Andre stared at the man's white clerical collar.

"Mr. Killian?" the priest asked in a pleasant tone. "I've come to bless the house." Before Andre could answer, Pat Killian was at his side.

"He's a friend of ours, Father," Pat said. "Won't you come in? This is Andre."

The two men shook hands.

Andre looked over to Andy, who had gotten up and come over to the landing where the others stood. "Father, I'm Andy Ferazua," he said. "Pleased to meet you." He offered his hand as well.

"I'm sorry to do it," Andre said, "but I've got to go. That's my pizza delivery truck outside, and I'm running late. Good to meet you, Father."

"Father Greg," the priest said. "Are you sure you can't stay and be blessed too?"

"Don't think I'm worthy of being blessed," he stammered, rushing now.

"I've really got to go," Andre said. "It was great to meet you," he said to Andy and Pat. "I'll surely tell Eddie about this. Hope to see you again sometime."

With that, Andre was out the door. Inside, the blessing began.

Outside, back in his Pizza City truck, Andre pulled away from the Killian's street. Good people, he thought. He rounded the corner, got back out on Academy Road and headed south toward his next delivery. Good people, but by the time they get to those pizzas they'll be cold, he chuckled. Oh well, that's what microwaves are for.

Traffic was light at that hour, and, before long, Andre had made his way to Route 1 South and had turned off at Oxford Circle. He searched the addresses on a side street for the one written down on his notepad. He found the right house after a time and pulled his truck up to the curb in front. The neighborhood was run down and old; he was a little apprehensive to be there. Andre shut off the engine, got out of the cab and went around the back of the pickup to the pizza oven. As he took out the three hot pizza boxes, he felt a vague sense of foreboding but dismissed it as ridiculous. He carried the pizzas toward the row house door. There were footsteps behind him then. No mistaking them. He started to turn around.

"Don't," an angry voice snarled. "It's better if you don't see us."

Andre turned around anyway to see two teenagers, one white and one black, coming at him. The young white man's face contorted, his lips curling as he raised his arm. He had a short wooden club in his hand.

Andre tried to get his arm up in front of his face to shield the blow, but he was too late. The club came down across the side of his head with a crack, and, instantly, everything went to black as he crumpled to the cement, the pizza boxes flying up high in the air before falling to the ground.

"Roll him over and check his pockets," the white kid said. While his partner began to check Andre for money, the kid with the club went to the Pizza City truck and started searching the cab for cash.

"He's only got $38 on him," the young black man reported.

"There's only a little bit more than that in here," the instigator hollered back from the truck. "Let's grab it and get the hell out of here."

The other kid rolled Andre over on his back, then walked quickly back toward the pickup truck. After a quick conference there, the two of them were gone, running off down the side street.

Andre lay face up below the leaden sky, his eyes closed. A trickle of blood ran from his mouth. For a good ten minutes, none of the row house doors of Oxford Circle opened, until, finally, an older couple who had ordered pizza opened their door and walked out to examine Andre, then went quickly back inside to summon help.

# Chapter 16

## *The Way It Was*

### Lois

*I*'ve seen the world change so much in my years. My parents took a trip down the east coast in a horse-drawn buggy with four of us kids in the eighteen nineties. A horse drawn buggy! Now, some of my great grandkids get upset when the microwave takes too long to cook their frozen pizza. Automobiles were invented before I was born, but we never saw one until 1911 when our neighbors the Albertsons bought a model A Ford. The First World War was just starting then, and, when Mr. Albertson went off to war, Mrs. Albertson had to sell the car. I've seen airplanes come to be. The telephone. Television. And the one constant in all of it is that people are people, no matter what the technology. Human nature is human nature. People don't change much. What drove people 100 years ago, 500 years ago is nearly the same as now. People want to feel in control. They want to acquire things. Maybe most of all they want to procreate, to pass their gene pool on and on to live for the ages.

And the truth drives people too. Sometimes the quest to know the truth about anything moves people to do strange things. That can get bridges built, planets discovered, or people to come together in love. If you live long enough, patterns in the way people are begin to stand out like contours on a relief map. You can see what they are, these people, even some of why they are what they are. The *perspective always comes easier when it's applied to other people, but some of what we see in the others we have to apply to ourselves also. And the truth can hurt too. Lots of times truth comes to us before we're ready to face it, like a forgotten appointment showing up at your door at 6 am. I have faced this: we learn from history that we did not learn from history. Why else would we still go to war?*

*It seems people have changed in one way. They are more impatient than ever. If it sticks, force it. If it jams, bang it. If it breaks . . . well, it needed to be replaced anyway. One of the things that hasn't changed is that men still don't do their fair share of housework. Women still get stuck with most of it, even when they're working. And housework is what nobody notices unless it isn't done.*

*Even my Charles did less than his share of the housework, although you could attribute that to the sexism of the times. But things were good anyway with us. We started out totally infatuated with each other, totally in lust and then love, and we built from there.*

*Before Charles came into my life, there was another gentleman caller. A guy named Bill Evans who moved to Duxbury from west Texas. He brought his boots and wild dancing and Stetson hat with him all the way to Massachusetts. Came calling at my parent's house a few days after he joined us at Duxbury High and had singled me out to say hello. He stood there in my parent's doorway, a crooked grin spreading across his brown face, and asked my father is he could "speak to Miss Lois Kenny." I heard his smooth drawl all the way from the parlor.*

*"Lois isn't accustomed to men callers. Whom shall I say is here?" I heard my father ask.*

*"Mr. Bill Evans of Texas," he answered.*

*"Well, Mr. Evans, I'll go see if Lois wishes to see you," my father said. When he came to tell me I had a visitor, a Mr. Bill Evans, my father winked at me. Then he went upstairs and left me alone to go to the front door.*

*Mr. Bill Evans just wanted to talk, but, like most smart men, he knew that good talking is the best way to wheedle your way into a woman's heart. And he tried to talk his way in. Tried for weeks* and months. Before Charles came along, I even did the unheard of for a young Duxbury lady. It was a scandal around home for some time. I ran away with Bill Evans for a whole week! Just up and snuck out one night and went on the road with Bill and his borrowed, without permission, yellow buggy and his father's borrowed, without permission, horse. It was spring break at the high school, so we didn't miss any school, but we sure infuriated almost everybody I knew. Especially father. Somehow, Bill had saved up thirty dollars, so we did it up right. Rode that yellow buggy south along the coastline from town to town, all the way to Providence, Rhode Island before we turned around. We'd ride all day, talking, sightseeing, occasionally stopping for something to eat or a bathroom. Then at night Bill would get us a hotel, separate rooms of course, and in the morning we'd meet to have breakfast at the hotel, and then we'd be off again.

Bill had this harmonica he'd play, and he wasn't too good. He played "Pop Goes the Weasel" and other songs he remembered from his childhood, but he missed more than a few notes.

One morning as we rode along the green ocean side on a dirt road with wispy clouds hanging over the rolling water, he told me, "I used to be able to play better. I haven't been practicing."

"Did you ever really practice it, the harmonica?" I asked from next to him on the buggy's rocking seat.

"Nope, but I think about practicing sometimes. That ought to count for something, ought to make me better somehow."

He went back to playing, then stopped to look at the harmonica. "This here's a working man's harp. It's my only one, and it's in the key of E. I heard somewhere that the key of E is the people's key, the most democratic one. Now you'd think a working man's harmonica would just naturally want to play 'Pop Goes the Weasel' without any help from me, wouldn't you?"

I held my wicker food basket on my lap with both hands.

Bill slapped the harmonica on his hand to clear the spit. "Say girl, don't you know how to sing along?" he wondered.

"I'm just concentrating on listening."

Bill started clapping his hands and singing, "All around the carpenter's bench . . ." He picked up the harmonica and played the tune again, bobbing his head and stamping his boots. The horse's reins lay between us on the buggy's seat, but our horse didn't need any guidance.

The sun climbed higher over the water as we rolled along the coastal road. The song over, Bill stuck the harmonica in his breast pocket. "You know, there's something about that song . . . something. It isn't really a children's song at all when you think about it. Every since I was about five years old, I've been trying to figure out who's really doing the chasing. Because they're moving in a circle like that, who says the monkey's after the weasel? Maybe it's the other way around. More than that, who the heck is the carpenter and what is he . . ."

"Or maybe even she," I interrupted.

"Right," he continued. "What the heck is he or she building? That's what I keep wondering. And where's the carpenter off to, leaving the tools just lying there while all this running around is taking place? Maybe the carpenter is sitting cross-legged on the bench watching all the commotion below him. The weasel makes some kind of sense, but I never figured out why a carpenter would have a monkey in his shop. Never understood that. Are you getting tired of hearing all this nonsense, Lois?"

I turned my attention away from the road in front of us. "I'm fine. I've never been happier." I meant what I said then, although it's hard to believe it all these years later.

There was serious hell to pay when we got back. But I didn't care. It was worth it. Somebody once told me if at first you don't succeed, then destroy all the evidence that you even tried. But that was impossible for Bill Evans and me. After all, we'd been missing together for a week. It wasn't worth the effort to try to cover that up, so we decided to tell the truth. All of it.

When our buggy pulled up in front of my parent's house back in Duxbury, Bill tied the horse to our big Cypress tree along the road and where our front lawn began. He obviously meant to come in with me. I put my hand on his arm.

"I don't think this is such a good idea, Bill. I think I should go in alone. You go home and hope for the best, and we'll talk soon."

*I'd barely gotten the words out of my mouth when my father and mother came running out of the house. I guessed that they'd been watching from the front windows.*

*My mother and father's arms were around me. "Thank God you're back," my mother cried. "We were worried to death."*

*My father gave Bill a stern look. "I strongly suggest that you get home to show your parents that you're O.K., young man. After that, we'll have some serious talking to do."*

*My parents pulled me along toward our front door. From over my shoulder, I saw Bill untying the horse and then climbing in our purloined buggy. He began to ride away, looking forlorn. I turned to my father.*

*"I swear, Daddy, he never touched me. Not once."*

*"He better not have," was all my father said then, "or I'll kill him."*

*"Amen," Mom said.*

*As went inside the familiar house, I knew I'd be grounded forever, but it had been worth it.*

*A few years later, I knew Charles was the one for me when I told him all about the adventure with Bill Evans and the consequences, and he just accepted it all. Love is like that. The Bible is right about that. Love is patient, kind, never jealous. Our saving grace.*

## Chapter 17

### *The Grapes of Wrath*

Andre awoke to muted sunshine in his eyes and two paramedics and a policeman staring down at him. His head hurt and his vision was a little blurry, but he felt all right otherwise.

"Can you move your hands?" one of the paramedics asked him. "Can you feel your feet?"

"Yes, I feel fine."

"His blood pressure is good," the other one said. "He seems O. K., except for a lump on the head."

"I feel fine," Andre repeated.

"Did you get a look at who did this to you?" the policeman asked.

"Two kids who look a lot like any other kids. One white. One black. I really didn't get a very good look at them. Sorry."

"Do you want us to drive you to the hospital to get checked out more thoroughly?"

The cop added, "That might not be a bad idea. I could take a statement from you later."

"Just let me stand up and see how I feel," Andre said. "If I'm with it, I'll give you the statement right now. Besides, I've got to get this truck back to Pizza City. Later on tonight, I'm supposed to help lead a book discussion at a library."

When he stood up, Andre felt pretty good. He talked with the policeman for a while as the paramedics packed up. The elderly couple came out of their row house.

"Are you O. K.?" the woman asked. "We heard some shouting and then saw you lying on the ground, but we were afraid to come out at first. So we just waited, then telephoned for help."

"Yea, we hope you're all right," her husband added. "We don't want anything bad to happen to anybody."

"I'm good. Thanks for calling," Andre said.

He finished the interview with the cop as the older couple went back inside. "If that's it, I really should be going," Andre said. "Thank so much for your concern and your help."

"We'll call you if we get any leads," the policeman said. "But I wouldn't hold my breath."

By that evening, Andre had a wicked headache that took four Motrin to begin to quell.


Margaret Dorris started the bidding from up at the wooden podium. "*The Grapes of Wrath* is Steinbeck's masterpiece. Maybe we should try to figure out why."

A woman in the audience at the Wrightstown library raised her hand.

"No need to raise hands," Eddie said from his seat near Margaret, Andre, Lois and Harry. "Just jump right in. We don't stand on ceremony here."

The woman in the green dress jumped in, hands down. "I just wanted to say that *The Grapes of Wrath* is such a good book because it's about human struggle and being a displaced person and migration and hopes for a better life in a new land."

Eddie uncrossed his short legs, stretched. He noticed that the woman was attractive, and, from what she'd just said, obviously smart.

"Woo Nellie," Margaret said. "You've just put your finger on some important aspects of Steinbeck's book. Let's zero in on some of what you've said and discuss.

"Consider the idea of being displaced. How many of us have been physically displaced like the Joad family or at least felt displaced at some point in our lives?"

Several hands in the small audience went up.

Andre surveyed the old library that had once been a two room schoolhouse at the turn of the century. The inside walls, plastered over, and most recently painted with beige, gave the library a warm look. Andre and his partners faced the largest open room set with folding metal chairs for the group. Behind the discussion leaders were the holdings, upright shelves crowded with unrelated books of all kinds. The original oak card catalogue still stood nearby the circulation desk in the smaller room. No computers needed here, Andre thought. His head still hurt. The artificial light stung his eyes, and all afternoon and early evening he questioned the wisdom of delivering pizzas in the city.

Andre nodded to an older man in the back row of metal chairs.

The distinguished looking fellow had on a checkered western shirt and a string tie. "I think all of us have felt displaced," he said in his pleasing baritone, "and many of us have been actually displaced.

"When I moved here from northern California fifteen years ago, I felt like a stranger in a strange land. The pace of life is so shrill here, nearby Philadelphia and New York. I was just overwhelmed by all the people. I've gotten used to it now, but I imagine I felt a lot like the Joads when they got to the fruit picking fields in California."

"Well-said," Harry chimed in. Maybe if he's touched these people, Steinbeck doesn't exactly suck, Harry thought.

"Here, here," Margaret agreed. She nodded to an earnest-looking and pimply faced teenager who still had his hand up.

"On the idea that hopes for a better life motivate us, I think that's universal," he said. "The Joads have nothing left at home in the dust bowl, and all the stories of the better life in California fuel their optimism and make them want to drive across country in a funky old vehicle so they can have a chance at that better life. They see picking fruit, at least at first, as the way out of all their problems."

The young man stood up from his chair. "That's why I'm here too. To better myself, to hope for something better. I think that drives a lot of us."

Eddie stood up too, looking right at the young man's eyes. "What's your name son?"

"Justin, sir."

"Well, Justin, you keep thinking like that son, and I'm sure you're going to find that something better," Ed said kindly. He stood for a while longer, smiling at the boy, and then they both sat down.

Andre saw that the woman in the green dress had something else to say.

"Part of Steinbeck's point is also that our dreams can disappoint us. I mean just look at what happens when Tom Joad and company get out west. Everything's so political and difficult, from who gets picked to pick fruit, to the abuses by the bosses, to the company store charging outrageous prices to their captive audience. It's a real awakening for the Joads."

"Yes," Margaret agreed, "we're getting it. The book is about what moves us and about how what moves us can be bittersweet and disappoint us, and it's about going on anyway, about surviving disappointment and trying to make things better."

He's a raving socialist, Harry thought in private reverie.

Eddie pointed to a young woman who sat in the back by the older man who had spoken. "You look like you have something to say, young lady. What's your name?"

"I'm Cindy Waller," she said, standing up. She was tall with long brown hair and wore a peasant dress and sandals. "I'm a student at Bucks County Community College, and we read *The Grapes of Wrath* in our novel class. I wrote a paper about how the novel is picaresque, about how it moves from the Midwest all along Route 66 to California and how that journey mirrors the movement and emotional growth in the characters."

Margaret moved back from the podium and sat next to her beloved Harry. "Wow, that's a mouthful," she said as she sat down.

"Holy snapping turtles, you're not kidding," big Eddie agreed. "Can you elaborate?" he asked Cindy.

She looked at the assembled discussion leaders. "Sure, I'd be glad to.

"When the Joads give up their old way of life and everything that's been secure for them, they're taking a chance on the journey to what they hope will be a better life. But they know they're risking all their past, that the trip is a roll of the dice where they can win, lose or draw. My paper is all about how their journey is outward as they drive Route 66 but also inward as they all take a chance on discovering a new life and new things about themselves."

The older gentleman sitting near where Cindy stood commented, "That's a perceptive young lady."

All the way in the front, Andre heard and agreed, "You're not kidding." His mental haze began to lift.

Eddie lumbered up to the podium, pushing off lightly on the cane Harry leant him as he walked. He felt every exertion of chopping wood.

"What always amazes me when I read John Steinbeck is how well he knew the human heart. Faulkner talked about it in his Nobel Prize acceptance speech, but I think Steinbeck understood it even better. Sure, he has his political agenda, but in front of everything else is his understanding of our hopes and fears, of what makes us tick. John Steinbeck loves his characters, warts and all, and that love of people comes shining through in books like *The Grapes of Wrath*. The man flat out understood the human heart."

Lois smiled behind Eddie's broad back. The same could be said about you Eddie, she thought warmly. Your heart is as big as your body.

As the twilight faded outside the Wrightstown library, the sunset a wash of pink and purple turning to black, they talked on inside in the warmth of the building. Light from the historic library's windows leaked out into the black yaw of the night with first stars emerging above.

# Voices,
# Inner Chapter Three

*Isn't Love What We've Been Making?*

## Andre

When I was working for a time, before the tunnels and the campus, my life was pretty stable. Stability can be an illusion, though. Anyway, I had some things going right in my youth, just as I came to some right things with my newer friends.

I lived for a time in a room I rented from a good-looking young woman named Carrie Kirby. We were platonic roommates for a while. The Doylestown house was her parents' place that Carrie managed while she was in college, and I existed to help pay their bills while I worked and lusted after their grown daughter.

Carrie was a wild child those short months and that now distant year. She'd bring guys home late some Friday or Saturday nights, really late, after closing and the bum's rush time when I imagined taproom lights came on harshly and she chose partners. It was the '70's, a long time ago. I'd hear her and her chosen one going at it in her bedroom, upstairs, just across and down the hallway from where I suffered so in my own rented room. I always wished I was the chosen one. Friday and Saturday nights often played hell on my so-called sleep.

One weekend night, late again, as I dreamed half dreams of Carrie, I heard someone walking quietly in the hall. This time, it wasn't the boisterous noise and clatter of Carrie and her short term lover unlocking and then coming through the front door, up the wooden staircase brashly, then shutting her door as barrier to the thin Victorian walls. No. This time Carrie came for me.

She let herself in. "Move over, roomie, I'm needing some love," she cooed in the dark. I smelled the booze on her breath even before she crept in bed.

"Awake, Andre? Have a pulse?"

Her cool hands were on me. "Oooh," she teased. "You feel pretty well-hung. Do you know what to do with that thing?"

"I'll show you," I growled. "Teach you to crawl in my bed." I smelled the Captain Morgan, heard her measured breathing next to me.

"I own this bed," Carrie said. She rolled on top of me.

For one night, one long languid night, I was in 1970's heaven, ever the fool, imagining some 1970's and 1980's future between us, if I could just tame her, reform her, reform myself. I even imagined beyond.

We never slept together again.

By the next weekend, she was back at it again with some Doylestown Inn stranger, back to squealing and kissing and sex noises down the too close hall. What kind of idiot imagines himself in love after one stolen night in a rented room? But isn't love why we draw every breath? Isn't looking for love the only damn reason we're put here, on this earth, for? Wasn't love what Carrie Kirby and I had been making?

Hell no. What in the hell did I know as a young man? What the hell do I know now? It's Lois Kenny who knows. Lois knows.

# Chapter 18

## *Descent into Madness*

### Eddie

Just because it's still standing does not mean it isn't dead. That's what my mother, God rest her soul, used to say. One of her many Mama Couchisms. I think she meant that looks can be deceiving. She's buried in St. Dominic's off Frankford Avenue, but my father wants to move her to be closer to where he is and because he thinks there's not enough room in the family plots. I told him we've got four plots at St. Dominic's, and that only three will be used for the rest of the family, but he didn't seem satisfied with that, and I haven't heard from him since. That was some weeks ago. I've invited him to a couple of our book discussions, through word of mouth you know, but so far no dice. We'll have to talk about it later.

Just last night I was back with the gang at Dagwood's. It was the tenth anniversary of the place, and I wanted to time things so that we could give the bar a commemorative plaque for all the help they gave us in the Mom and Pop Killian golf outings and in the parties at Dagwood's afterwards. Pat Killian and her Andy were there, of course, as were all the brothers and their wives, and the Di Javon brothers too and the younger Killians' cousin Kathy and of course a ton of people for the anniversary party. You could safely say the place was packed. When it came time for me to present the plaque to the owner of the bar, Pat Killian had to stand up on a chair and holler to get everyone's attention.

She said, "Yo, everybody, listen up! My buddy Eddie Couch has something he wants to say on behalf of the Killian family. Listen up!"

The proverbial sea of faces at the downstairs bar at Dagwood's turned toward us. Somebody turned the music down a couple of notches. It was time for me to speak. Earlier, I'd tried to convince Pat to do it, but she and the brothers felt I should do the mini talk because I'd done so much work for the benefit every year. So there I was.

"When someone means so much to you, as Mom and Pop Killian did to all of us," I said, "then you do something to cherish their memory. If you've got a lot of money, you can do something spectacular, but when you don't, you can still do something from the heart. That's what the Mom and Pop golf outing and benefit are for us: something we do from our hearts to cherish the memory of Mom and Pop. And Dagwood's bar has helped us for seven years now. That's why we're back here again to honor that help," I continued, feeling a little nervous. I looked at the faces. Most were smiling, and, when I realized that, I felt better. I stood up a little straighter and stopped leaning on my borrowed cane, setting it against the bar instead.

"I've got this here plaque from the Killian family and from me, and in just a minute I'm going to give it to Ed, the owner here, but there's something I want to say first.

Let's all bow our heads for a moment. We all know Mom and Pop are smiling down on us from up in heaven, but let's take a moment to think about what we're doing here. We're honoring two people we love whom we lost, and we're honoring all the people here who love each other and who remember." I stood up even straighter. "Father, we offer you our prayer of thanks for all your blessings." Someone turned the music, a song called "Wind Beneath My Wings," down even lower. "And we ask from you that you help keep us all healthy and happy so we can continue to appreciate this beautiful world you've given us. Thank you, Lord, for letting us know Mom and Pop Killian, and thank you for everything you've given us."

Almost everybody at the downstairs bar clapped. Patty took a flash picture of Ed, Dagwood's owner, and the plaque and me, and then all the Killians and a lot of people at the bar clapped again.

Tony Di Javon laughed and yelled "Speech, speech!" and I hollered back, "That's all the speechifying you're gonna get from me." As the high school yearbooks often say, a good time was had by all that night.

So it goes, Vonnegut says. So my memories and my demons formed me. My fall from grace with Ellen, the affair, all my many failures.

We'd settled into a good routine, our book discussion group, all of us staying at Margaret and Harry's, at least for a while. A discussion offered every week at the Wrightstown Library, not too far from the community college, and all of it paid for by the National Endowment for the Humanities grant. Uncle Sam at work. Those were happy days. So why was it that my old problem cropped back up, came back with a renewed vengeance, just when I had so much reason to be cured?

It began with restlessness when I slept in my borrowed bed at Margaret and Harry's house. I'd toss and turn, never really sleeping deeply, and I'd get up to pee every hour or two. But that wasn't the half of it. I'd lie wide awake, trying to force myself to sleep, and the more I'd try, the more anxious I'd become. My mind ran full speed ahead, worrying about every imaginable problem, large and small and trivial and momentous, until I couldn't tell what was worth worrying about and what to let go. It got to the point where I couldn't sleep at all, and, if I did nod off momentarily, my sleep was nightmarish and disturbed. Once, Lois heard me calling out and came out of her borrowed bedroom next to mine to see what was wrong. It must have been after 3 am. She kept the light off, but I could see her looming over me, lit by the weak moonlight falling through my window. She had her hair down and flying around her head, and she wore her long pink nightgown.

"What's wrong sweet boy, what's wrong?" she wanted to know.

"I must have been dreaming. I didn't mean to wake you."

She smiled warmly. "Not to worry. Now what's the problem?"

I rolled over to face her, then reached for the tableside lamp's knob. My room brightened to a yellow glow. I saw Lois blink. "I haven't been sleeping. I can't seem to shut my mind down at night. Maybe it's the medication I'm taking: I am on a ton of antibiotics and a strong decongestant for the sinus infection I'm fighting . . ."

"Maybe it is the anti-depressants you're taking. Maybe it is something more," she said, concern written in the soft lines on her face.

"You know?"

"Andre told me a while ago."

"Would you have known something was up if he hadn't said?" I asked.

"You know me, Eddie. Of course I could tell you are fighting off some dark cloud. True friends always know."

"I should have figured, Babe, I should have told you a long time ago."

She held my hand. Her skin was warm to the touch.

Lois smiled her grandmotherly smile. "It doesn't matter. What matters is getting you better. You will get better, but you may have to face whatever it is that's dragging you down."

"Sounds good to me," I said. "Thanks for checking on me."

"Thank you for being the person you are, Eddie. You're a special man with a heart of gold." She bent over and kissed my clammy forehead with the softest brush of her lips. "Goodnight, big guy."

"Goodnight," I said, hearing her pad away out my door in her slippers.

I shut off the light. I heard echoes of Paul Simon in delirium.

> *"Why can't you sleep, sweet boy; sweet boy why can't you sleep?," I seem to hear Lois ask in a voice so soothing to the fevered brow of my burning psyche that it cools me on the spot of my previous infidelity, so soothing that is feels to me like floating in a rented glass-bottomed raft on a sandy-*

*bottomed river in the New Jersey Pine Barrens, so clear and so cool that I can see green water nymphs dancing on the tumbling always-moving downriver white and black pebbles above the rock and ever-flowing clearwater polished grains of crystalline, blonde sand, smooth fragments of polished stone, infinite fragments that are both smaller and larger than other perfect parts of the coherent whole fabric of nature, the molecules inside the hairy fibers, inside it all, woven parallel to and part of the larger whole cloth of warmth and certainty in the cold chaos, of the bigger picture, of the raw sense and composed pattern of it all, of the planned miniature ship inside the bottle God provides but makes so damn small, so damn small, the green nymphs dancing so simply, their invisible but real translucent wings beating in the stronger pulse and current so that, when I float over them, a clear, plastic bottomed dirigible appearing inverted and unlikely to the nymphs and piloted by a massive sleeping captain of non-industry, furthermore guided by the one who seldom sleeps except on water and with two mating crimson dragonflies entangled on his green Bavarian fedora, with his arms limp at his sides, his palms open to the dappled tree-cast sun spots that dance too on his rough hewn and sleeping inner hands. I don't sleep a lot, in case you're wondering, because, quite likely, we'll be dead a long time. I don't sleep a lot because of what I've done.*

The demons didn't come back until the following night, but, when they did, they did with a vengeance.

*Let it all go. Go to sleep, just let it go. But I'm afraid to drop off. Afraid I'll never wake up, never survive. My heart is racing. I feel like I can't breathe. I just keep thinking about how I need a car but can't afford one. Just keep thinking about thinking. Worrying about worrying. Thinking about worrying. Worrying about thinking. Thinking about worrying about thinking. Stop it Ed, just stop it. Relax. Breathe deeply, slowly. You've got to sleep. Let it all go. Just let it go. You'll drive yourself crazy unless you slow your mind down. Just sleep. Sleep. Drift away. Come on. You can do it. Shut it all down.*

But I couldn't let go. I spent another tortured night, replaying all the many failures in my life and all the things I should have done differently. When you're seeing through negative filters, your view of the world is distorted. My view that night was blue and purple. I couldn't see all the many positive things that should have kept me going. My beloved kids. The good times in my marriage. My teaching business techniques to people who wanted to learn. It was all invisible to me. I tried not to call out or moan as I flopped over and over in my borrowed bed, lest I bother Lois again. I crept quietly out once again to use the bathroom. I didn't want to wake her. When dawn came breaking through the window in harsh light, I got out of bed. I hadn't slept at all. My bare feet felt the cold touch of carpet. Looking down, I saw the white crescent of a toenail on the dark rug.

The day dragged on and on through yawns and the swirls and eddies of my confused thoughts. I don't remember much of it, but I remember hanging on until late night, when I could try to sleep again.

*God, here we go again. The wind is howling against the walls and window, and my mind is spinning around and around in a vortex of medication and anxiousness and paranoia. It's been more than two whole days, more than two whole nights. Please, God, let me sleep. The shingles on the roof must be blowing off. The window panes are rattling, but I've got to let it go. Instead, I see my father in the bleachers at a little league game. It's 5 to 4, and we Giants are behind, ninth inning, but my normally stern father smiles and waves to me as I swing two metal bats in the on deck circle. Billy Weiss is suddenly out on a ground ball to first; there's still one man on second and two outs now, and it's all on me. I take my place on the right side of the plate, batting left as he'd taught me. The ball looks small as hurtles toward me. I let it go. "Strike one!" the umpire yells. "No batter, no batter, no batter," the catcher sings as he throws the ball back. The next on is right down the middle. I lash as hard as I can. I crush the ball on the sweet spot of the bat's head and take off down the first base line, hearing my father yelling in joy. The ball tails right and over the fence but just to the right of the foul pole. Jack Power ahead of me trots back to second and I return to the plate. "He can't hit," the catcher chants. Their pitcher winds up and the ball is on its way but drops lower and lower, crossing the plate below my knees. I let it go. "Striikke three," the umpire yells, "you're outta here!" "But it was low!" I yell and argue, and, when he walks off, I kick dirt toward him with my spikes. "Sore loser," the catcher says. "Get a life," someone from my own bench hollers. Still I cannot sleep. Please, God, please. On the ride home, my father says nothing, doesn't play the radio, and the quiet tension is like a thunderstorm about to hit. I'm off to the bathroom in bare feet. Still no sleep. I've got to shut my mind down. Shut it down. Cover all this with softness. Dawn comes hard again.*

Lois and Andre are both at my bed and are talking, but for a moment I can't respond. Then the words come, "I'm O.K., I'm O.K. I'll be down in the kitchen in a few minutes. I'm O.K." The two of them, my friends, leave. I am most definitely not O.K. I cheated on my wife, my Ellen, with another woman so long ago. Or was it last year? I fell.

Somehow, I ride the crest of exhaustion and fake my way through another day, holding on again to the lifelong habitual promise of night through the high seas of daytime guilt and nonsense. It's as if my daytime life is some mad cartoon, not real. The evening came, as it always does, although I was surprised I'd lived to see it again. After saying goodnight to Margaret and Harry and the crew, I rode the magic carpet ride of my bed on toward oblivion again.

> *I cannot take it any more. My body and my mind cannot take it. Something has to give. My heart pounds, the pulse beats in my neck, and I am suffocating. All I can see is an endless parade of things wrong with my life. My tee shirt is soaked in sweat. My wife is screaming at me, "You stupid son-of-a-bitch, I loved you with all my heart, and you blew it all by never letting me do things my way!" I'm saying, "But we always do what you want. Almost always." She's not hearing. She's slamming the door, slamming the door on us and leaving. And it's all over. It's all over. It's all over. And I can't get my breath. Surely, my heart will explode. I can't control any of it any more. Can't make it through this night . . . but it's another tequila sunrise, and there's some blood and bile on my bedcovers. They're all standing beside my bed. All of them. Lois in her bathrobe, Andre in some borrowed p.j.s and looking concerned, Harry with a stubble of beard, and Margaret without her wig on and wearing a Japanese housecoat. "Come on sweet boy," Lois is saying," get out of bed and get dressed. You're going to the hospital." I fight through the sotted depths of my consciousness to try to force the word no, but I'm too far gone to respond appropriately. I am living in my cartoon. It is of my own making. I broke sacred marriage vows. Please, God, cover this. Cover all this with softness. Forgive.*

I remember nothing of the ride to the hospital, but, on the way out of Harry and Margaret's car, I remember Andre supporting me under one of my arms and Harry under the other. Lois and Margaret walked quickly ahead. I remember both women were dressed and made up as if it were a normal day. Margaret's best wig was carefully in place. Where had they found the time? My feet shuffled and sometimes dragged along the sidewalk as we came toward the white and red double doors to Saint Mary Medical Center's Emergency Room.

Two ladies at the reception desk greeted my entourage and me.

"I think he needs treatment," Andre told them.

"I know he needs treatment," Lois added more succinctly.

One of the ladies asked, "We'll need his insurance card. He can talk can't he?"

"I can talk," I said, gathering all the will I could, "but, but I'm not making a whole lotta sense."

"Let me help you with you wallet," Lois said, then reached into my back pocket. She produced my expired HMO card, relic from my teaching days, and handed it to one of the ladies at the desk.

A nurse in greens came over. "Sit here, please," she said, motioning to the chair by the reception desk. "Roll up your sleeve."

"How's his pulse?" Margaret asked after a moment.

"It's rapid and shallow. What are your symptoms?" the nurse asked me.

"I'm dizzy," I said. "I'm not breathing right." I looked to my Babe for help. "I'm not thinking clearly."

"Nurse," Lois said. "He hasn't slept for days. I don't think he can take much more."

"I understand," she answered. "But you will all have to wait in our waiting room until we call Mr. Couch back." And wait we did.

The sea of sitting faces began to spin around me. I reached out for Lois' hand and found it. She looked over from where she sat next to me and smiled reassuringly, the many fine lines on her face softening when she smiled as her skin tightened. Her brown eyes shone luminously, but then her face began to spin, too. Nausea. I closed my eyes. Time passed and Lois held my hand. When I looked around again, the others, my friends, were milling around the crowded waiting room. There weren't enough of the scalloped blue plastic chairs for everyone. I closed my eyes again to stop the room from becoming a merry-go-round. Time marched on. No idea of how long.

"Mr. Edward Couch," I heard as if someone was calling from way down a tunnel. "Mr. Couch," please come to the admittance desk.

I was up and walking somehow, my friends surrounding me.

"You will all have to stay here," another nurse said. "Mr. Couch has to go back alone, but we'll keep the family informed of his treatment."

First Lois and then Margaret kissed my cheek.

"See you soon, big guy," Andre said.

This nurse took me back into the Emergency Room, supporting me along the way under my right arm. We went past people on stretchers in the hallway, past rooms with their curtains drawn and with muffled voices inside, until we came to a little room with its curtain drawn back open.

She gave me a weak smile, then handed me a flimsy gown. "Sit on the bed please," she said, "and take off all your clothes except for your underwear. Your shoes can go on the chair here with the clothes." Still the cartoon played on.

She left, pulling the curtain shut. My head spun as I struggled to get undressed and into the gown. I was just fumbling with the awkward ties in the back when a young doctor pulled back the pink curtain and came into the room.

"I'm Dr. Chris Alyub," he said, looking at the chart on the clipboard in his hands. He had dark hair and wore glasses, and, when he looked up from my chart, his expression seemed one of genuine compassion.

"So you're dizzy and confused?" he asked.

"Yes, sir."

"You don't need to call me sir. We're going to start an I.V. to get some fluids in you, and then I want blood work, an EKG and a CAT scan of your brain. Sound O.K.?"

"Yes, sir," I answered. "I mean yes." It was an effort to form the words. Another lady came in just before Dr. Alyub left my room. She asked me to lie down, then started the I.V. in my right arm and drew blood from my left. "We'll be back soon," she said. "There's a button on this cord on your bed. I'll wind the cord around your bedrail. I'd like you to push the button when you see that your fluid bag is getting low, all right?"

"Okay."

> *I ride the hospital bed to madness. Faces come and go and look over me and ask questions, but I'm unable to respond. The broken parts heal hard, I keep singing to myself. The broken parts heal hard. Pray for me Lois. Pray for me Margaret. Pray for me Andre and Harry. You're all I have. The broken parts heal hard. Hard. The I.V. bag keeps dripping and is changed, and still I cannot respond. I want to sleep. But I can't. If I do drift off, I am certain I will die. As it is, my heart pounds in my chest then slows down and races high again. I cannot breathe right. The broken parts heal hard. A young Asian girl, a candy striper, comes in. "We're going to take you for your CAT scan." And my hospital bed is moving down some corridor. Someone moans. Someone else cries out in pain. We go past a woman on a gurney whose facial bandages are soaked through with blood. We are the broken and wounded ones. There are millions of us everywhere, and the broken parts heal hard. Pray for us, Lois. Pray. I see acoustical tiles above us. Their dots and dimples and broken pieces roll by overhead. We stop.*

"I'm going to put a blanket over you," the Asian girl says sweetly. "Don't be alarmed. It's just that we have to go outside and then on a lift into the CAT scan trailer. "We're remodeling, you know. You can understand me, can't you?"

I nod.

> *I am someone who floats somewhere between this bed and the ceiling tiles. I am water stained and brown. The wind is blowing against my wall, rattling the windows, and the shingles on my roof are flapping loose. My faucets are dripping. There is mold and dust and bacteria in my air ducts. My car is ten years old and likely to break down at any time. There's mold on the caulking in the shower and around the bathtub. I don't have enough money to keep my family alive. I have no job. Someone who doesn't know me*

*is going to take pictures of my brain. I know what they are going to find. Please, God, let me be O.K. I'm flying in Winchester Cathedral. The roof shingles are flapping in the wind. How can anyone justify the Crusades? Flying in Winchester Cathedral. Crosby, Stills and Nash. Pray for me, Lois. Ceiling tiles are swimming overhead. Pictures of my brain. Chemotherapy. No will. What about my children, Lois? My brain. We stop again. Ellen.*

The technician at the door of the trailer called down, "We're not ready. Mrs. Votto just came in and we're running behind. It'll be a while."

"Mr. Couch, I'll just leave you here for a little while," the young candy striper says. "Are you warm enough?"

The wind comes in from the open end of the corridor where plastic sheeting flaps and fails to keep out the cold. I nod yes. Then I am alone on my gurney bed in a hallway below the dirty tiles.

*So many people have died in the name of Christ that I can't believe it all. What would He say? I have no control over where my mind goes. I know only that if I sleep I will surely die. Eddie. Carol. My wife. What have I done to my family? The broken parts heal hard. Pray. I'm cold and the ceiling tiles are multiplying and dividing above. Pray for me. I can't even do Eddie's third grade math homework. I've lost it. Don't sleep. But we're moving again. My bed bumps against an unpadded wall. I'm guided by a young girl who doesn't know me, and an old woman with pallid color is wheeled by. Winchester Cathedral. Pray for me.* "Can you help?" *my angel says, and I reach forward to grab the side of the lift rail and pull with all my might. She pushes. The gurney bumps over an edge and onto the lift. It's cold. The technician pulls a lever. The lift complains as it groans up.* "We've got to get it fixed," *the technician says.* "I called maintenance three times today." *The car, the faucets, the roof, the bills, my brain, we've got to get it all fixed. The two slight women struggle to bump my bed over the lip into the trailer after the hoist has stopped a little too short. They eventually get the gurney lined up beside the padded table ahead of the scan machine. "Can you help?" they're asking me. "You'll have to help." My brain. Pray for us all. I move the rolling stand with my I.V. bag closer to the gurney. I sit up, collapse, collapse the railing and then slide over off the gurney onto the CAT scan table. I hear someone say, "Oh, God" from back in her monitor booth. I see her looking at the last images from the patient before me up on the computer monitor. "Oh, God," she mutters quietly. "It's a big one." Then louder she says to my angel, "I've got to run this tape inside. I'll be back." I hear her feet on some metal step ladder rungs. Then my angel and I are alone. She is not the one I worked so hard to seduce. She is not the seduction that haunts me still.*

"It won't be long, Mr. Couch," she says. No, I think, I'm afraid it won't be long. Our lives are a rush and then they're over before we do what we want to do. It won't be long.

*And it isn't long before the electric motors move the table back until my head is in the halo of the white machine. My brain. "Lie still," my technician says. "Stop breathing." I wonder what she will say to herself about me. We'll all lie still soon enough. The machine surrounds my head and shoulders, whirrs and makes noises as if something were spinning around inside. "Breathe," she says, and the table moves further under the halo. "Lie still." Whirrs and chirps and humming. My brain. My mind. Third grade homework. I've lost my mind. Sometimes you have to lose your mind to find it. "Breathe again." The table moves ever so slightly. "Stop breathing." We'll all stop breathing. Pray for us, Andre. After awhile, I can't take it anymore. "How does everything look?" I manage to ask. "Lie still," she chastises.*

*"The pictures aren't up on my screen yet."* I can see my Asian angel in the control station next to where the technician sits. *"Besides,* she continues, *I'm not a doctor. Your E.R. doctor will get the report to you. Now stop breathing..."* Pictures of my brain.

When it is over, it's not really ever over. After we got me back on the gurney and got my rolling I.V. pole lined up, the two ladies pushed me out toward the trailer door and the lift outside. Rolling by the control station, I looked at the computer monitor and saw two gray masses in an outline of my scull on the screen. Too small to be my brain. Too big to be any good?

### *Pray for me.*

The lift groaned down, jerking once before it bumped the pavement, and this time the two ladies got me off the metal pad while the cold wind blew our hair around in thatches and cow licks. My little angel pushed me inside the building as I held onto the I.V. pole. "Thank you," I called back behind us. Thank you, I think. Dark stained ceiling tiles again rolled by overhead. Then I was back in my room.

Lois was waiting there. Apparently, she'd talked her way into the portals of the E.R. as ambassador of my "family." Power of persuasion, I thought. She paced back and forth, her long gray hair back in pigtails, her brown eyes alight with hope and concern.

"Hey, big guy!" she called. "Long time no see."

"Hey, Babe."

"Any word on his condition?" Lois asked the candy striper.

"The doctor will be in soon with his test results," was all she said. She pulled the pink curtain shut as she left. I managed to say thank you as she left.

"Babe, I saw something in my brain," I said. "The picture was up on the screen when we left the scan room. There was something there."

She brushed her hand against my forehead, pushing back a forelock of hair. "Whatever it is, we'll get through it," Lois said. "Even if it's bad news, we'll get through it together. I'm not going anywhere."

The curtain opened, and the same nurse who'd drawn my blood and started my I.V. came back in. "We called your family doctor," she said. "He said it's O.K. to give you this."

"What is it?" my Lois wanted to know.

"It's Ativan. It will help him sleep." She moved to my right side, then squirted the air and a little fluid out of her needle, unhooked my fluid line and shut it off, then put the needle in the receptacle and pushed. I felt a slow sensation of sticky warmth flow in my arm.

"We're going to let him go home soon," the nurse said.

"But what's wrong with him?" my Lois demanded.

"Dr. Alyub will be in soon." She left the room, curtain open.

"Babe," I struggled to say. "Could you hand me that urinal bottle from the counter," I asked, "and then leave me alone for just one minute?"

She did as I asked, and then pulled the curtain shut. "I'll be right out here," she said.

I'd no sooner lifted my gown and half filled the bottle under my blanket when the curtain flew open.

"He's going to the bathroom," I heard Lois say, too late. Young Dr. Alyub stood before me.

"Go ahead and finish up," he said.

When I had, he took the yellow bottle from me, setting it by the sink. "You can come in," he called to Lois. He had a smile on his face.

Lois stood beside me.

"EKG, CAT scan, blood work, everything's pretty well normal," the doctor said. "You have unspecified weakness, and you're dehydrated," he said. "The CAT scan showed a big time sinus infection, so you're going to need strong antibiotics for several weeks. I think your exhaustion and many of your symptoms have a strong emotional component, so I suggest you see a counselor or someone to talk things out. But the bottom line is that you're going to be O.K." He stood, waiting for a reaction.

*Yes!!!*

"That's great," I said. The tension flooded out of me. "Thank you Dr. Alyub."

Lois smiled that reassuring smile. "Yes, thank you Doctor. We'll see that he gets the help you recommend." She took the prescription that he had written, putting the small piece of paper discretely in her blouse's pocket.

"You can get dressed now," Dr. Alyub said. "You need to read and sign the discharge instructions on the table," he said, pointing to a clipboard with papers attached to it. "If there aren't any questions for me, I'll send the rest of your family in. Good luck to you." With that, he was gone beyond the curtain. Lois held my hand. I felt lighter and lighter by the moment.

In the car ride back to Margaret and Harry's, the drug began to take over. My eyes closed and opened as I weakly fought it off. I saw a slow stream of cars and trees and houses going by the car, or rather us going by them, and then my eyes would close and the stream would stop until I forced them again and the stream flowed freely.

Back in bed at Margaret's house, sleep was waiting for me in the covers. The faces of my friends came and went, but, mostly, sleep finally came, welcome and familiar.

*The fine film "Forrest Gump" begins and ends with a single feather floating. In the beginning, the white feather roils above where Forrest sits on a city park bench, riding city air currents, falling and rising as cars and buses go by and as the wind blows through the trees in a park. Eventually, the single white feather lands on Forrest's shoe. In the end, after Jenny, Forrest's lifelong friend and eventual wife, dies, leaving him with their son, Forrest Jr., Forrest sits by a row of mailboxes at the bustop as his son is about to go away to his first day of school. And, after Forrest Jr. boards that bus and leaves in a cloud of diesel smoke and dust, Forrest is alone again. There again is the single white feather, blowing off in the wake of the bus, blowing on toward some other destination. Floating. I am the feather, blown on currents of destiny and fate and accepting the wind, following it wherever it may flow. Rising, darting sideways, falling and rising again. I am movement itself, floating without worry. Floating. I am that feather and nothing else.*

In the days that followed, I got slowly better and better. I did cognitive therapy and took my medicines and went on long walks with Andre and Lois. Took two steps forward with one step back. But always two steps forward. I learned to accept.

*I am a feather, nothing more, and nothing less. The breeze carries me, and I am light. I have learned to float and fly without even trying. I let the wind carry me.*

# Voices,
# Inner Chapter Four

*Fooled Around and Fell in Love*

## Eddie

What are the odds of finding it? Finding it the first time? Love, that is. Well, I found it the second or third real try. But I was already married and so I lost that one real love. It started like this, goes like this...

We were just two ordinary people, Ann and I, who happened to work at the same place. Both married with kids, both attracted to each other from the first, both knowing that this innocent playing at falling in love would never go anywhere because of commitments, family, love, ethics. Yet it did go somewhere. Somewhere terrible and strange and deep and wonderful too. See, in those early days, when I was hammering away at the Master's Degree, the key to the lock of teaching business at the community college, I also temped on non-class days to help Ellen and me with the bills, tuition, life. I met Ann at a computer technology place that I got assigned repeatedly. It was 20 some techs making computers work, making software run fine. She was the diamond in the rough, the Mona Lisa of lower Bucks County. She was more than my old, troubled heart could bear or handle. She was perfect, with a soft, round-oval face, splashed with small freckles on slightly sun burnt pink and creamy skin, with robin's egg blue eyes that danced with light even under florescent light and office nonsense furnishings. Ann was so much smaller than me, a trim 5' 6" with smallish, perky breasts, the loveliest can I'd seen, long, long legs carrying a shorter, firm torso, and chin length, fine, elegant brunette hair. She dressed impeccably in outfits that accented her quite nice figure. A siren she was, but I think, in retrospect, it was her voice that got me: a half-baritone purr that lilted, fell, rose earnestly, sounded out words so lovely that the words themselves ceased to matter after a few lines. Her voice snared me. Nor was I blameless.

It all started with some innocent flirting, simply enough. I think we were both kidding in the beginning, playing around with pretend futures we'd make up, secretly, in stolen moments while others scurried around in tunnel vision. Within weeks, it had become as serious as a heart attack, at least as far as I'm concerned. It went like this, so long and not so long ago.

I stepped into her little office, pretended to have official business in my hands, looked over my shoulder out into the thankfully clear hallway.

"How was Carrisa's Confirmation?" I asked, waiting for an answer. That voice. "Party at your place afterwards?" Wait for an answer. Wait three seconds, look out to the hallway again. Her voice thrilling me. "Very good." I put the papers on Ann's desk, freeing me to stretch my hands.

Hallway still clear. "You're probably a good Catholic woman, faithful and all, and I'm a good Christian man, so we can't have a thing right now, damn it." I looked her straight in those blue pools of eyes. Strongly. She looked up from behind her seat behind the metal desk that separated us, surprised. Her eyes are azure, that fathomless robin's egg blue. "But I have an idea," I went on, stumbling for words. "We'll just outlive our spouses. Have a wild affair when we're in our 60's or 70's. I'll still be able to make whoopee in my 70's," I stammered. "At least I hope to. No shame in that." I stepped back two steps. I was just inside Ann's doorway, seeking retreat, safety, something. Seeking.

"I can't believe I just said that to you," my voice cracked baritone. I looked around, eyes on eyes gone in an instant, just as quickly as real moments are shared. "I apologize. It's you're voice that's driving me crazy. Your voice and your laugh. I love your voice. It's great."

As I left, I imagined Ann heard my footsteps receding down the long, hard tiled hall.

"Damn," I guessed she thought, "that's as close as he's going to come to spilling it. This one needs care." Words like that seemed to be right for us then, for who we are, who we were.

We couldn't wait until our 60's or 70's. I wrote her a poem and put it in her mailbox, sealed up in a company envelope. A poem so honest and real that the words tore up out of my gut, up my mind's mouth and seared the pages. The next day, there was a single yellow rose on my borrowed desk. We were in bed within a week, in bed repeatedly in hotels during luxuriously long lunch hours, during the last hours I'd steal away from some of my night classes, telling Ellen that class had run a little long, that I'd stayed after, too, to work on papers in computer labs on campus, all the while worrying or half welcoming the possible discovery of love bites or the scratches of a passion I'd never known. Perhaps I'd never known it like that because it was stolen, secret, just we two stealing away from our separate families, separate lives. But I don't think so. I think it became love, a love so sad and desperate and thrilling that it had to be real. I know it was real. I know it. She's out there somewhere, living her separate, long resumed life without me. She knows it too.

# Chapter 19

## *Harry and the U-boat*

Harry and his fellow Civil Air Patrolman Maj. Greg Weiden were playing cards in the air patrol barracks in Point Pleasant, New Jersey when the call came in. It was summer, July 11, 1942. Harry had been certified as a navigator before he volunteered, although he didn't have his pilot's license; Greg Weiden was an experienced air patrol pilot. A German U-boat had supposedly been sighted by a private pilot flying some 65 miles east of the Point Pleasant beach. Major Weiden and Harry were to investigate.

The two men suited up, used the bathroom, then marched out of the aluminum Quonset hut barracks toward the airfield. When they reached their Grumman Widgeon aircraft, Harry pushed the wooden blocks away from its tires, and Greg Weiden climbed into the cockpit. He began manipulating the controls as Harry walked around the plane to watch for the correct function of the flaps and rudder, part of their pre-flight checklist. After a few minutes, Maj. Weiden started the engine. The Widgeon's single prop spun faster and faster until the engine caught with a blast and momentary black exhaust poured from the exhaust for a few seconds until it cleared to nearly invisible color. Harry climbed over the wing and took his seat behind the pilot, belting himself in and putting on his goggles. Soon they were rumbling down the black ribbon of runway and pulling up into the warm air. As the Widgeon clawed up higher and higher toward cruising altitude,

Harry looked down to the right and then his left, the two views where the plane's fuselage didn't block his sight. Below them, the Atlantic Ocean spread out like a favorite blue blanket, successions of nearly straight white lines marking the waves as they advanced toward shore. The warm wind pouring around the plane's second windshield felt good on Harry's face.

The sun straight above, they flew smoothly through a few patchy clouds that cast small shadows far below them on the blue water. Harry saw a patchwork of different shades of blue and green that indicated the water's different depths. When Greg Weiden turned around for a second ahead of him, Harry flashed his friend a thumbs up sign. Margaret's Harry, then a handsome young man, watched the instruments in front of his second seat as they flew on toward the point where the Nazi sub had been sighted.

It wasn't long before pilot Greg Weiden saw something under the water in his forward vision and turned around momentarily to Harry, pointing up ahead and down to where a dark cigar shape lurked under the bluish green ahead of the plane and to their left. Harry again gave Maj. Weiden his thumbs up sign. After the pilot turned around, he banked the Grumman Widgeon gently to the left and began descending. A small depth charge was mounted under each of the plane's wings. Harry's instruments in the second seat area included controls for dropping the charges, so he had to coordinate carefully with Greg Weiden in order to have a chance of hitting the submarine. The warm wind whipping his face as the plane dropped lower and lower, Harry set his arming dial for 75 feet below sea on the right charge and for 100 feet of depth on the left. The underwater silhouette was clearly visible ahead of them now: a long black shape that appeared almost motionless below the water. Up in the front seat, Weidon leveled off the plane's altimeter at 60 feet above sea level. He turned again to Harry and shouted, "On my count" into the wind. He turned forward again.

"Ten, nine, eight . . ." Harry heard. "Seven, six, five," came through the wind. "Four, three, two, one, now!" Maj. Weidon yelled from ahead of him. Harry hit the right side release button in that instant, and the plane got a little lighter and lifted up a few feet as the charge fell away.

"I'm circling so we can watch," Weidon yelled. Harry felt the Widgeon bank steeply and come around to the left. To his right, he saw the charge falling close to the water, but, as the plane turned, his view was blocked. They made a complete circle and came back over their drop site. Harry leaned to his right, then pointed down to a spot in the water below. "There," he hollered, "right there," he said as Greg Weidon turned halfway around to look. Down on the blue-green water, a circle of white bubbles and roiling water welled up, and, following fractions of a second later, they heard a muted boom. The circle of disturbed water widened, spread rapidly, and in its center a dark oil slick rose and spread out too.

"We're coming around again," Major Weidon yelled and again the plane banked left. With his plane lined up perfectly once more, Greg Weidon used his sight line to time the Widgeon's pass over the slick on the water. "On my mark," he shouted.

"Ten, nine, eight, seven, six," Harry heard through the wind. He put his finger on the left side release button. "Five, four, three, two . . . one, now!" Greg Weidon shouted. Harry hit the release, and, again, the plane rose up slightly as the two men heard the depth charge whistle away below them, dropping to the sea. In the seat of his pants, Margaret's Harry felt the airplane bank left and begin to come around to the drop point. He felt as alive as he'd ever been.

He and Greg Weidon came around in a big circle toward the oily, dark stain on the sea below. Harry saw what looked like chunks of debris popping up in the stain. "We got him," he yelled convincingly to the pilot ahead. Greg Weidon turned his head around for a moment.

"Good shooting, Harry," he hollered approvingly. "This is one for the history books."

A civilian plane sinking a Nazi sub, Harry thought as the plane turned back toward the mainland, to New Jersey. That's something.

But as they flew back over the blue-green waters and the lines of waves, he began to think about what it all meant. Somewhere below the sea, they were leaving dozens of dead men, actually, probably more like boys, he thought, leaving them to a watery grave. And for what? No doubt they believed in honor and duty and country as he did, and what it got them was killed. Bombed from the sky above by a couple of men who felt the same way they did, who had more in common than in difference. Were it not for a madman in Europe, they might have been friends had they met. Time and chance happeneth to us all. He remembered the Bible verse. Save for accidents of birth and circumstance, one of those boys down there could have been me, Harry thought. Sometimes it all seemed so arbitrary. You are born to a place and stay there or find another place, and where you are and the people who happen to be there too color almost all of what you are and what happens to you. A few hundred miles in a different direction, hell sometimes even a few feet or some small distance, as in the case of the dead Nazis back behind them in a watery grave, and everything might turn out differently. You might turn a different corner one day and meet someone who will become your spouse, changing the course of your whole life for the better. Your submarine might be running deeper, and the depth charges might explode harmlessly above. It was all so weird. If you had a deep religious faith, everything seemed guided by a divine hand, and Harry saw the comfort in that. If you didn't believe, it all seemed so random.

Harry rode behind Greg Weidon through the smooth air. Their Grumman Widgeon's engine droned steadily on, their propeller pulling them certainly back to the mainland. On the water below, the shadow of their plane followed them, spreading wider over the blue green water as the plane moved on above.

# Chapter 20

## *Feeling Good, the New Mood Therapy*

The Wrightstown Library had seldom rock and rolled like this. Margaret Dorris was on a roll, and Lois Kenny wasn't far behind her.

"David Burns isn't just teaching us a desirable philosophy," Margaret chanted from the wooden podium, her best wig on straight and her brown and severe knit suit pressed professionally, "he's showing us how to be happy!" Lois, who stood beside Margaret, nodded her head in agreement.

A man from the small semi-circle of participants stood up from his metal chair. There was no discernible part in his wild gray hair; for a man of fifty or so, his face was heavily lined, but his eyes were the deepest shade of blue light. "I read *Feeling Good*, and I liked it, but I have a hard time distilling the main ideas. Can you folks help?"

Lois held out her hand, palm open, a gesture of welcome. "What's your name, young man?"

"Kristopher. Kristopher Bart," the man said. He took an awkward step toward the front of the circle, toward Lois and Margaret and the rest of the National Endowment for the Humanities book discussion gang behind them, so that he ended up standing in the middle of the circle, uncertain where to go.

Lois' long hair was out of its braids, and it fanned out over her shoulders front and back. Her brown eyes and her white hair flashed the light from the central multi-light globe over them on the library conference room's roof. "Well, Mr. Bart," she said invitingly, "I thought you'd never ask. We old ladies like to talk," she teased.

"I should let you know, Lois," Margaret interrupted, "that Mr. Bart is a poet and a teacher at the community college. A damn fine one at both tasks, I might add."

"A poet," Lois savored the word. "So much the better. He'll understand all the more about feelings and their relationship to thoughts.

Dr. Burns is saying that *all* our feelings are a result of thoughts," Lois continued from her place by the podium next to Margaret. "Every single emotion, helpful or otherwise, comes from our thinking. When our thoughts are realistic or positive, our feelings are too. When our thoughts are unrealistic or negative, our feelings get distorted."

"That's what he's calling 'Cognitive Distortion,' isn't it?" Kristopher Bart said from the middle of the circle. Two new recruits, football fans Tony and Steven DiJavon, sat in the circle, listening intently.

"When our thinking is inaccurate or misled, our feelings get distorted too as a result and that impacts our lives, can make us experience negative feelings and even depression because of errors in our thinking process," Bart continued. His head bobbed and nodded in empathy as he spoke.

"You got it!" Eddie couldn't help hollering from the back of the room.

"The first big distortion we're often guilty of," Lois said, looking down at her impeccably handwritten notes, "is All or Nothing Thinking."

Kristopher Bart walked back to his seat and sat, running his hand through his thick gray forelock of hair. "That's something we do all the time," he said.

"Anybody care to explain?" Lois wondered.

Stephen DiJavon answered. "I'm new here, but I read the book. From what I recall, 'All or Nothing Thinking' happens when we see things in black and white categories. If our performance falls short of perfection, we feel we're total failures."

"Right," Margaret agreed, "that makes us feel lousy because we almost always fall short of perfection. Instead of giving ourselves credit for what we've done, we focus on not becoming the absolute thing and beat ourselves up. So we haven't become rich and famous from our painting; what we have done is achieved a local reputation and a lot of enjoyment."

Lois nodded, "Life is often about in-betweens, not all or nothing states."

"Then there's 'Overgeneralization,'" Eddie added from the back. "Sometimes people see a single negative event as a never ending pattern of defeat."

"I'm a roofer now," Tony DiJavon said. "If I break through the sheathing on someone's roof and I say to myself 'I'll never get this job done right,' that's an overgeneralization, isn't it?"

"Absolutely," Tony's brother said.

"Without a doubt," Lois agreed. She turned and called Harry, Andre and Eddie up to the podium so that all five discussion leaders stood beside each other.

Andre, in his Sunday best clothes borrowed from Harry, looked dapper and relaxed. His hands touched gently at the sides of his borrowed and freshly pressed black slacks: his hair was greased back. "My favorite is the 'Mental Filter,'" he said.

"As you probably know, that's when we pick out a single negative detail and dwell on it so much that our whole vision of reality is darkened, like a drop of ink that discolors a whole glass of water. That's a 'Cognitive Distortion' we've got to guard against or we miss so much else of the glass of water and of *reality*," he said, drawing out the world reality.

"Another thing we do is to 'Disqualify the Positive,'" Andre continued, his fingers tapping gently, inadvertently, against the sides of his pants. "We sometimes reject positive experiences by claiming they 'don't count' for one reason or another. We maintain a negative belief that is contradicted by our everyday experiences . . ."

"Dr. Burns is right," Harry agreed. He rubbed his reddish nose for a moment with the back of the knuckle of the index finger on his right hand before he continued speaking. "Just yesterday, Maggie here," he said, pointing to Margaret, "complimented me on the good job I did putting in mulch around the back of our house. That's great, I thought to myself, but she just wants me to do more yard work." Harry paused to smile a jagged smile at Margaret who beamed back a knowing grin. "In reality, Maggie only complements me when she means it, and she sure does tell me outright when she wants me to do something, so I should have taken the compliment for what it was: a compliment. I ought not to have disqualified the praise."

"I sure do tell him like it is," Margaret assured the small audience. "Any of you have other 'Cognitive Distortions' from David Burns' book that you want to try out?"

The woman sitting next to Kristopher Bart, a petite and dark haired woman with the whitest skin, spoke up. "I'm Mary Bart," she said, "and one of Burns' distortions that I'm guilty of is 'Jumping to Conclusions.'" She didn't move from her seat, but her voice, reedy and high and genuine, filled the small library conference room. "One type of 'Jumping to Conclusions' I do is 'Mind Reading.' Sometimes I arbitrarily conclude that somebody is reacting negatively to me without bothering to check this out.

For years, I thought Kristopher's mom was angry at me for not wanting to move to Massachusetts to be nearer to them. When I finally worked up enough courage to ask her about this, she told me that she and my father-in-law had been having problems, and that that's why I sensed hostility in her. Turns out, it had nothing to do with Kris or me. I'd been assuming I could read Mom's mind." Mary looked at the discussion leaders. Eddie's eyes met hers.

"When I was in high school," big Eddie said, "I ran for junior class president against a girl named Tracy Caulkins. She was pretty, a cheerleader and popular, and she'd been the freshman and sophomore class president, and everybody figured she'd be a shoo-in to win that year too." Eddie looked upward for a moment, saw the fine cracks and webbed lines in the library's old plaster ceiling, then looked back at Mary, then the group, and continued. "You have to understand, I was a gawky kid with glasses and hush puppies, while she had long blonde hair, blue eyes and was sharp as a tack with a personality to match. Anyhow, we had this special assembly to give our vote-for-me speeches, and, after Tracy's usual upbeat talk, I launched a surprise on her and on the whole school. Some of my friends were in a rock band. At that time, there was this popular song you may remember called 'The House of the Rising Sun,' and what we'd done was to parody the lyrics with all kinds of references to the school and to Tracy and so on. We'd been practicing in my friend's parent's garage." Eddie's eyes looked around the room.

"So when it came time at the assembly in the school gym, we played the song. We had the amplifiers and the speakers and the drum set all put together in advance, and I sang the twisted lyrics to our 'House of the Steak Well Done' right there at the public address microphone while the band played bravely behind me. Most of the kids in the wooden bleacher seats went nuts, stamping their feet and clapping and cheering, and I thought I could see Tracy scowling off to the side of the gym. When I finished singing, the kids gave me a standing ovation. You can guess what happened next."

"You won the election?" one of the DiJavon brothers called out.

"You got it," Eddie said.

"And you figured that the Tracy girl held a grudge?" Lois asked supportively from near where Eddie stood.

"You got it, Babe," Eddie said, "I thought I could 'Read' her mind. For years I figured she hated me."

Mary wondered out loud, "What showed you that you'd 'Jumped to a Conclusion?'"

"Yea," her husband Kris agreed, "what was the breakthrough?"

Eddie smiled his knowing smile, his face beaming like he used to so often, chuckling inside to himself. "I went to our 10 year reunion. My wife Ellen and I were still together at the time, but she thought I'd have more fun if I went alone. I had a couple of drinks there, worked up the nerve to talk to Tracy, who was still gorgeous as ever, and she told me flat-out that she'd never held anything against me. That she'd been glad all those years before to get out of student government, that my winning was a relief. She'd only gotten involved with the elections because her parents wanted her to . . . All those years I created scenarios in my head that were false. Wasted all that emotion. So the point is, we can't really know what other people are thinking unless they tell us or show us."

"Dr. Burns is right when he says we go awry trying to read minds," Lois agreed. "And there's another way we jump to conclusions. Sometimes we engage in his 'Fortune Telling:'"We make the mistake of anticipating that things will turn out badly, and we feel that our predictions are already-established facts.

It's always possible that things will turn out well, and since we can't predict the future, it doesn't make any sense to fortune tell that things will be a mess. A negative assumption like that can turn our attitude negative and make it *more* likely that something will be a disaster. Why would we want to do that?" she asked the group. "Yielding to our fears when fortune telling can lead us to false conclusions that unfortunately turn out to be self-fulfilling prophesies."

"Whoo, Nellie," Eddie teased. "Can you put that last idea in plain English?"

"One more time with feeling," Andre agreed.

Lois looked approvingly at her two friends. She'd come to look at them as if they were two of her own sons, Eddie fat and awkward, compelling, warm and with a heart unlike any other, and Andre, battered by the world but not broken, his lean look not of someone starving but of a coyote who'd survived the roughest years and come into better times. "I just meant that if we predict that we're going to fail, we're more likely to do just that than if we admit that we flat out *don't know* what the future will bring. Ness pa?," she asked, then moved closer to her friends.

"Got it," Eddie said.

"Who's got another one of Dr. David Burns' 'Cognitive Distortions' from **Feeling Good**?" Margaret asked the assembled mass of half-a-dozen people. She pulled the skirt of her brown suit straighter.

"I do, I do," Tony DiJavon chimed in, and, as he did, he caught himself wondering what a good Italian kid from south Philly was doing in the outer reaches of the suburbs, in a hundred year old library that used to be a schoolhouse. And with his brother yet. He fought the odd thought and forged ahead. "I like the 'Magnification (Catastrophizing) or Minimization' distortion because it's two problems for the price of one," Tony said.

"On the one end of it, we exaggerate the importance of things. If we goof up, we blow the screw up out of proportion. Or maybe we take someone else's achievement, something that we'd have liked to do, and make it seem bigger than it is, exaggerate the other person's accomplishment." Tony felt good. He felt he was making sense to this group of strangers. Andre and Eddie, whom he of course recognized from the community college roof, when they came to his door to invite him here, were his only entree into this world of books and ideas. It impressed Tony that the two stowaways had been able to track him down. It impressed him more when Andre and Eddie flat-out begged him to join the group, at least for one try, explained that the little book group was desperate for the right kind of participants. "Do you mean people with a pulse?" Tony remembered that he'd joked that day in his living room.

"The other end of this problem, the one that makes Burns call it the 'binocular trick' as well, is 'Minimization,'" Tony continued. "That happens when we inappropriately shrink things so they appear tiny. We might shrink our own desirable qualities when we're depressed or thinking negatively. Or we might minimize the other person's imperfections if we're trying to be kind. Either way, the truth gets lost."

"Well, said," Harry chimed in. "Catastrophizing can get us into real trouble because when we blow something up in importance all out of relation to its true meaning—maybe we get a flat tire in the rain and wonder why go on living if things like this are going to happen—when we make mountains out of molehills," he said, "that gets our emotions all riled up past the point of what's reasonable. When we get all worked up over nothing, we do unnecessary damage to our psyche. Once, when I was mining in

Central America, I thought I was going to literally die when I found a leach attached to me. I got myself so worked up that I kept expecting an infection and sure death for days, weeks really, after we'd removed the thing. Nothing happened. Nothing except that I worried myself half to death for far too long for nothing. Wasted energy."

Lois pointed to Harry. "Amen," she said. "Another related distortion of Burns' is one I'm often guilty of. That's 'Emotional Reasoning.' You all know that one. It's when you assume that your negative emotions reflect the way things really are. The logic of 'Emotional Reasoning,' if you want to call it logic, is 'I feel it; therefore, it must be true.' I feel like I'm talking too much now, and that you're all tired of listening to me; therefore, you must be sick of hearing me. Right?"

"You know we love you, Babe," Eddie reassured.

"You're sick of hearing me talk because I feel that way, right?" Lois went on.

"Wrong," Kristopher Bart said from the audience. "We're not sick of hearing you at all, or, if we were, it would be because we *actually* were tired of hearing you, not because you *felt* that way."

"No wonder you're a poet," Lois agreed. "You not only send messages, but you *get* them too."

"He gets it, that's for sure," Eddie said. He moved closer, then put his hand on Lois' shoulder. "This guy remembers what he's read in **Feeling Good**."

"There are times when it's more important to forget than to remember. And more difficult . . ." Bart said.

"A Honeymoon is the period between 'I do' and 'you'd better.'" Mary interrupted her husband.

Eddie caught on. They were playing profound: having fun. He could play too. "These days, when roll is called in Congress, sometimes you hear "Here" and sometimes you hear 'Not guilty'!"

Stephen DiJavon joined in. "Thanks to the interstate highway system, you can now drive coast to coast without seeing anything."

From next to Eddie, Lois joined in. "Never cut what you can untie," she said with a wicked smile.

"All right, children," Margaret scolded, her satiric tone of voice showing that she was actually enjoying the game, "Can we get back to Dr. David Burns' book?"

"O.K., Mom, O.K.," Eddie responded. "One of the 'Cognitive Distortions' that's caused me a lot of pain is Burns' 'Should Statements.'

We think of 'should' judgments as being part of our conscience, as something that keeps us morally in line, but judgments about what we 'should' do or 'should' have done can hurt us," Eddie continued. His hand fell away from Lois' shoulder. "In the past I've tried to motivate myself with should and shouldn'ts, as if I had to be whipped and punished before I could be expected to do anything. I 'must' do this or I 'ought' to do that judgments are really the same thing. The emotional result of these sorts of judgments is *guilt*."

A young man in ripped jeans and an Army fatigue shirt stood up quickly from his chair. "What the hell is wrong with guilt?" he demanded to know. Eddie noticed the multiple earrings in the kid's ears and the annoyed glare in the young man's eyes. "If it wasn't for feelings of guilt, and for having a conscience, people would be running around doing all kinds of stupid things," the young man said. "There'd be even more rapes, murders, thefts and you name it without feelings of guilt to keep us in line."

The kid was clearly angry, his posture defiant, his voice a snarl. "Guilt serves a purpose," Margaret answered curtly. She was surprised by this change in the tone of their discussion. "But I think Eddie is talking about excessive guilt and excessively harsh judgment of oneself."

"Yea," Eddie said, "think about what happens when you direct 'should' statements toward other people: you should pay me the money you owe me; you shouldn't have called me a moron. When you direct shoulds toward others, no matter the circumstances, you feel anger, frustration, and resentment. Same thing when you make the judgments toward yourself. These negative feelings are no good for us. They cause all sorts of problems mentally, even physically.

"Do you want an example?" Eddie asked.

The youngster stared at Eddie and his partners near the podium. He wiped his nose with the back of his hand. "Sock it to me," he said in a surly tone.

Eddie looked straight at the kid's eyes, met his gaze. He saw the shaved sides of his head, the dyed purple ponytail drawn back behind his head. "Suppose you're like a lot of us," Eddie said, "suppose your frequently look into your past and mope about your mistakes. Maybe as you review the financial section of the newspaper, you say "I sure as hell shouldn't have bought that stock because it's gone down 10 points . . ."

"Is that the best you can do?" the kid interrupted. "Some hypothetical?" He was still standing, his hands on his hips, a heavy gauge silver chain dangling from one belt loop and disappearing into his pocket.

"Just hear me out, that's all I ask," Eddie said. "You have to find a way out of the should trap," he continued patiently. "Ask yourself, 'At the time I bought the stock, did I know it was going to go down in value?' I'll bet you'll say no. Now ask, 'If I'd known the stock was going to go down, would I have bought it?' Again you'll answer no. So what you're really saying is that if you'd know this at the time, you'd have acted differently. To do this—to have acted differently—you would have to be able to predict the future with absolute certainty. Now I ask you, can you predict the future with absolute certainty? Again, your answer must be no. So, son, you really have only two options: you can either accept yourself as an imperfect human being with limited knowledge and realize that you will at times make mistakes, or you can *hate* yourself for it. I've had to learn to accept myself as an imperfect human being who is going to screw up sometimes. I can't hate myself any more. My health won't stand up to self-hate about what I should have done last week or last year. Do you get it?" Eddie asked softly. All the while, while he talked, Eddie's thoughts darkened, turned within.

*I don't have the words. Don't have the words to say how much I loved my Ellen. Earned love. How much I loved*

*Ann, my one love of passion. How I loved two women and lost them both. Lost it all so badly.*

"I guess I do," the young man said flatly and then sat back down, startling Eddie out of twisted reverie. "When we're telling ourselves what we should and shouldn't have done, we're making a useless judgment and beating ourselves up about something that's in the past. But wait a minute," he said, rising out of his chair again, "don't we have to learn from past mistakes so we don't have to keep repeating them. Isn't judgment a part of that? A way of gaining knowledge?"

"Judgment can help us," Eddie said, almost spitting out the words, "but it has to be realistic. *If,* and that's a big *if,* if I'd known the stock would go down and I bought it anyway, then maybe I realistically *shouldn't* have bought it unless I like losing money. If it's a *realistic* negative judgment, fine, we can learn from it, but the thing is, those negative judgments are hardly ever realistic. Usually, we're just beating ourselves up unnecessarily for being human or for circumstances beyond our control. Check me out on it, you'll see." He almost convinced himself.

The young guy sat down to stay. He seemed to be thinking.

"One thing I can't stand when people do it," he said, "is Burns' 'Labeling and Mislabeling.'"

"So you have read the book?" Margaret couldn't help saying.

"That's just what I mean," he said from his seat, "its damn labeling. You've mentally labeled me as someone who doesn't read the book before a discussion, labeled me as a loser. Am I right?" he demanded.

"Perhaps you are," Margaret said, recovering nicely. Maybe I've assumed too much. Could you explain what you get out of the 'Labeling' distortion to the rest of us," she deflected, using the years of practice as a teacher, and, more recently, as a librarian.

"Most labeling," the young man said, "is just an extreme form of the overgeneralization you all were talking about earlier. Instead of just describing some error you've made—like 'I forgot to pick up the milk you wanted'—you might attach a negative label to yourself: 'I'm a loser.'

"It's even worse, I think, when you do that to someone else. When somebody's behavior rubs you wrong, you attach a negative label to them: 'He's a goddamn louse,'" the youngster continued.

"Yes," Harry chimed in. "Mislabeling is unrealistically describing an event or person with language that is highly colored and emotionally loaded. The philosophy behind it is 'The measure of a man is the mistakes he makes.' If a golfer misses his putt on the eighteenth hole, he might mislabel 'I'm a born loser' instead of realistically saying, 'I goofed up on my putt.' Labeling yourself or someone else in this way is not only self-defeating; it's irrational. Your *self cannot* be equated to any *one* thing you or someone else does. Your life is complex and ever changing flow of thoughts, emotions and actions."

"Here, here," Lois agreed. "We're more like a river than a statue."

"Yes," Harry went on. We've got to stop trying to define ourselves with negative labels: they are overly simplistic and wrong. You breathe, don't you?" Harry asked the group.

"Of course," Mary Bart answered.

"Would you think of yourself *exclusively* as a breather because you breathe or as an eater because you eat?" Harry asked rhetorically. "That is nonsense, and such nonsense becomes painful when you label yourself out of a sense of your own inadequacies.

"It's just as bad when we label others. When we label other people, we inevitably generate hostility. A boss sees his occasionally irritable secretary as an 'uncooperative bitch.' He feels this label is true and so resents her and jumps at every chance to criticize her. She, it turn labels him 'an insensitive chauvinist' and complains about him at every opportunity. Around and around they go at each other's throats, focusing on every weakness or small imperfection as proof of the other's worthlessness. Labeling distorts the truth and causes harm." Harry concluded forcefully. He again rubbed his red nose with the knuckles on the back of his right hand.

"Damn straight old man," the young grunge kid said from his seat in the library conference room.

"O.K.," Lois said. She glanced at the old schoolhouse clock on the beige plaster wall behind the audience. "We need to wrap things up by nine o' clock. Who's got one last 'Cognitive Distortion'?"

Andre, who had been silent for some time, spoke up. "How about 'Personalization'? That's the one, you remember, where you see yourself as the cause of some external event which you were not in fact responsible for."

Tony DiJavon could hold back no longer. "That one is the mother of all guilt!! When I was young, I got some bad report cards, some with a note from the teacher saying I was not working up to potential. My Mom would say 'I must be a bad mother . . . Look how I've failed . . .' But I was already in Junior High School and High School. I was responsible for my own actions. I was choosing to screw up. It wasn't my Mom's doing at all; in fact, she was my rock. She and Dad were doing everything they could to support my school effort. So Mom was 'Personalizing' when *I* failed. She was feeling guilty for something she had only slight *influence* over, not *control* of."

"Good," Lois said. "Any questions? Comments?" ***Never cut what you can untie***, she thought to herself.

Eddie, meanwhile, struggled again with his old demons, could not run from them.

*Damn the lies. Damn myself. Love's sweet damn agony. Ellen first for the years, for better or for worse. I made it worse. I loved her. Loved her everyday. But I loved Ann more. And I couldn't commit to her because of Ellen. My family. My sad, separate life. So I lost Ann too. Lost them all. Lost. Your life can change with a kiss. A bittersweet kiss.*

# Voices,
# Inner Chapter Five

*Once in a Lifetime Love*

### Eddie/ Ann

## First

Ann was inside of me from the beginning. The first time I saw her, at the temporary job's office Christmas party, I knew I was in trouble. Those eyes; that voice. My old fool's heart never had a chance. It was lust/ love at first sight. She had this kind of graceful movement in a crowd of co-workers, a completely confident social manner. She had a body to die for, all womanly curves and light in her blue eyes that spoke individually to each person lucky enough to have her attention, my Bucks County Mona Lisa. Before the open bar in New Hope was no longer open, before the last of the thank you cards and presents for the staff were gratefully opened, I'd already written her a poem in my head. She has lynx eyes, I mused. Haunted blue not yellow/ has furry pads/ that never sink too deep/ in snow/ she catches my heart/ leaves the remains/ behind some brush/ so the crows/ would never see. I had it bad.

Ellen and I were on the outs then, so I was especially bruised and vulnerable, but Ann was clearly the real item, a beautiful woman outside, and, I learned in time, on the inside as well. I was out of my league again in the life of romance, but happy as a lost dog's owner chasing Ann down, always seeing just flashes of her up ahead, around the bend, always calling her name in my head. Come here to me, Ann, come back to me for the first time. Don't run. Come to me.

Ann was married too, had kids, had a separate, perfectly fine life, but I used every resource within my power to get into her head, her heart. Passion is like that, can make fools of us all. And even though she was committing adultery too, sinning with me, because of me, just as I was, Ann seemed somehow less responsible, somehow more pure than I'll ever be. Love made me a fool; sex made me love; I made us happen, but Ann loved me back, at least for a while, the most delicious wild grape tasting time my lips have ever felt, my body fluttering with her in every pulse, every heartbeat and every breath.

She deserved better than stolen hours in hotels, than stolen walks outside the computer place I'd been assigned repeatedly to work temporarily while trying to keep my separate family going, but that's what we had. That's what we carved out for our stolen brief, intense life together, punctuated always by what we had to go home to, the separate lives cast long before, hardened concrete that could not bend without shattering into dust. That's all we had, and it was enough.

Ann stood before me in an antiseptic white hotel room that first time. She had emerged from the bathroom in some silky red kimono robe and glided over rented white carpet to stand in front of me, stopping to purr her mouth just a few inches below mine, her eye light dancing seductively just a few inches from my own as she looked up.

"We're like virgins," she purred. "Teenagers."

"Speak for yourself," I said. What had I done to be facing this beautiful, seductive woman, I remember wondering. How has my luck changed, and what will it cost me, what bargain?

Ann smiled shyly. She reached to pull my hand out of my pants pocket where I didn't know I'd forced it, and, in the process, her red kimono opened. She was naked underneath, and, as she put our hands downward, palm to palm, rubbing skin, I saw her small, perfect breasts swing free underneath red fabric. I saw the skin above her collarbone flush pink just above her soft neck as she stepped to me.

"You're no virgin, are you?" she cooed seductively.

"Not by a long shot," my voice croaked back. I felt heartbeat and pulse begin hammering in my neck.

"So maybe you'll show me some things," Ann suggested. Come to me, won't you?" she asked, taking both of my hands now, turning them upward with her own, sliding them in the opening V of her robe to her creamy soft belly skin and ever upward to her firm breasts.

I felt the puckered, pebbly skin circling her nipples, traced my fingertips in slow ever shrinking circles until I touched only her hardening nipples with my eager thumbs, the balls of my thumbs matching the buds of her swelling nipples in size.

"Come with me, Eddie" she said, moving one hand down below her robed waist to hold her own. She led me to the bed, holding hands, leading me to where the freshly-made bed awaited, covered with the whitest sheets, folded back and ready to receive us, we strangers who wished to be one.

Ann's red kimono dropped to the floor in front of the queen bed, and lithely, naked and as curvaceous and fine as Guinevere sliding up on her white horse, Ann slipped underneath sheets, blankets. A window air conditioner hummed, and my slow heart pounded fast in my chest.

"Come to me," she repeated from our bed, watching me take off my clothing in a scattered hurry, pants and shirt falling away, blue boxer shorts thrown aside, shoes gone to somewhere. She looked at me the whole time, light dancing in those wonderful deep pools of eyes. I think she liked what she saw as I stood beside the bed, my compass standing at full attention, arms and chest and back tense. At least I flattered myself so . . . She was a goddess in those days, so, surely, I must be a minor god. I was in the bed. Where we belonged.

"You can do anything you want with me," Ann teased. Then, "Please."

We began kissing and licking and touching then, hungrily, as if this was always meant to be, prelude to falling into her for so far and for so long that what we made together was not just practiced lovemaking but something beyond me responding to her woman goddess' body and mind, responding to her beautiful, velvety curves and smooth, electric skin, beyond those blue eyes that narrowed while I filled her up again and again, eyes that never, not ever, not once lost sight of me at all, woman's voice that whispered and encouraged and demanded and thanked and told secrets in my ears.

## Chapter 21

### *Frozen Grandpa*

### Eddie

"Do gooders" are funny people. They never cease to find causes, no matter how obscure, to align themselves with, sure as I'm Eddie Couch. Our Margaret was always finding new and important causes to fight for or against, and her Harry was no slouch either. One morning, as he read the paper at the breakfast table in their house, while Andre, Lois, Margaret and I wandered around the kitchen and shot the breeze, Harry let out a belly laugh that vibrated the Venetian blinds over Margaret's kitchen sink. It was the kind of laugh that's infectious, that takes over, that dominated Harry until he couldn't laugh anymore and tears came to his eyes and streamed down his time-worn face into his stubble of beard. "Unbelievable," he kept muttering. "Unbelievable."

"We've got to help out this frozen grandpa." Then: "Margaret, how many of those Silver Pass airline tickets do we have left?" Harry wondered.

"There are two," Margaret answered knowingly. "Two and one United airlines ticket we earned with the mileage plus club through all our credit card purchases."

Margaret, Harry and I struggled uphill in the snow, deep in the Colorado Rockies. I looked down at the news clipping Harry had cut out and that I now held in my hand, and an ice ax in the other. The *Philadelphia Inquirer* headline read: "Trying to avert possible thaw for frozen 'Grandpa'." As I hiked, bringing up the rear behind my two friends, I read the article again, struggling to see the words as I took each uphill step. I cursed and blessed the luck I'd had in being picked to come along while Lois and Andre kept the book discussions going back in Pennsylvania.

Boulder, Colo.—This college town is a cool place, but it hasn't been cool enough lately for Bredo Morstol, a Norwegian of downright glacial mien.

The wind and weather, and now balmy breezes, have played havoc with the wooden shack where Morstol's remains reside, and the thaw was threatening.

Morstol's been dead since 1989; but nine years ago, his grandson, Trygve Bauge—a proponent of freezing the body so that when science figures a way to bring a person back, the body will be there—brought his frozen body to the family property in Nederland, a town of 1,500 outside Boulder. He packed his grandfather's body in 800 pounds of dry ice and put it in the shack.

Then Bauge was deported because he lacked the proper visa.

A friend of Bauge's, Jerry Nuessle, said Bauge has returned to his native Norway and another body, that of a Chicago man named Al Cambell, has gone on to more formal cryonic storage in California.

Leaving, as Nuessle calls him, "Grandpa..."

"About every two weeks we bring dry ice up to him," said Nuessle, 45.

This week, the shack that houses the ice-enclosed stainless-steel coffin began to complete its years-long slide into collapse.

Another Bauge friend went on the Internet, asking for help. An afternoon disk jockey in Denver saw the plea, and rounded up donations of a new, prefab shed and free labor. "People donated everything from ice cream to Stone Cold Ale," said Garner Collins, the station's promotion's director.

About 10 people trekked up to Nederland, at about 7,000 feet, last Wednesday to begin building the new shed, he said.

Brooke Svoboda, Netherlands's research assistant for zoning and planning, said that local officials were satisfied as to the legalities of keeping a body on the property.

"It's a storage shed," he said. "And, well, they're storing something there."

The reading while hiking had been difficult, but I couldn't stop a smile from spreading broadly across my face as Harry and Margaret and I struggled up the poorly marked trail through the deep and brilliant white snow that sent sapphires of sunlight glinting at our eyes. We were, most assuredly, going to help save Grandpa. This was why I'd swallowed my terror of flying and come here high in the mountains. The snapped chain of our lives was being repaired, the links of friendship coming together for Andre and Lois and I, Margaret and Harry repairing us until we were one chain unbroken again, whole jewelry. Frozen Grandpa was dead, to be sure, but he needed us. Who among us is not afraid to no longer exist, to die? Surely, we knew that Trygve Bauge's Grandfather Bredo was not likely to be resurrected or unfrozen and repaired in the near future, but the force of life, to preserve or restore life is so strong that it's in every cell, in the very core of our being. I walked upward, leaning on my rented ice ax, the replacement for my cane, cursing my weight but celebrating my freedom. As I folded Harry's newspaper article and put it carefully in the liner pocket of my heavy coat, I heard the crunch of snow under my rented climbing boots, the sound of popcorn crunching on a hard kitchen floor. My breath came in heavier and heavier clouds, hanging suspended and visible for a few fractions of a second until each exhale became vapor. Margaret and Harry kept having to stop to wait for me. I couldn't keep up.

My wife Ellen was never one for poetry, and she hated snakes and all insects, was forever calling on me to catch spiders or thousand leggers and flush them down our john, one of the only heroic things I got to do in our relationship, but she had a favorite poem that showed how much she, and the rest of us with her, appreciate life and mourn its passing. We are afraid of what we do not know. I remembered most of the poem in my head as I walked toward a decaying shack in the mountains near Boulder, a shack with a metal coffin and a frozen Norwegian inside. It was "The Black Snake" by Mary Oliver that my wife was so fond of... "When the black snake/ flashed onto the morning road/ and the truck could not swerve—/ *death*, that is how it happens./ Now he lies looped and useless/ as an old bicycle tire./ I stop the car/ and carry him into the bushes./ He is as cool and gleaming/ as a braided whip, he is as beautiful/ and quiet/ as a dead brother./ I leave him under the leaves/ and drive on, thinking/ about *death*: its suddenness,/ its terrible weight,/ Its certain coming. Yet under/ reason burns a brighter fire, which/ the bones/ have always preferred./ It is the story of endless good fortune./ It says to oblivion: not me!/ It is the light at the center of every cell./ It is what sent the snake coiling/ and flowing forward/ happily all spring through the green/ leaves before/ he came to the road."

 I missed my wife, but our relationship, too, had come to the road. And it was my fault. Ambition can kill too. Sexual ambition. Lust. The affair with Ann, all my demons came down to ambition. Ellen and I had come to the black snake's dead end road, and I had brought us there. The same road that Bredo Morstol had traveled before he'd flown the friendly skies to America. Keeping him on ice was the least I could do.

 When we walked into the little town of Nederland, a town of only six or eight blocks of local streets, none connecting back to Boulder, I wondered why the residents of these neat, Scandinavian style homes, each with a small and tidy snow-covered front yard, even bothered with cars. Yet there were cars outside of many homes. Mostly old 1970's American models, remarkably well preserved. How in hell had they gotten there? If Timothy Leary's head can orbit in space, I thought, why should cars with nowhere to go surprise me? It didn't take long for Margaret to find someone to get directions from.

 "You're the third of fourth group to go up today," this kindly old gentleman with a handlebar mustache said, "it's a regular work camp up there. All this to fix a shack!"

Directions in hand, or really in head, we set about finding a store in Nederland, someplace that might sell ice blocks. It hadn't occurred to us that Nederland's only grocery store had had a run on ice,

"Sold the last blocks an hour ago," a ruddy complected and pimply faced teenage clerk told Harry. "We don't do much ice business here in Colorado when winter's still hanging on. It's those whackos who want to keep Grandpa cool . . . Did I say 'whackos,'" he apologized, "I only meant those concerned out-of-towners like yourselves who want to help."

"Thanks for the help," I said.

"Have a nice day," our teenager responded.

An hour later found the three of us exhausted and sweaty in our heavy hiking clothes, victims of the fierce and beautiful light bouncing off the snow that blanketed everything around like a heavy and undulating outdoor quilt of white. Up ahead, on a flat plain of snow, we saw a group of people milling around what looked like someone's abandoned backyard tool shed. Even from a distance, the people working and carrying boards, saws, hammers, levels, bags of what must have been nails looked as if they'd been transported from a Grateful Dead concert. There were bandannas and jackets and shirts with skulls and crossbones, and loose flowing and funky heavy clothing made the theme. The shack itself was tall and narrow. In another life, it had been painted green. Its "A" shaped roof made sense, all the better to shed snow, but years of heavy wear had curled the dirty brown shingles, and several shingles were missing. I saw holes in the sheathing in places and rotted looking support beams underneath. The double swing doors to the shack were open; someone worked on a hinge where the left side door was leaning badly at an unnatural cant. Inside, we saw the sun-starred glint of the stainless steel coffin resting on what looked like two hobby-horse carpenters' stands.

Margaret took off her red skier's cap. Harry, in the habit of the long-married or long unmarried, straightened out her wig a little bit until he was satisfied. "There it is," he said affectionately. "Good as new."

"This is what we came here for," Margaret said. "The spirit of adventure," she said, taking in deep draughts of the clear and cold Colorado alpine air.

"There's no place I'd rather be," I said and was surprised that I really meant it. I didn't mind sounding like John Denver.

Harry nodded, moving away from his hairdresser's position. "Let's have a great day helping out," he said, the timbre of his voice charged.

"It'll be our own damn fault if we don't!" Margaret Dorris said.

It wasn't hard for me to imagine our frozen Grandpa saying "Amen" in Swedish. It isn't hard to imagine anything if you really try. There are crocodiles in cornfields, and television shows really are the commercials for how we're supposed to live, while the commercials are the shows for our entertainment, and the TV set is a primordial campfire moved indoors, drawing our eyes always to color and light. And in life there is always death and eating and excrement and joy too, and it is all so brief that we had come to the temple of Bredo Morstol, who had a 1 in 20 billion chance of cheating death, so that we could be truly alive while we were living. That is all anyone can ask. Sure as I'm Eddie Couch.

# Voices,
# Inner Chapter Six

*Only Once in a Lifetime Love*

### Eddie/ Ann

### Second

It's the oldest story in the world. It's the purest story too. Love is. Whether is comes once or never, it is what we live for.

Heart to heart. We lay heart to heart, Ann and I. We loved each other with fire. We moved together as if all time were just our time, this time together. We moved in heat and fire.

Ann's hands moved all over my body, touching skin. We were skin to skin, tracing every sensual outline of each others' bodies, every curve, every nook and cranny. We are heart to heart in our temporary bed, stealing love; we are one and the same person, moving strongly together, becoming one. She touches my face. She puts her hands behind my neck and pulls my face up to kiss her long and languidly as she moves on top of me as if swimming strongly up current in a river of sexual ebb and flow and rushing passion wearing away stones that were our old hearts, now worn away to pebbles, then sand moving always, incessantly, toward the ocean of us, where all rivers flow with power and time, elemental flow and grace. I love her. Love her back with all my being.

I touch Ann's face with charged fingertips, run my fingers down her hot neck to gently grasp her collarbone as she moves above me, her legs inside of mine, parallel, me inside of her, velvety, warm and wet. Her hair fans down from her red and smiling face as she breathes me in and out. My hands cup her creamy, round buttocks, and I roll us over, me on top now, moving, laughing, panting, whole.

We have two hours of joining together as if one of us couldn't exist without the other one. Our fear of waking as separate strangers, waking to separate already cast-in-stone lives, is swept away completely by our passion, leaving us two of the sanest people on the planet, rid of our separate minds.

After kissing, cuddling, me still inside her, I fall asleep, Ann's velvety body spooning over in front of me, still skin to skin, female breasts to male chest, hearts together. I dream Ann's long leg is draped over mine, dream that she laughed, curled closer yet to me so I could feel the warmth of her, the length of her, along my entire body. I sleep fitfully, alternatively lightly, for fear of dallying too long and being missed at separate home, alternatively deeply, for dream deep moments where Ann and I rock again together amid disappearing night stars and white sheets, making love with her again and again until we feel our shy bones and blood and organs waltzing away together in a spasm of spiraling tickertape and bright colored ribbons, the bursting red bouquets of our dream parade, never, no never rained out. I dream memories of love so thick we have to brush them away from our faces like tears and laughter and new spider webs. Love is why we do it all, risk it all: what we live and are willing to die for. Love is all. I know this now. I just hope I have learned this in time to save my soul. Ann knows this truth and has moved on to living it without me, but what we shared together was real. Real as rain and sweet remembrance.

# Chapter 22

## *"My Dinner with Andre"*

After we were back from helping to preserve our adopted, frozen Norwegian relative, something even stranger happened to us all. We got invited to a dinner party. It wasn't just any dinner party; it was the kind that could only have happened in America in the very late 1990's, when the century was about to draw to a close and when people were already making plans for end of the millennium celebrations aboard ships or in fancy New York hotels or atop the Space Needle in Seattle, although there was debate about when, exactly, the decade ended. Was it December 31, 1999? Did we have to complete the year 2,000, making the new century begin January 1, 2001? Would all our computers freak out because of calendar programming only set up to deal with dates to 1999? No matter. These concerns would happen with or without Andre, Lois, Margaret, Harry and me. What couldn't happen without us was the party.

You just *have* to be there, Academic Dean Crane enthused to Margaret one afternoon at the community college library, its roof newly fixed, its false ceiling area vacant save for an occasional bird or bat that might find its way in. We were between book discussion dates at the Wrightstown library, and although we'd planned a talk about T.S. Eliot's *Four Quartets* for the near future, that date presented no conflict. Besides, the Dean was Margaret's boss.

"Of *course*, you'll *have* to bring Harry," the Dean continued, her thick, reddish hair curled perfectly, her voice as smooth as molasses. If they comes to my house, *I* control the circumstances, she thought, no more turkey carcasses and cats. "And what about those lovely vagabonds you're taking care of?" she continued.

Margaret swallowed hard, expecting a change of heart about the college's surprising willingness to forgive and forget the trespassing and the thefts. Instead, Dean Crane surprised her.

"Why not invite those three also?" Dean Annie Crane asked. "It might be so, well, *so interesting*." So it was.

I've never been the type to socialize much, except with family, and, when I lost it all, job, wife, family, friends, after I lost it, I didn't socialize at all. When Margaret came home from work and said to Andre, Lois and me "Get out your dancing shoes for next Saturday night hob-knobbing with the elite and effete of Bucks County academia," I had my doubts about the whole deal. But, when you've lost it all and regained only a little, like the little immense love I had for Lois that was nothing at all and all of everything, you figure you've got nothing to lose, at least socially.

"We're in," Andre said for us all. "Where to? Wherefore? Who, where, why, what, when and how?" he teased.

Margaret had come to welcome Andre's warmly satiric manner. She gave him a crooked grin. She hiked up the waist section of her bright pink pantsuit. "At Dean Crane's house," she answered. "You'll get the rest of your inverted pyramid news story on the scene." Her grin turned wicked. "Say, Andre, did you know that the Quakers invented the whole concept of large scale prisons here in the east?"

I saw Lois' eyes meet Margaret's, the look of an older, understanding sister to her younger sis. As usual, we were sitting around Margaret's and Harry's kitchen table, drinking black tea. Harry was somewhere outside, puttering around. The green birds-eating-pink watermelon wallpaper, the yellow, flower-embossed linoleum floor had become familiar and welcome, but I knew this place couldn't be home forever. At some point, we three vagabonds would have to move on. Would we move together? Where was there for us to go? I had gotten used to living with uncertainty. Lois obviously had long ago learned that chance is a constant and was beyond worry. Andre, who had survived living in tunnels while others lived in $350,000 suburban mansions not a mile away, could change colors as easily as any chameleon. Life was a traveling pageant parade for us, and we were entertained.

The dinner was like no other I've ever attended. A guy like me, an Eddie Couch first from the west and of late of northeast Philly, just doesn't get a chance to get together with a group of educated people who talk about stuff other than the Eagles, Phillies, Flyers and Sixers, or cars or corruption in the city government or the damn city wage tax. This was different all right. It was one thing to get drawn into and enjoy book discussions, another to drop right into the politics of relationships we didn't understand.

Dean Annie Crane had a Ph.D., a great wardrobe, and a pretty nice house too. When we drove up the long, gated driveway in Margaret's battered sedan, the house spread out before us like a two-story country club framed by the bug-splattered windshield. The sun still cast enough light for us to see the covered front porch, the white columns that framed the front doorway and held up the porch roof, the elegant outdoor chairs and recliners that sat protected around the front of the house. The front lawn was immaculate green, the landscaped trees, shrubs and hedges perfectly shaped. Later, we saw the backyard tennis court and pool and the little white cottage that had been a gardener's house in earlier times. What went on inside was a bit less organized than the orderly grounds.

First off, there were a lot of new people for Harry and Margaret and us three homeless literary critics to assimilate. Annie Crane met us elegantly at the front door, her man, a live-in lover from Connecticut, Margaret had informed me, in tow. Both of them looked professional and completely at ease in their high class habitat as they ushered us into the house and gave us a quick house tour, answering our questions along the way. The place was impressive, to say the least. Although it was quickly apparent to all of us that Dean Crane's man had been drinking a fair bit, his voice was just a little too loud and his ruddy complexion just a little too red, Arthur, for that was how the Dean had introduced us, seemed in complete command of his mood and faculties. He looked smashing in his powder blue suit and with his thick, reddish hair and beard. I wished, quite suddenly, that I'd worn something fancier than Harry's borrowed and too tight turtleneck and sports coat. At least Lois had talked me out of wearing my customary sandals, convincing me instead to borrow a pair of Harry's black dress shoes just a size too tight. Andre was similarly decked out in Harry's temporary hand-me-downs, but somehow he carried it off a lot better than I.

We found the others sitting casually in an uncasual first floor family room. There were two crushed velvet salmon colored sofas, a matching love seat and matching overstuffed chairs. In the awkward seconds while everyone uncomfortable seems to wear an idiotic grin, and in the minutes it took Dean Crane and her Arthur to introduce us all, to do the requisite handshakes, nodded heads and "it's so nice to meet yous," I surveyed the topography and realized that there were at least five more people I didn't know, four men, one new woman.

"Ah, a familiar face," Margaret said to one young man who sat in one of the plush chairs, a tousled lock of his dark hair falling over his forehead. "It's good to see you off campus, Mr. Shakarchi," Margaret concluded. I loved her for having the moxie to wear the same pink pantsuit three days in a row. I think we all loved that her wig, so obviously artificial, was in perfect place.

The young man answered, "You know it's Michael to you. We're all in this teaching business together. Librarian, teacher, it's all the same at the brain ranch." Something in his voice irritated me. Regardless, we all made our way to Annie and Arthur's formal dining room.

As fate would have it, I got seated next to Michael Shakarchi, tenure track candidate in English at Bucks County Community

College. He of the quick witticisms and the practiced flick of black forelock hair . . . No matter, I thought, there were plenty of others to concentrate on. In particular, I had to fight the tendency to stare at the younger man that Dean Crane had introduced as her brother-in-law, the one who resembled a younger, leaner and sickly version of Arthur. This one sat at the head of the long cherry wood dining table, looking gaunt with belief. His skin was pasty white; his Hawaiian print shirt hung loosely from his shoulders. I saw the back of his head reflected in the glass panels of the dining room hutch: his mousy hair was unkempt and patchy. His eyes caught mine unaware, looking too long at the obvious.

"Yes, you're right, Mr. Couch, is it, there's something wrong with this picture." There was a bite in his quiet voice. "I'm Jonathan Laney, and I've got Aids." Jonathan sat up a little straighter.

"You see, my almost sister-in-law is not only the Dean of the community college, but she's also heavily involved in the movement and its publications. Annie here is one hell of a woman."

Jonathan turned to his left, where an impeccably groomed Puerto Rican man, easily 15 years Jonathan's elder, sat completely at ease in his dark blue suit, its front opened to reveal his bone white shirt and expensive gray tie. "This is my lover Louis, Mr. Couch."

Louis nodded at Andre, who sat on my right, and me.

"My ex-lover perhaps," Jonathan continued. "Things have gotten complicated. You see, Louis married a *woman* last year." The way he said woman was full of disdain. "They have an infant daughter who now has Aids. Sadly, it touches all of us."

Arthur Laney's cheeks got a little redder, but otherwise he seemed unaffected as he sat at the opposite end of the dinner table and listened. He smiled at his brother as Annie Crane brought out a gleaming silver tray of appetizers, miniature stromboli and tiny pigs in blankets, setting the steaming food in front of Jonathan.

"Dig in," she said cheerfully. "Dinner's almost ready. Nosh."

"Mrs. Kenny, Mr. and Mrs. Dorris, Andre, Eddie, this is Bill Ernheart," Arthur said, his voice booming. "Bill is a lawyer who worked for a Governor down south," Arthur continued, sounding as if he were doing a Chamber of Commerce promotional for his guest.

"It's not really so impressive," Bill offered. He too wore a suit and tie. "The Governor's dead now, and I find myself unemployed.

"Oh, yes," he added, almost as an afterthought, "I have Aids too."

Andre and I exchanged surprised glances.

"Oh, my heavens," Lois said, sucking in a breath.

"Come on now, eat up," Jonathan said, offering the snack tray to Louis and the others on his left side.

"I may as well tell you, I'm Warren," a distinguished looking man to our right said. "I used to be the Vice-President of First Federal of Bucks County, but I took the golden handshake to get out while I still had my health. I'm H.I.V. positive. Our Jonathan's right: it touches us all."

"I don't know what to say," Margaret commented. For once, I truly believed, she was speechless.

Harry too sat mute and almost motionless, except for his nervous habit of pulling the bristly hair inside his right ear. His face seemed to me to be a craggy canvas of concern, his eyes wide with surprise.

"And while we're giving backgrounds," the woman sitting next to Dean Annie Crane's empty chair said, "I may as well throw my proverbial hat in the ring." I saw what I took to be a tired, resigned flatness in her eyes, despite her impeccable dark blue business suit. "I'm Beverly. I was a nurse at the Aids Hospice in Newtown," she continued. "That is until I burned out taking care of wasting patients: I guess I never learned how not to care too much. So now I'm an ex-nurse. I bought into Bucks County Office Window Cleaning with Bill and his Southern Governor law money. Have you heard of us?" she wondered.

Lois shook her bemused head "no."

"A shame," Beverly went on. "When I'm not doing the logistics of cleaning windows or arguing with Bill, I go to dinner parties and make nice," she said. She looked at Michael Shakarchi with a provocative glare, her eyes unblinking and now intense.

Just then Ann Crane came back into the dining room. "How are those appetizers?" she pretended to care. "Dinner will be out straight away, as soon as Arthur gets his butt out in the kitchen to help me with the serving trays. But there's something you should know," she said, turning especially to Margaret and Lois and our little exotic dinner group. There's something I think that young Assistant Professor Shakarchi wants to tell us, something he wants to reveal. I believe it's the reason I brought you all together tonight. It's not something having to do with the college or his teaching but his person, his soul."

The way Dean Crane spoke and the preceding revelations lets us all know, I think, what young Mr. Shakarchi was supposed to say. In particular, Lois looked at me uneasily, using her body language as if to say "why are they forcing dirty laundry to be aired in such a public display?" My thoughts were perhaps more direct: you don't shit where you eat. Before I could know that we were right, Arthur Laney rose to help his almost wife. On the way by, he put his hand briefly on his brother Jonathan's shoulder, a gesture as natural as April rain.

"We'll find out what we need to know in good time," he boomed and then left, disappearing behind the swinging half-doors to the kitchen.

Michael Shakarchi seemed to feel the social pressure mount. His hand brushed his thick and fallen black forelock back up over his forehead more stridently now. He surveyed the table demographics. "I don't have to tell you all a damn thing," he muttered in an irritated tone. "What business of it is yours what goes on in my private life?"

Andre surprised me by speaking, his rising voice so close to my ear. "Trying to define a person's essence is like enclosing a wilderness of feeling within a wall made of words," my friend told the professor.

Holy shit, I thought, what's Margaret gotten us into? I didn't have time to answer my question, because Bill Ernheart had been a lawyer for too long to let Andre have the final word, and Warren hadn't become the ex-Vice President of a bank for nothing.

"'It's *interesting*,'" Bill said smugly, "how throughout history there have been truth tests for the innocent and the guilty." He stopped to wipe the pigs-in-a-blanket grease from his lips with a linen napkin. "Most of the methods relied unknowingly on the psychological principles of the modern polygraph. For instance, one lie detection method involved giving the suspect some rice to chew. After a time, the suspect had to spit out the rice.

"Care for some snacks, Mr. Shakarchi?" Bill Ernheart interrupted his own runaway train of thought. "An innocent person could spit out the rice easily, but a guilty one was expected to have grains of rice stuck to the roof of his or her mouth and tongue." Lawyer Bill chuckled out loud. "Can you imagine? The technique was sound: it relied on increased sympathetic nervous system activity in the presumably frightened and guilty person. Fear dries up the saliva, and that, in turn," Bill argued, "caused grains of rice to stick in the mouth." He smiled sardonically at the young professor. I felt I was watching something I shouldn't see, and I thought of Babe. Why should she be subjected to this modern mind game, she who had survived so much already? Maybe that was the point, I concluded. She had survived it all by never running away.

"There was another depraved variation," Bill droned on, grease still smudging his upper lip unbeknownst to him. "This more frightening technique involved placing a hot knife blade briefly or not so briefly against the tongue. An innocent person wouldn't be burned, but a guilty person would feel immediate pain, again because of the relative dryness of the mouth."

Margaret could stand it no longer. "You sure it wasn't because of diarrhea of the mouth?" she interrupted. You go girl, I thought.

"I've got a better one," Warren, who may or may not have been condemned to die, said to the assembly. I heard dishes rattled around in the kitchen.

"Don't start any good gossip without us," Dean Crane's lilting voice called out from behind the partial doors.

"Listen to this," Warren said, leaning forward, then accepting the snack tray from Beverly who had revived it from where it died. "This Persian King had a primitive but functional technique for detecting liars," Warren continued between eager bites of miniature stromboli. "Everyone knew that the King had a very special donkey, one that had the ability to tell an innocent person from a guilty one. When a crime was committed, or, when somebody refused to tell the truth," Warren said, chewing, looking at Michael Shakarchi, "any suspects were gathered in a hall next to the room that held the donkey. According to the rules, each suspect entered the room alone, found the donkey in the pitch dark, and pulled its magical tail. The donkey would do the rest! If an innocent person pulled the tail, the donkey was said to remain silent. If a guilty person pulled the tail, the donkey would bray out loud. In reality, the donkey's tail was dusted with graphite. The *guilty* person would emerge with *clean hands* because he or she wanted to avoid detection. The wise King knew that a person with clean hands was guilty, and he proceeded with swift and terrible punishment."

"Pretty witty," Michael said, not trying at all to hide his annoyance. "I can be witty too. Have you ever heard this one?"

He glared at Warren and Bill. "Discontent is the first step in the progress of man or a nation. How's that for profound? I read it in a fortune cookie that came with my underpaid professor's solo dinner of take out Chinese last night. That's pretty good, isn't it? That's the kind of thing an off duty academic is supposed to say, right? The right kind of witty repartee? Or maybe you'd prefer to pry farther into what's none of your business—my private life?"

I felt like crawling under my seat, and I was sure my friends felt the same. There came a silence gone on too long, broken only when Arthur and Annie came back to the dining room bearing large silver trays of food. Places were made on the long table, and, when the gleaming covers came off, steam rose off the tray of multiple golden brown Cornish game hens, rose over the huge mound of white mashed potatoes, rose in evaporating curls over the perfectly steamed snap peas and broccoli and cauliflower.

"Why don't you just tell us, Michael?" Dean Crane asked invitingly as she gestured with fingers of her right hand cupping toward her palm for plates to be passed to her for serving. "It's not as if you have anything to be ashamed of. Look at Ellen Degeneres. She came out on national T.V. of all things!" The Dean sounded proud of her Helen Reddy-like sister.

"Yea, what would it hurt," Arthur added from next to his almost wife. "Jonathan and the others could only help. And just because Annie and I and some of are guests are straight doesn't mean we can't understand."

Michael Shakarchi's hair was back down over his eyes. He pushed it back aggressively, then looked around the table at what had become an inquisition of sorts. "What is it with you people?" he asked, his voice almost breaking. "Can't we change the subject?"

"Yes, let's do," Lois said soothingly. "How about aesthetics? John Keats said a thing of beauty is a joy forever. But what is beauty, that's the rub."

Jonathan spoke for the first time since his confession. "If the old poet were alive today, he probably say something like, 'A cool-looking web site can be a magnet for millions!'"

Andre laughed out loud. "Touché," he said admiringly. Most of the tension of the previous moments seemed to dissipate.

Arthur offered a toast: "Here's to a duck that swum a lake and never lost a feather; maybe this time in another year we'll have our shit together!" We all began to eat, although I noticed that Jonathan only picked at his food. Unfortunately, the tension came back. They just wouldn't let it alone.

Bill Ernheart picked up the chase. He looked at Beverly, who avoided his eyes, then glanced back at Michael Shakarchi. "Maybe you could just write it down on a napkin and pass it around," Bill joked. He served himself a game hen while he waited for a response. He was the only one who had not passed his plate.

Michael Shakarchi's eyes bore down on lawyer Bill. "I tell my students that writing is easy: all they have to do is stare at a blank sheet of paper until drops of blood form on their foreheads. My job is to make the drops of blood smaller. It's an old saw."

"Despite that, I'm not writing down anything tonight," he finished.

"A pity," lawyer Bill replied. He shoveled some mashed potatoes onto his gleaming plate.

Beverly grew tired of holding her tongue. "You're my partner, Bill, so I can tell it like it is. Sometimes you can be such an asshole. I've read that lawyers have a higher than average divorce rate. Now

I can see why. Good food," she concluded, looking over to Dean Crane and Arthur, hoping to divert the conversation. "Delicious."

"Yes it is," Lois said, smacking her lips. I'd noticed her turning her hearing aid down earlier and so was surprised she'd heard the whole exchange. Babe never ceased to amaze me. We all seemed to welcome the chance to move on. My friends anyway.

"Very good," Andre said. He'd put his napkin in his shirt collar, and my buddy looked to be enjoying himself as he ate heartily, looking dapper in Harry's borrowed togs.

"Say, I'm writing an article about writing," Assistant Professor Shakarchi said. I gathered he too was trying to start again. "It's a list of quotes about the craft that I'm putting together for my students . . ."

"Always the quest for tenure," Annie Crane interrupted, laughing.

"Anyway, one of them is 'The art of writing is the art of applying the seat of the pants to the seat of the chair'. It's by M. H. Vorse," the young teacher continued.

"I like it," Harry said in his raspy voice, suddenly putting his two cents in. "Have you thought about what Maggie taught me about Joseph Conrad? He said, 'My task is, by the power of the written word, to make you hear, to make you feel-it is, before all, to make you *see*. That-and no more-is everything.'"

"I like it," Michael said. He brushed back that infernal forelock, began to eat. "Can I get the source from you and Margaret after dinner?"

"Sure thing," Margaret said. "That what we librarians are for."

"I've got one," Louis said. "I know you've heard it before, but it's so true. Just ask my Jonathan. 'A picture drawn with words, a specific, vivid example may be worth a thousand or more words of explanation.'"

"Like the pictures of your wedding," Jonathan interrupted.

"That's not what I meant," Louis said, his dark eyes shining.

I ate my meal, heard Andre's lips smacking next to me.

"What's your daughter's name?" Annie Crane asked Louis from the head of the table, sadness lilting in her voice.

"Victoria. She's beautiful. We're hoping she lives a long life."

"With contemporary treatments . . ." Arthur started to say, but then his voice trailed off in sadness.

"Just look at Magic Johnson," Andre said through a mouthful of game hen and broccoli.

"Whatever we conceive well, we express clearly," Jonathan said. "It's Nicolas Boileau. It's for you Michael."

"Thank you," he said simply, as if he could take the quote in and remember it instantly.

His hair in place, he said "Writing and rewriting are a constant search for what one is saying, according to John Updike."

"Seems like I've heard that one before," Arthur said. He coughed a little, his face growing redder than before.

"Bless you, sweetheart," Annie Crane said to her lover, her almost husband. "Want some more vegetables?"

"I'll take some," Lois said. "And I've got a quote for our young author. 'Originality doesn't mean saying what no one has said before; it means saying exactly what you think yourself.' James Stephen, if memory serves."

"It serves," Michael said. "Thank you."

Maybe it was because he was through eating. Maybe it was because being vice-president of a bank and then suddenly having nothing constructive to do got to him. Maybe it was the uncertainty of living with HIV. I don't know. But I do know that Warren, who had been silently eating for a time, jumped back into the conversation with a vengeance. He went after Michael.

"Professor Shakarchi, 'you don't write because you want to say something; you write *because you have something to say.*' It's F. Scott Fitzgerald. Now, do you have something you want to say to us? It's better this way, you know. We know anyway. Saying it will make you feel better."

I was shocked that such a distinguished looking man could speak so much invective in between his words.

Warren went on. "'Easy writing makes for hard reading.' Ernest Hemingway. Tell us Mr. Shakarchi. Don't take the easy way. Get it out into the open. It's why we're all here."

Michael Shakarchi put down his fork, stopped eating. "I've got one for you, Mr. HIV positive. Henry Wadsworth Longfellow said 'what an artist asks of his audience is not so much to *like* as to *listen*.' So listen to me. My sex life is none of your damn business."

"It would be if you were stupping students," Dean Crane reminded.

"I'm not that stupid," Michael shot back, then remembered who he was talking to and softened his tone, "I mean I would never do something like that."

Lois always had a sense of propriety, a saving grace. She came through again, breaking another silence gone on too long where the only sound was of people chewing, silverware clinking on plates, and people's very breath inhaling and exhaling. "Ralph Waldo Emerson said, 'Some books leave us free, and some books *make* us free.' We're going to be discussing T. S. Eliot's ***Four Quartets*** next week in our discussion group. It will be our first poetry. What do you folks think of it?" she asked earnestly.

"It's a profound book," Margaret said quickly. "The way the four poems resonate wisdom and play off each other is marvelous. The man may have been neurotic as hell, but he sure could write about the limitations of language and the limits of experience . . ."

"Here, here," Michael interrupted. He looked straight at Louis, who returned his glare. "Here's another Eliot line. 'It's not wise to *violate* the rules until you know how to *observe* them!'" We all sensed that Michael had imbued the quote with all kinds of double entendre'.

Babe came to the rescue again. "We were going to discuss a book we'd all read called ***I Am a Most Superior Person***. It's edited by William Cole. But the egomaniacs inside, although funny, are just too unbalanced, we decided." Those wise brown eyes looked at me, the eyes of a nearly 90 year old fawn.

"What do you say big fella? Which quote is your favorite?"

I was momentarily derailed. Lois Kenny had a way of doing that to me. "All that gallimaufry amazes me," I said. I wished I'd brought my cane to lean on as a prop. "I'd say all the egomaniacs in the book could be divided into either geniuses, blowhards or leg-pullers, except that those categories don't mutually exclude. I guess my favorite quote comes from Frank Harris, a 19th-century writer and blowhard. He said, 'Christ went deeper than I, but I have had a wider range of experience.' But I'm also partial to the novelist J.P. Donleavy, who'd only shelve books written by him in his library!"

Michael Shakarchi couldn't stay out of the game for long. "There might be some people here who should make it into the book, the way you're describing it." He looked to Louis and then at the others as they talked and ate.

"I love it when egoists are actually named for their own strain of self-love," Harry chuckled, his face an atlas of road lines and places been. "Shelly Winters says that her Italian lover boy actor Vittorio *Gass*man used to, 'grab me in his arms, hold me close—and tell me how *wonderful* **he** was!'"

Harry doing Shelly Winters was a wonder in itself. Never put down a man whose clothes you wear, I had to remind myself. "Sometimes, the egoists are just banal or boring. Colin Wilson said, 'I want to be remembered as the greatest writer of this century . . .'"

"Guess what?" Margaret interrupted, "He won't be. Neither will Theodore Dreiser whose dying words were, 'Shakespeare, here I come!'"

I noticed a pretty sizable tan fleck of Cornish game hen hanging on Margaret's ruddy cheek, and I was ready to alert Lois to give Margaret the high sign when Margaret took away my chance by speaking.

"Henry James was a classic blowhard when he said, 'I know everything: one has to, to write decently.' What is it with these puffed up guys?"

Andre smiled wryly, a 52 year-old cat with a canary he was about to take into the mines to check for poison. "Henre' Balzac was like an old time boxer. He believed that in order to write a great book, a writer had to be celibate."

My friend from the tunnels paused to survey his audience. "Whenever Balzac was lucky enough to bed a woman, he shouted, 'There goes another masterpiece!'"

Dean Crane and her Arthur laughed out loud. Arthur poured himself another glass of the inevitable Merlot that came from the preset bottle nearest him.

"What an ass," Jonathan said.

"Me or Balzac?" Andre wondered.

"Balzac, of course," Jonathan answered reassuringly. He looked like shit.

Michael, ever the professor on the rise, asked, "Do any of these guys at least vindicate their narcissism by throwing mud at one another?"

"For sure," Margaret answered. "Maugham said that hearing Yeats read his poetry was 'as excruciating a torture as anyone could be exposed to!' Evelyn Waugh said that, if Joyce was dying of anything, 'he was dying of vanity.'"

Annie Crane's almost brother-in-law Jonathan had to ask it again, although this time in another way, "Were all of the people in the book such assholes?"

Being out of the loop, lawyer Bill and banker Warren had been refreshingly silent as they ate and drank.

"Not at all," my best friend Lois said. "Some of them are delightfully vulnerable, just like all of us. Think of the biographer Lytton Strachey who wrote *Carrington*. During World War I, a lady asked him why he wasn't fighting for civilization. 'Madam,' Strachey intoned, 'I *am* the *civilization* for which they are fighting.'"

"That's vulnerable?" Warren asked, then said, "Please pass the wine" to Beverly, who complied.

"Maybe not that one," Lois admitted, and then, in a shock of private recognition, noticed Margaret's face ornament. She pantomimed a motion of brushing her cheek for Margaret, pretending the action was literal and for herself only. "But think about this."

Harry got boldly up out of his chair and picked the piece of bird off Margaret's face. Here was a woman who had grown beyond the need for shame.

"Go on," Margaret said.

Babe went on, big sister to the woman who was herself a grand dame'. "Just when you expect these nabobbing naifs to be oblivious to the fatuity of their self-regard, or to be repulsive megalomaniacs whom we should avoid at all costs at dinnertime, just then some of their one-liners subvert the goal of hating them."

"Say what?" Andre shouted, kiddingly.

"Translation?" Dean Crane asked. She was obviously enjoying herself immensely.

Lois knew how to translate. She knew a lot of things. "Well, for starters, I think Rudolph Valentino was being appealingly ironic when he complained that 'I am beginning to look more and more like my miserable imitators.' And how could you not want to hug Winston Churchill when he warned, 'History will be kind to me, for I intend *to write it.*'"?

"I've already got a date," Louis said boldly.

"Don't go there," Jonathan warned.

Lois hadn't grown up in tenacious New England for nothing. "Think about Juan Peron, Argentina's political legend. He wasn't known for his subtlety was he?"

"Not by a damn sight," Michael interjected.

"Well, I think he wins some points for his corner when he said, 'If I had not been born Peron, I would have liked to *be* Peron.' So you see my friends," Lois said charitably, "a lot of these alleged arrows of egotism can be easily translated into something else." She sounded satisfied. "I think I'll have a glass of that wine myself," she surprised us all.

Margaret, too, was satisfied that her face was free of debris. After Harry had sat back down, she put her hand in his. "The Frenchman Jules Renard flagged an important epistemological truth when he observed, 'I find that when I do not think of *myself*, I do not think at all.' Who among us can't say the same?"

"Right," Michael Shakarchi chewed. "Who the hell needs Descartes, anyway?" Lois sipped her Merlot. In past years, the conversation would have floated right over my head, barely rippling what hair I had left, but now, thanks to the book club, I got the gist of everything. The gist is all that matters anyhow.

Dean Crane was too good, too savvy to sit quiet for so long. "Here's to egomaniacs and all the rest," she raised her glass, her curly red hair a mass of body around her smoothly rounded, enticingly freckle-marked and grinning face. "Here's to the tongue-in-cheek brio, not ego, in Sir Thomas Beecham, the conductor, when he said: 'I'm not the greatest conductor in this country. On the other hand, I am better than any damn *foreigner.*'"

"Tongue in cheek?" Louis teased.

"Forget about it," Jonathan said. He raised his glass weakly.

"I'm sitting here thinking . . ."

"And eating too," Harry said.

"I'm sitting here thinking that we could divide these statements and how we feel about them into divisions of labor," Margaret said.

"How so?" I asked.

Margaret was nobody's fool, I knew. "Egotism seems to *charm* in entertainers, *daunt* in writers and artists, *offend* in politicians . . ."

"Yes!" Harry agreed, finishing her thought. "And *persuade* in chess masters." He was through being Shelly Winters. "Remember what Bobby Fisher crowed before he whipped Boris Spassky on T.V. in 1972? He said, 'Everybody knows I'm the best, so why bother to play?'"

"Maybe so," Arthur surfaced, "but bravado didn't help Gary Kasparov the time he got his clock handed to him by I.B.M.'s Deep Blue."

Lois looked thoughtful, her hands folded in front of her on the table. She'd eaten her fill. "Even the Puritans knew that ego could be a positive driving force. I think it spurs us to do things, even to be creative. The key is to moderate it like every other explosive thing in life. Ernest Hemingway used to say he felt as if he'd used up too much of his vital force on an early life well and frantically lived, that he not saved enough vitality for middle and old age. But I think a lot of us have had amazing lives, even early on; I know I have. There's no reason for us to extinguish like Hemingway did. Sure, maybe our lives haven't been all ambulance driving on the Italian front or Safaris in Africa or Tarpon fishing off Cuba, but think of all the amazing places you've seen already, the curve of green leaves, the whispering of water over gray stone, the places you call your own, all the people you've loved who've loved you right back. I think in old age we have to be explorers, as the story goes. Even the ones with Alzheimer's. All of us. We should skydive or bench press 200 pounds or end up living in the library roof. If we are not driven to something, *we are not us at all.* We're simply taking up space until we are driven to do what we do. Love can move us farthest of all."

"Amen, Babe," I said. She never ceased to startle me.

"Alice Roosevelt Longworth's father said he always 'wanted to be the corpse at every funeral, the bride at every wedding and the baby at every christening.' That's how strong his desire to be noticed was," I said.

Andre liked that one. I remember that he said so and told us one more quote before the conversation and the dinner turned. "The journalist A.J. Liebling had a zesty line," my buddy said. "'I can write better than anyone who can write faster, and I can write faster than anyone who can write better.'"

I'm no writer, but I remember thinking that that's how Andre and I had lived our separate lives: we had tried to live better than anyone who had lived a faster pace, and we had tried to live faster than anyone who had lived a better life. Something like that. I'm not saying it so well. Anyway, things changed that night.

Beverly kept pouring wine; dishes were cleared; from somewhere in the bowels of Dean Crane's kitchen a huge crystal bowl of chocolate mousse and a service of small dessert cups appeared. The remainder of the evening held so much promise. I don't remember exactly what ex-southern governor's ex-lawyer turned window washing magnate Bill said, but it was something too blunt and too pointed to ignore.

"Why don't you just give it up, Mr. Shakarchi?" It was something like that. But I remember young Professor Shakarchi's response like it was shouted through a bullhorn into my ears.

"All right, you *assholes*, I'm *goddamn gay! I'm gay*, isn't that what you wanted to hear?" he screamed out. Michael Shakarchi stood up abruptly, a trickling rivulet of sweat running down the dark skin of his temple. He threw his wine glass directly into the mound of chocolate mousse, sending a volcanic spray of spattered mousse out and over the table. He stomped out of the room without his jacket, which still hung on the back of his dinner chair, slamming the house's front door a moment later. We heard a car start outside and then the sound of tires spinning, gravel spraying. Then nothing. Nothing but breathing.

"Well, I never!" Lois finally exclaimed. Harry wiped a little chocolate off his forehead and tasted it. "Umm," he said approvingly.

"Damn it, Bill," Annie Crane said. "Now you've gone and done it."

There were flecks of chocolate in her red hair. If I'd squinted enough, she'd have become a strawberry malt. "And no thanks to you either, Warren," Dean Crane said sternly.

"More wine?" Arthur offered. He seemed to suppress a burp. I watched Michael Shakarchi's glass encrusted wine goblet sink slowly into the dark mass until it too, like the Titanic, propellers roiling helplessly in the air, slipped undersea for the long and final count.

Hospitals are always so damn antiseptic. Annie Crane had nurse-maided her almost brother-in-law Jonathan, along with Arthur's help, as well as any two people could, but now their care and the care at the local hospice in Newtown, where Jonathan's elderly mother frequently visited, was not enough. The wasting had taken over, and so St. Mary Medical Center in Langhorne it was. Margaret and Harry went along for the visit. I couldn't bring myself to do it. They told me what transpired. And I believe them. They've never given me any reason not to . . . Quakers may get the better of you in an argument, but they don't lie . . .

The way they told it, Jonathan had slipped pretty rapidly into an almost vegetative state. When Margaret and Harry arrived, Margaret in her blue work suit usually reserved for special days in the library and Harry dapper in his Sunday best and a tie, there was a room full of visitors in the private room Jonathan's mother had arranged. They said he lay almost motionless in his hospital bed, propped up with blue pillows, surrounded by his mother, his brother Arthur, Annie Crane and a young male nurse in whites who attended to Jonathan and whose nametag read Chris. When the young man was through checking Jonathan's vital signs, he took off his latex gloves, and, with a weak smile, threw them in the red flip top bin marked sharps and waste. "He can hear *every* word," was the only thing Chris said before he left.

Apparently, when Jonathan awoke to see his mother's and the others' faces, he was in pretty good spirits, considering. He was polite and thankful that Margaret and Harry had come. He told his guests a Charlie Brown cartoon story from his childhood.

Sitting up straighter in his hospital bed, he described Charlie Brown, Linus, Lucy and Pig Pen out trick-or-treating on Halloween. "After the kids came home," Jonathan said meekly, "they dumped out their paper sacks of candy onto a table. 'I got snicker's bars, lolly pops and tootsie rolls,' Linus reported happily. 'I have Pez, Mallo bars and Milky Ways, lots of other stuff,' Lucy bragged. 'I've got all that and some Unicef pennies and an apple,' Pig Pen exclaimed.' 'Well,' Charlie Brown said sadly, 'all I've got is a rock.'

Jonathan looked at Annie Crane. She saw the veins under his temples through his thin skin, like blue lines in Bleu cheese. "I got a rock," Jonathan said finally.

"You sure did, sweetheart," Dean Crane said.

"I want you the hell *out of here*!" Jonathan's mom shouted suddenly at Annie, her face growing instantly red. Margaret and Harry told me they felt uncomfortable as it got ugly.

"Come on, Mom, for Christ's sake," Arthur tried to make the peace. "Can't we put away old jealousy, old wounds? We're here for my brother, after all. Can't we all please get along?" His ears and neck turned scarlet too, and this time it wasn't drink.

"What the hell did I do?" Annie Crane snapped back, incredulous.

"All that damn politically correct involvement in the *movement*," her almost mother-in-law sneered, "all that bleeding heart posturing. It makes me sick. He's not your *son*! Why don't you get the hell *out*?" she repeated.

Margaret and Harry told me that Dean Crane was crying quietly when she and Arthur left the room. "We'll be back," Arthur told his brother. "Don't you worry."

When the silence in the room of four people was louder than the silence of the space between stars, Louis came marching in, his tan face aglow, grinning, holding his hand out to take Jonathan's hand, a much younger Puerto Rican young man trailing behind.

Hand in hand, Louis told his lover, "Everything will be all right Jonathan. God will take care of you."

Margaret had to turn away. Tears rolled down her wrinkled cheeks too.

"Jonathan, my love, this is my new boyfriend Joseph. I wanted him to meet you." The younger dark skinned man moved toward the bed.

Jonathan' eyes opened wide, his wet pupils the size of glassy dimes. He gripped Louis' hand tighter. "Even when my arms are empty, Louis, I'll still be holding you. *I'll still be holding you.*"

## Chapter 23

### *Lois on the High Trapeze, a Fictional History of the Wallenda Family*

Think about your brother-in-law. Imagine your entire family around the dinner table at Thanksgiving. Start with your brother-in-law as he's pouring wine. Consider all his positive assets, his good intentions. Consider all the things that make you want to dump gravy over his head.

I know you don't know me all that well, but we are all at the circus together, so it won't hurt for you to indulge me for a while before the real showstopper is on. Think about your sister now. Study her as she finishes her third glass of wine; think of all the stupid disagreements you've had, the quirks of hers that have made your stomach churn since you two were children.

Think about your husband. Don't worry, he's not paying attention; he's yapping to his brother. Reflect on his moods, his rages, his beer addiction—the whole shebang. Got the picture? Good. Now imagine this. Close your eyes and breathe deeply if it helps. Think about all of you at the Thanksgiving table, sisters, brothers, in-laws, spouses, all of you, forming a human pyramid. Seven of you, arranged in three distinct tiers, only you're not on the ground: you're on a wire about the width of a ring finger, and you're three building stories above the floor, and the person on top, maybe it's you, is standing on a chair. There's no safety net below. To live, your family has to work together, to synchronize every step perfectly while walking precariously from one end of the high wire to the other. One screw up, one failure to counterbalance one of the nagging little jerks from the brother-in-law, one petty jealousy between you and your sister remembered, one bad night with your husband, heck, one little hiccup or coughing jag and . . . And it's curtains for all of you.

Oh, yes. I forgot one more thing. You have to do this act perfectly not once, but seven days a week, for years, all over Europe and America. You eat and sleep and dress and travel together, hating one another, loving one another and handing each other your lives over and over again, cheating death. You see, my mother and father took us kids to see the Wallendas once, drove us all the way to downtown Boston and spent money we didn't have so we could see how our lives and deaths depended on getting along. Mom and Dad were already elderly then. All of us kids were really adults by then, and lots of us had families of our own. It was the late '40s after World II had ended and my own son had come home. Our trip to the circus was the last thing that our whole family did together before time and distance got in the way.

> *Ladeez and Gentlemen! You are about to see* **Circus History!** *The remarkable* **Wallenda** *family is astonishing the World with a Here- tofore Never Done seven-person pyramid on the high wire . . .*

This is all you need, right? There you are with your kids and your mortgage; you've got your overpriced popcorn and soda, and all you want to do is sit back and enjoy the circus before it all ends and you've got to go back to work Monday morning, but some old lady named Lois sitting behind you is chewing your ears off with her life story. Well, I'll be quiet in a few minutes, I promise, but there's a couple of things I can tell you that will make what you're about to see, astonishing though it is, even more astonishing. You see, I can know the future, for I have lived a long, long time. If I can go back some decades, a time traveler, to sit behind you at a circus, then I can tell you what happens in the future.

The Wallendas, you know, are the ones who made The Pyramid famous. They brought it from Europe to America in the '40s, and the pictures of their special trick made people's eyes go wide. The world covered its collective eyes 15 years later when the Wallendas fell apart in Detroit. It was the horror of horrors: Karl Wallenda up there dangling pathetically by his one foot, his pelvis cracked, his ex-wife's niece clinging to his silks for dear life, two other in-laws dead on the ground below, Karl's own son paralyzed for life. You're probably wondering how any survived, but it's not that simple to say, you see, because . . .

> *Ladeez and Gentlemen, the daunting task of the seven person pyramid demands the total concentration of our tightrope artists. We **Need Complete Silence** in the arena!*

I'll whisper now. Not to worry, I won't ruin it for you. There's no ruining what you are about to see. You see, the more you know about this trick and these high wire artists, the more amazing they are. When Mark Twain was born, Haley's comet blazed through the sky, and Haley's came back the year he died. I saw Haley's myself. It lit up the sky in a fireball so bright that you could read the newspaper outside at night, but even that doesn't compare to this family, the Wallendas. This is a family that loves one another, maybe loves each other too much. They no doubt have rivalries and arguments, fights that were never quite worked out, just like those in your family or mine but the difference is, for the Wallendas, each of those little spats can emerge in the most innocent of ways and kill them all.

You know how hard it is to keep a family unified. That's what the Wallendas have to do up there. They must be a team of **one**, one tribe, just like when they were children in Europe. Sure, you say, they're all adults living in America now, some of them have kids of their own, for sure, and maybe that's a stupid illusion these days, to be completely together. One thing is certain: the act has cost them years of trouble and anger between them, between the ones who held onto the illusion like a foot on a wire while dangling and those who gave up the illusion before it could ever really become reality. Sometime before tonight they all came to the realization that there was only one way to do it right, a way no other family could ever even consider. The one thing that could keep them all together is the one thing that also might destroy them altogether.

Yes, you know. It is The Pyramid. The Seven.

*We're proud to present the sen-sa-tional **Wallenda family** performing their **Death-Defying** maneuver high above us all.*

Pay attention to their lips moving up there on the tower. They're praying, all of them. In the name of God, if He can hear them. They're assembling now. It'll take a lot of paraphernalia: three heavy crossbars, long balancing poles for each of them, and a metal chair. What's that for, you ask? Just you wait. It's damn complicated, but I'll tell you, once the flying Wallendas are up there, you won't care a whit for details. Your heart will be in your stomach.

Here goes the lead man, stepping out onto the wire. He's a Wallenda in-law, married into the family, and he never walked the wire in his life until the Wallendas seduced him into this high adventure a few years before. It's easier not knowing anything, they told him over and over, no bad habits to break. Just do *exactly* what we tell you, and we'll all be all right. But I doubt he believes them, not for a minute, not the way he's up there praying like the Pope after fifteen cups of coffee. The worst part of it is that he's just like us: he won't get one glimpse of anything, not one look at the amazing Pyramid or his fate, because everything in the world that makes up his destiny is going to happen behind his back.

He's far out enough on the tight rope for the next one to place two hooked and padded braces over the lead man's shoulders from behind. And who is it, you wonder, that goes out next? He's the kind of strange being the Wallendas fear most of all on this earth. An outsider. He's a non-family member, a necessary but feared seventh member of the team. I imagine that whenever he watches the Wallendas play with their children, he must feel the blood drain from his face and must wonder, what if *I* must be the one who makes the inevitable mistake that will make orphans of these beautiful children? This is not a far-fetched notion, I'm telling you, for one reason because the outsider broke his leg falling off a wire once, and now he has to support the 350 pounds of pressure that each man on the base of The Pyramid has to bear. I hear tell that the others have to keep an eye on the outsider to make sure he's in bed at a decent hour and not off sweet-talking the circus dance girls in their revealing tights. He's got to be watched: he's an outsider after all.

A beautiful dark complected woman is next. She's a slip of a lady, but muscular, and, although she's from a circus family, she never dreamed of going out on the high wire until one day when she met one of the Wallenda brothers at age 17 and married him six weeks later. She realized within a few months that she had so much to learn and so little time to learn it in order to go up where her beloved went every day that she ended up in the hospital from a fall and a miscarriage that almost killed her. But now she's back, in Detroit, and she's standing on the pole that the first two men support, they, in turn, on a high wire stretched tight, the faces of all of us, the little people below, looking several stories up, where The Pyramid is assembling. To them, we must seem as small as guppies, as insignificant as hundreds of tiny fish among the millions of fish they've flown above, if they see us at all, that is.

> *It is absolutely imperative, ladies and gentlemen, for the safety of our artists, that there is to be **POSITIVELY NO** flash photography while this next trick is in progress.*

A Wallenda brother toes the wire now, third man of the four man base, the brother who ran away at age 13 and never came back to the Wallendas except to visit until now that the family has assembled itself out of chaos into the most perfect unity of all, more perfect than any of Aristotle's unities even. Yoking his life to the lives of the others is enough. But who can help doubting whether the second-guessing of his steps on the wire or his posture up there is justified or whether, rather, it is the life-long squabbling of brothers who love each other too much. You see, the older brother who is about to attach himself from behind is the very same one who always teased his younger brother, the brother that younger son always thought got favored treatment as father Karl Wallenda's first born son. Odd isn't it, how we can end up with our fate tied and yoked to the very same thing we have run away from.

Next comes the last man on the base, the stocky, well-built guy who is bearing the padded brace that is now connected to his younger brother ahead of him, now that's it has been picked up from the platform where it rested and attached muscle and sinew and blood to blood. This Wallenda has been a star in his own right in Europe, and you'd think he'd have been in charge of it all by now, now that he's in his forties, but instead he's glad to be under the command of his father Karl again. He's swallowing the bile that others might feel because he is so glad to be rid of the loneliness he felt on his own and to be *family* again.

This one is the handle of a living horsewhip. Movement, no matter how infinitesimal, will ripple and curve through The Pyramid back to him, always to him. He must be strong. He must be able to dampen and absorb that sudden force and movement, kill any waves in the whip, or else they'll roll back to the others while they're still rocking and rolling from the first wave, high wire surfers caught between wave caps and white, wind blown froth. You want to know how the handle of the whip sleeps at night? He pushes his bed against a wall so he can wedge against something solid and hence won't be able to jump out of bed with his arms flailing, dead certain that he's falling to earth again, like he did in Europe, when he fell so badly that he took two ribs through a lung and spit blood for days as if it were red mucus from some cold he couldn't shake. He has taken the place of his former self, the one who never dreamed of falling without a net.

Say, there's the eldest Wallenda daughter, getting off the railing on the second level of the platform and stepping out onto the narrow crossbar that her sister-in-law now supports on her shoulders. Watch now. This oldest daughter Jenny is a daredevil. Before the Wallendas dared to try The Seven, she was the family star, jumping over one of her brothers, clear over him, and landing on a thin wire 30 feet above the ground. She'd let a brother stand on her shoulders and walk with him standing there all the way across the high wire. Jenny's done things that no woman acrobat has ever done before. She's ripped tendons everywhere, broken her hip, her tailbone, herniated disks in her spine, and still she comes back. But Jenny quit the family once, some 12 years before, betrayed them, those are her very own words, by leaving the act, walking away. But now she's volunteering for the most dangerous position of all: riding the executioner's chair at the pinnacle of The Pyramid, nearly five stories up, with no hope of a saving grace if she, or anyone else, falls. Watch now.

Watch the sinews and muscles beneath their bright colored silks carefully. It's Karl Wallenda himself, the leader of them all, the one whose passion has led them to risk their lives, one for all, all for the one, The Seven, each and every day. He reaches out from the platform firmly and just balances the metal chair on the crossbar behind his oldest daughter. She takes a precise step backward and gingerly lowers herself into the chair, the overhead lights glistening off the sparkles in her jet black hair. Karl Wallenda is in the spotlight now, a flood of purple light projected up from the side of the center circus ring where the high wire apparatus is strung. He tucks his shoulders into the padded brace, suddenly bearing the 150 pounds of pressure he has to support, yoking himself to his daughter-in-law on the second level of The Pyramid. Now she's stepping deliberately, ever so carefully, onto the crossbar connecting Karl Wallenda's eldest and youngest son. Where is Karl's youngest daughter, you want to know? I'll tell you. His princess, his little girl, his secret favorite all grown up, is in a wheelchair. Her vertebrae are crushed; she's paralyzed from the waist down. A horrible fall in practice. She's probably somewhere here in Boston, or is it Detroit, in the audience anyway, her heart in her throat, wishing she were back up on the wire.

You're right, Karl Wallenda has a hell of a profession. He must maintain his cool for every second of the 34-foot-long oddesy across the tight rope, must be aware of every faint leaning, must know each minuscule loss of Zen harmony, must correct it as Zen master, with the slightest tilt of his body or the calmest verbal command; he must never betray even a hint of the terrible terror that no doubt screams through his heart and soul, that has cost him a daughter and so much more. It is Karl Wallenda's job to father and mother them all, heal them, put bandages and salves on their mental and physical wounds. He must hold them all together, even the ones he cannot forgive who walked away all those years ago. He's the pilot of the plane. Their very lives depend on him. Perhaps not everyone was praying. Perhaps not Karl . . .

Oh, the ignorance of those who say that high wire walking is not a sport. Tell me, where is the line that separates the two? Teamwork? Balance? Agility? Athleticism? Strength? They must be joking. This family has all that and more. I doubt even the great Jesse Owens could do what the Wallendas do. Closer still, I'm sure Mohammad Ali would have fallen before he fell. From 30 feet up, he would not have gotten up as well as he has risen.

*Absolute **quiet** in the arena, please!*

We'll have to whisper now. They are all in position now, and the spotlights track across their faces and bodies, clad in bright silk outfits, the men in silk pants bulging with long muscles, the women wearing skin-colored tights over their powerful legs. Before they start across the perilous walk, the handle of the whip yells out, "Ready?" The stridency of his voice tells everyone that it is a command, not a question. Ready or not, here we go.

We know how they do it, or at least we think we do, but **why?** Why in the name of all that is holy are they doing a damn fool thing like this? It can't be just the money. Don't worry, you say, you doubt that even the Wallendas know.

I am old now. I've lived so much longer than you. I don't know the answers to all the big questions that cry out to be answered, but this one I think I've grown to know. I'll tell you why.

It is family, clan, ancient tribalism. The reason is the will of one man becoming the will of all of them: the reason is Karl Wallenda. Let me tell you what I've read about this guy. Let me tell you what I know. He's up there in his 60's now. He can't be more than five foot five. If you think you're watching a spectacle unfold now, up on the hire wire, wait until you know more about Karl Wallenda. That's a spectacle and a pageant parade all in one.

Who would have ever thought that this altar boy would run away to join the circus? That this little serious runt who was getting straight A's in school would just vanish one day to join the charlatans and hucksters of a two-bit circus in Europe? Acrobat comes from the Greek *akrobatos* <*akros*, high, and *bino*, to go. Little Karl would go high. But first he had to pay his dues.

Karl was disillusioned, like so many of us are, and he was suffocating at home by the time he was a teenager. His grandparents were rich landowners who had disinherited his father for running off to marry a gap-toothed and illiterate peasant woman and for having two little boys with her. And, guess what, when Karl was four-years-old, his father flew the coop, leaving this poor mother with two boys, and her rosary beads, her savvy and her saints to pull her through. Karl's mother had a switch she wasn't reluctant to use, and her sons were *certainly* going to get up before dawn to sell vegetables from their garden in the town square, and they *certainly were* going to hustle from there to school where they *certainly would* get good grades, and they *certainly must* run from school to the rectory to do their jobs for the priests, and, finally, they *certainly should* hustle home to their glorified shack so they could do their homework before starting all over again the next day. And when the garden quit producing, they *would* scour the countryside with their mother in their delapated truck, buying and selling produce out of the bed of the truck so that *her* two boys could someday go to the university and reclaim what had been taken away from them all by their father and their grandparents.

But Karl Wallenda had grown up smart, and he'd been tithing to himself, stashing a small portion of his pay, what was left after paying mom what was expected and after paying the priests kickbacks of half his pay, stashing his nest egg in an old sock in his battered chest of drawers in the room he shared with his brother, next to the bed they both had to sleep in.

Those priests wouldn't have approved, he knew, but then they taught his mother to tell him that movies are immoral and circuses a perversion, so, when the rag-tag circus came into town for a weekend, Karl drained his sock plus interest and ran off with the pagans. Imagine, for a second, how fantastic that must have been for a 16-year-old boy. Imagine how delicious that taste of freedom. For a few minutes until young Karl realized he'd made a terrible mistake... Unfortunately, or fortunately perhaps, Karl was just as stubborn as he was smart, so he never went back, *no matter* how many times the circus promoters stole from him, *no matter* how many times people sent clandestine word to him that his mother and brother forgave him, and still loved him, and wanted him back in the fold. *Never, no never,* did he return to Mama, *never no never* did he return to their God. Instead, he climbed up the ladder from snack vendor, to barker, to carpenter, to mechanic, to head of vehicles, to stilt-walker, to clown to the promoter's man Friday, for god sakes, all by the time Karl was 18. Why is the question at hand. Why? Because he was a diamond in the rough of peanut shells and sawdust and animal dung, an honest, good-looking, humble, trustworthy and smart young man in a circus full of casualties of life.

Unfortunately, circus ladders are made of rope. They sway and fray sometimes, sometimes snap right in your hands. Whenever one broke, Karl wondered: could this have happened; would they have ripped him off again and again if he had a family, a *family*? This was what he'd given up in his bargain with Lucifer. *Family*, the most important thing of all. He'd traded it for freedom. Could he admit his doubts about the bargain? Whom could he tell? Name it hubris, name it sin or pride or dignity or balls. What he'd do,

Karl decided, was to get out from Lucifer's thumbnail by building his *own* circus. He'd build his own *family*, bound together as tightly as a fist, a clenched fist that a lonely man could hold up to the sky and pump in anger . . .

Sometimes when a man is angriest, he meets his softer side. Karl was in his late twenties when he met her. The love of his life. She was gorgeous, and she was flying the trapeze, just as he had begun to. Her reddish-brown hair and creamy smooth skin fascinated him. And how about this? Her father, at the tender age of 16, the same age Karl had been when he too left home, escaped using a circus rope over the stone wall of the seminary he had been compelled by his mother to enter, leading that poor lady to have a fatal coronary when she heard that her own pious son had overthrown God and his family for the trapeze. Sounds familiar, you say? Yes it is. And get this, the future Mrs. Wallenda's own brother would eventually have 15 children, all grown up in the circus life. You're right, I agree. She *was perfect* marrying material for Karl Wallenda. So it was.

> *One, two three, STEP. No room for anything in their minds save for those three numbers and God. They are a third of the way across. Absolute silence. Absolute.*

Of course they were opposites. Don't married couples, when they are truly in love, like my Charles and I surely were, don't they call that constant pulling east, the other pulling west, don't they call that balance? Isn't that what love is? She was temperamental, but soft and dependent sometimes, he a thinker, philosophical, aloof, dependable beyond hell or high water. When they pulled against each other, as in a tug-of-war, it only made them stronger. What did it matter that she already had two kids from a previous lover. So much the better for Karl's dream: two fingers already for the family fist, an automatic tribe. Their first daughter was Jenny; they kept adding fingers and building toward The Pyramid from there.

You understand, now, don't you? The high wire act was inevitable. It just *had* to be. It was more than a metaphor: it was

Karl Wallenda's life. One step off of the platform, and it was impossible to retreat. Impossible to turn around and take that one step backward to safety. Safer to take 30 more steps to the other side and not look down. No net. No, not *ever*. So you see how it began. Karl couldn't crawl back to *Mama*. He needed a partner up high to do the tricks he'd come up with, to do the tricks that brought money when people's eyes opened wide, that brought the money that let him build his fist of family. He sounded the alarm to his wife loud and often: never trust outsiders. *Family* is all. But Karl was the first to pick up gypsies or hitchhikers in his red '44 Ford stake-body truck. He'd feed and shelter them, teaching them to go up on the wire in all those little towns, but, often as not, they'd run off, take his secrets of rigging, take his original tricks to another circus, and always it broke Karl's young heart. Mrs. Wallenda thought he was out of his skull when Karl first broached the subject, first demanded that it come to pass, and her previous children were too young to object, so the inevitable came to pass. They became Karl's partners on the high wire. Who else was there to trust? I'll ask you that, sure as I'm Lois Kenny. Who else but loved ones is there to trust?

> *One, two, three, STEP. Nothing but three numbers and God or disbelief. Almost halfway across.*

See Jenny Wallenda atop her chair? She was *up there* as a fetus! Her mom would girdle her abdomen, suck in her breath, dress herself in baggy skirts, then go up on the wire, climbing on Karl's strong shoulders, letting her young son scamper up on hers. Imagine it. Eight months pregnant. Performing through numerous pregnancies. She lost a baby once when she fell off the trapeze. Within days, she was back up high. Tell your husband that one. One evening, her contractions started while her son was balanced on a chair on the crossbar pole between her and Karl. "Karl, my God, I am in pain," she cried out. "Hold on!" was all he could think of to say.

She held on like a trooper, finished the performance, and then, in a tiny clinic in a little town in Europe, she gave birth to the last of the fingers of Karl's fist: a final boy. "No, more, not ever," the village doctor said, and then he tied her tubes after Karl reluctantly nodded his head. They were a family. They groaned up the hills on Europe in an old Ford truck, its wooden bed loaded with bears, monkeys and a mountain lion, its wide cab stuffed with teenagers, diapers, toddlers, milk bottles, infants, printed circus flyers, junk, Karl often sitting at the wheel with a baby on his shoulders, pulling on his hair to hang on around the curves ahead. They'd pull into a little town, unpack the tents and tights, put bear crap in bottles to sell as a cure for baldness, put their brightly colored advertisements in wide-eyed children's sweaty hands; there were tent stakes to pound into the ground, seats to be set up, sometimes two shows a day.

The little kids had the job of getting in everyone's way while the family busied to get ready. That is the way of things, you know. At night, when there was enough money, all of them, save the animals but sometimes one or two of the animals too, would collapse at home: a rented room in a local boarding house. Sometimes the clan of the uncaged bears would sleep outdoors. Once, Karl nearly lost his private parts to the swipe of his water-hating bear's claw when both of them went down to a river on a hot day to bathe. This is how it was, I've read. Do you want to know more of the story, or would you prefer to just watch and swallow air? Go on, you say?

*One, Two, Three, STEP. God or no God.*

If you live out of a truck, you give up some things. Cribs, for instance. Karl's fist kept growing, but it lost fingers too. A baby girl rolled off the bed of the Ford, struck her head on the ground hard, then died. Karl's first and best wife was so distraught that she vowed to never again be so careless. She wrapped and padded their next baby girl up like a cocoon whenever the child rode in the bed of the truck, but this one wriggled too far under her clothings and suffocated. They found her blue and lifeless after a long summer drive to the next venue. The years passed, a collage of happiness and grief. The Wallendas learned what too few of us know: it's not bad to be sad. Emotion is the hemostat of life, an instrument of self-correction: when we are happy or sad, our feelings are not frivolous; they have meaning. When Thomas Jefferson revised his original phrase in the Declaration of Independence from "the pursuit of property" to "the pursuit of happiness," he doomed generations of his believers to chronic discontent. Karl Wallenda and his family learned that sometimes it's important not to have fun. They learned that chasing property and seeking happiness are *not* the same thing. After a while, two of the boys ran away, beaten down by the relentless tent-raising, wire-walking, tumbling, cage-mucking regimen, all under the stern eyes of a father and step-father who didn't care about having fun. Time for play? They must have been joking. Karl Wallenda didn't conscience play; he didn't really believe in friends. You give, they take, he'd say. Work and family are your only friends: everything else is just heartache.

Where did they run to? Yes, you've got it. To another circus. When they came home to the traveling show, it was just to visit. When one of the remaining kids fell during a show and broke ribs and a clavicle, doubt clouded Karl's clear sky mind. Maybe he was too hard. Maybe he'd scare away his whole family or lose his children to death if he kept taking them up high, dragging them along on his merciless ride. But what choice did he have? Their life's savings were all in the circus. His hand cramped when he wrote the letter so long overdue. He had not held a fountain pen in years.

The three youngest ones were going to have a real home. Go to a real school. One day, Karl did the hardest thing he'd ever done: he went home to the mother he'd run away from all those years ago. She looked so much older, but otherwise the house was the same. She asked no questions, nor were any unasked ones answered. She hugged them all a long time, cried between hugs. Karl was respectful, polite: he offered her the three youngest children, and, that very day, the Wallendas split up.

A year later the only telegram he'd ever received arrived at Karl's circus site. He read it, then crawled under his truck, sobbing inconsolably. His wife had to tear the message out of his clenched fist to find out what the telegram said. Their youngest child had been run over by a bus back in Karl's hometown. Another finger cut off.

You're right. The whole thing would just be so incredibly sad, except that it's an amazing testament to human will. Karl gathered up his two surviving children, livid with himself for opening his fist into a hand and allowing *family* to scatter like flakes of dead skin, furious at God for tricking him into softening when he knew all along that to be hard is to survive, tricking him into warmth and forgiveness and then smashing him to the ground. His worst fears were confirmed. Justice, fairness, laws in this universe are lies unless men make them true. The only law out *there* without our making new ones was the law of suffering: no matter what a man does, no matter his intentions, he will pay for what he's done seven times over. That's what's between man and fate unless other men come along to help. And if that's the way things work, Karl reasoned, if death was lurking everywhere, for the saint and sinner alike, then the only thing to do was for *family* to stick together, go down together if fate decreed. But, goddammit, Karl thought, if they had to go down together, they were first going to *go up* !

> *Look now. Here is where they stop, dead center on the wire halfway across. Here is where they must forget every wound that's happened, every wound along a scar. The past is gone. They must trust one another absolutely. Absolute quiet.*

Pray they have been perfect. Pray they are one, because if someone is leaning when Karl calls, "STOP" then God help him; that person is going to have to hold that position come hell or high water, hold force while Jenny Wallenda slowly, carefully, rises from her seat and ever so gently lifts her foot up onto the chair . . .

> *Hush now. She's standing to her full height, her full glory above it all, awash in colored lights, her costume sparkling, her eyes alight.*

If Jenny could talk to us now, she'd tell us at this moment that she feels an awareness, an aliveness in every *cell* of her body, something she can't feel anyplace else on this whole earth. The ones below her would tell us that purity courses through them too: their aches and pains, their arguments, the bills, the bearshit, the tragedy, all gone completely *gone*. There's a purity in their stillness, the most terrible and divine of purities, beyond what you or I can ever know. This is the gift their father gave them. If we don't get that, we'll never understand him; maybe we never will anyway. To us, putting our children through danger, that hardship, why it's unthinkable. Just imagine asking your kids, yes your son and daughter sitting right there next to you, just imagine expecting them to be *up there*. But then, we've never felt this moment, this moment up above us in the spotlights.

I've been around all kinds of people—athletes, poets, workaday Joes and Janes—and I tell you that there's an essence to this *family* that outstrips them all. Karl Wallenda is all of us enhanced, an atheist who understands the *concept* of God but still *hungers* for the reality, the proof. He keeps climbing up *there*, toward that absolute, no matter how many times reality, gravity, knocks him down. I believe he's *found God*, even if for only minutes, right in the clutches of all the con artists and hucksters, no, really *above* them, and he has passed what he's seen on to his children. The magical place of healing. Purity like nowhere else on earth.

> *Look now. See how still The Pyramid is. Only the slightest human quiver. Here, borrow my binoculars. See, only the faintest human shaking in their calves and their biceps. The rest is God. Up there.*

It was in the cards, you say, that a guy like Karl Wallenda would end up in a country like America, this shining light on the hill. He'd give up his beloved circus. Make some real money for a year or two. Hook up with Ringling Brothers. Go back to Europe a wealthier man, his own man. How could he have known, you wonder. How can any of us know? We have no Oracle at Delphi. We have only the flickering shadows of television sets, campfire substitutes, that have learned how to lie.

The *family did* months of running and leaps on the wire, did rope jumping, somersaults and baton jumps that other walkers judged as being insanely dangerous, and, when the big time promoters in Europe began to pant for them, and just after they returned triumphantly home, financially security so surely just ahead, the fist opened again. In the space of months, two fingers, then three, then four up and walked away. The grown Wallendas were suffocating, they said. They had to strike out on their own. There were only the parents, Jenny and one other of the kids left. Karl was stranded in the middle of Europe, his heart breaking, his marvelous act up in acrid smoke, the fist of his *family* shattered, bleeding. Young Jenny and the remaining ones couldn't help judging those who walked away, though they still loved them, as traitors to the only cause that mattered. Jenny ached to prove the defectors wrong on the one place it mattered: up *there*, on the high wire. And Karl, you're asking? How did he take it? Let me tell you this. Aristotle said that comic artists must "accommodate themselves to the wishes of the spectators," must please their audience. By his definition, much of the history of high wire acts has been a comedy: people being shown what they expect to see, at the expense of progress. This ***man, Karl*** Wallenda, would veer toward a theater of high trapeze confrontation. He would find an eager, impatient audience. He would find us. Find me, Lois Kenny, right down in my soul.

> *See, now. They are more than halfway across. Look, now at how the wire, no matter how securely tightened, bends under the weight we all must bear. Think of it. We are all defying death, each and every day. The artist is what we are. Only heightened. More so.*

Karl towed the family's new silver, tear-drop shaped trailer to a walnut grove in Spain, where the landowner didn't care if a trailer parked on his vast land. Yes, you're right. Karl did what he always did. He went back to basics: he set up a low wire, for practice. His

Jenny was ready for the big time, a natural. His remaining son had much to learn. For nearly a year, under both a blazing Mediterranean sun and Karl's critical eye, Karl's last hope, his remaining son, walked the hot wire from dawn to dusk, fearing the stick that Karl used to bang his feet when he erred, hating, yet loving every second of the attention and the pain. Months in a walnut grove, no electricity, bathroom or lights, the four of them, no animals, no shows, nothing but black bread and lentil soup and practice and the heat . . . When his father finally judged him as ready, the four fingers drifted through Europe again, all but destitute, sleeping in the trailer in rest stops until the inevitable knocks from police who saw them as vagabonds woke them up and forced them to move on. The Great Wallendas! Imagine . . .

# Chapter 24

## *Searching for Debbie*

## Eddie

B ack from the mountains of Colorado, back from our collective pasts, we were together again in Margaret and Harry's kitchen. My tea bag floated in the cup in front of me like a drowned mouse, its string tail flopped sadly over the lip of my hot mug. I can't remember ever being happier. Margaret was holding forth. Something about how she meant to complete the book she'd been working on before she'd left English teaching for the library. My psychiatrist, Dr. Benwish, had quit his practice to become a part-time English teacher in New Jersey and to write mystery novels. On our last session, he'd said, "Ed, I want to let you know that this will be our last session."

"Was it something I said?" I inquired.

"It's not you, Eddie. I gave notice two weeks ago," Dr. Benwish told me. "It's that I'm sick of the paperwork, of malpractice premiums, of being sued. That and I'm sick to death of hearing about other people's problems." He sighed deeply, resigned. Then he asked me if I knew any Literary Agents!

So, I'd lost my HMO rent-a-shrink, but I had what I needed now around me. Lois, on my right, had traveled so much farther into the emotional depths of falling and getting up again. She drank her tea at this oval kitchen table, kept the conversation moving, kept all our hopes for whatever the future held alive.

"Margaret," she said. "Perhaps you should spell out very specifically what the book is to be about." She paused for a long sip of hot English Breakfast tea. "If you can express it clearly to others, you'll know what is to be done."

Harry stole an askance glance toward me, as if to say 'here we go!,' and his lady love warmed to the task. "You all think you know me," Margaret said, her forehead shining below her gray helmet of wig, above those intense eyes, lucid and clear. "We'll, let me tell you," she warned. "There are three "ME's." She grinned a wicked smile, the fine wrinkles around her eyes dancing. "There's the "me" *you* think I am; there's the "me" *I* think I am; and there's the real "me" *God* only knows!"

"Ain't that the truth," Harry teased. He covered Margaret's hand, resting on the yellow table top, with a battered one of his own. She smiled that knowing smile, prompted by the touch of the long familiar skin.

"We'll, anyway," Margaret said, "My book was going to be a breakthrough in teaching syntax and punctuation. I came up with mathematical symbols for most of the coordinating conjunctions. It's brilliant. My students knew the math symbols, and they vaguely knew the seven coordinating conjunctions that form compound sentences, but they had next to no idea of how to structure around and punctuate those glue words."

Andre rose from his straight-backed chair, its feet scraping over Margaret and Harry's yellow linoleum floor, walked over by the coffee pot to the kitchen sink. "How did the symbols work?" he asked, pouring a refill from the permanently—stained glass carafe.

"It was magic. The one they use the most, the *and* conjunction, is an equal sign, isn't it?" Margaret looked up from the table for Andre's approval. "When you say, 'I woke up, and I went to work,' you're putting *equal* emphasis on both ideas, on both independent clauses. And equals an equal sign," she concluded.

Andre sat back down in a rumpled slump. His matted hair and dull eyes showed me that he'd gotten up too early. And early it was: still only 6:32 a.m. on Margaret's red numbered digital clock, though who knew how accurately she kept it set. 6:30 in the morning, and here we were discussing a yet-to-be-written and most likely never to be completed book on coordinating conjunctions and their mathematical equivalents! Older people get up early. Thus it goes.

"Do tell," Harry said. He'd sunk a U-boat all those years before. Perhaps he could sink this theory and do his lover a favor. Perhaps, if her theory floated after being depth charged, it deserved to sail on.

"Yes," Lois agreed. "Go on."

I removed the drowned mouse from my cup, set it in a napkin, then balled it up while the white paper covering leeched to brown stain. The tannic acid in my cup tasted bitter: I'd let my tea steep too long, but the biting flavor in the bottom half of my mug tasted good.

"We'll, it's pretty clear that a *but* is a less than sign," Margaret said, looking around her table for consensus. "If I say, 'I really love Andre, *but* he stole my purse,' I'm putting all the stress on the second idea. The *but* says that my first clause idea is outweighed or < than the second clause idea. Ness Pa?" Margaret demanded.

"We're with you," I said. I'd learned long before to give Margaret plenty of latitude when she'd built up a verbal head of steam. I rocked back in my chair, inadvertently knocking my half a bagel with Philadelphia Cream Cheese made-in-Ohio onto the yellow floor. I'd give my right arm to be ambidextrous, I thought as I bent to pick up my mess.

Margaret gave the ring of white cream cheese on her floor only a cursory glance. She had bigger fish to fry. "I think *yet* is a less than sign conjunction too. When I say, 'I'm a happy camper, *yet* I've got a bagel stain on my floor,' I'm telling you that my happiness is *less important* than the damn stain. *Yet* is a < sign too!"

"How about for?" Andre prodded.

"For he's a jolly good fellow," I said, mopping away the last of my circle print art off the linoleum with the enshrined wet blob of my mouse teabag.

Margaret, as usual, was undeterred. "*For*, quite obviously, is an *equal* sign too," she said, dragging out the *eequilll*. She had a way of speaking in a tone of voice she reserved for situations like this when she deemed that her true genius was being underappreciated by the rabble, the general public, us. "If I say, "I'm happy, *for* I'm in love," I'm using *for* as an equator, similar to the subordination conjunction *because*. I'm saying the *equivalent reason* why I'm happy, the equal cause, is because I'm in love."

"Come again?" Andre sputtered. Harry excused himself to go to the bathroom. Coffee flows. Prostates swell.

"It's simple. "I'm pregnant, *for* I had sex repeatedly."

"Four times?" Andre teased, smiling his wicked, Clarke Gable gone homeless grin.

"Let's move on, shall we?" Lois appealed diplomatically.

"Yes, let's," Margaret agreed. "*Nor* is an equal sign too. 'I won't give up this theory, *nor* will I quit writing this book.' I equally won't do both things."

"What!" Andre repeated. "You equally won't do both things?"

"That's a fact," Margaret said. She stood up as Harry came back to his place at the kitchen dissertation exam, lovingly pushed in his seatback after he sat down.

"Thanks, Maggie," Harry said. Then, "How about *so*?"

"Glad you asked," Margaret smiled conspiratorially. "I need help with *So*. *So* is a cause and effect linking conjunction, but what the hell mathematical symbol fits that?" she demanded of us.

We looked around at the littered debris of an unplanned breakfast, the best kind. It *was* both the best and worst of times. Mostly the best, I thought.

"I don't know about *so*," Lois chimed in in her singsong voice, the New England cadence of sounds I could listen to forever, "I don't know about *so*, *but* I've got *or* figured out!"

"Clever girl, Babe."

"*Or* is a less than or equal to sign," she said excitedly. "I will live to be 100, *or* I will die trying! Either the first idea is given equal stress if I make 100, or the second idea, the *dying* gets star billing if I don't!"

"Yes!!" Margaret enthused. "You've cracked the code!"

"Amen," I said.

"Just write the book, then we'll let you know how it floats," Harry growled.

"You know what?" Margaret said, smiling through the pretended venom in her words. "There's been an alarming increase in the number of things you people know nothing about!"

A silence came over the room. It often did when Margaret had the last word.

Andre came back into the warm kitchen from the frosted grass outside. He carried the *Bucks County Courier Times*.

"Fork it over," Harry said. "It's my subscription."

Andre made a big ceremony, giving Harry the front pages of the paper with a bow to royalty, then distributing sections of the news to we other three among the breakfast discussion club.

Pages turned, rustled. Tea and cups were filled and refilled. Toast bred in Margaret's toaster; her microwave hummed and timer bells rang. It didn't take long for the outside world to come in to the kitchen.

"What an outrage," Lois started. "This sweet old man died because we live in a society so technically advanced that you have to pretend you are on a *rotary* phone in order to get a human being to talk with." She pointed to her section of the rumpled paper.

"There you go again," Margaret accused, "ending with a preposition! Well, I never," she teased, imitating Lois' New England expression.

"Tough toma*toes*," Lois countered. "Read your George Orwell. 'Politics and the English Language.' He says break any of my grammar rules rather than say anything 'outright barbarous.'"

"Nanny, nanny, boo, boo," Margaret countered.

Lois wasn't deterred. "Come on now, old lady, this is serious. This article's about a local man who died in part because of that damn newfangled Voice Mail stuff."

"Hot pota*toes*," Andre exclaimed. He looked at Harry for male-bonding support.

"Do tell..." Harry said. I almost put my two cents worth in but thought the better of it when I was sure that Lois was serious. She paraphrased her news article for the club.

"Apparently, some old guy who lived alone in Levittown started having stroke symptoms yesterday. He started to panic, then did the right thing by calling "911.""

"So?" Margaret prodded.

"So he got *Voice Mail!* Apparently that's what you get when the lines are busy. Disgraceful," Lois spit out. "Here's this poor man pressing numeric buttons on his phone, 'If you think you need immediate help, press 1; if you know your emergency company's extension, press 2; if you'd like to leave a message, press 3; if your situation is urgent, press 4; if you'd like to receive automated emergency medical technician care, press your home phone number, starting with the area code, now.'" Her normally tranquil brown eyes hardened to barely open slits circled by a latticework of fine skin wrinkles.

"Here's this poor old guy having a stroke, and the emergency phone system is jerking him around with *Voice Mail!* Just picture it: he falls to his kitchen floor, clutching his head on the way down as he crumples. The phone receiver clatters on linoleum, then scoots away, pulled back by the elastic cord. The man *dies*, right there on his kitchen floor, a floor just like this one," she gestured sharply to the floor below. "This man *dies* just as our technology tells him this. It's the last thing he hears. '*If you have a rotary phone, please stay on the line . . . an operator will answer.*' Then the damn phone rings," Lois allowed herself a rare profanity, "and there's an answer, but it's too late. Too late. Our man dies! *Voice Mail!*"

"That's ridiculous!" Andre roared. "Typical of how the world's gone to hell in a hand basket. We're so smug about computers, cell phone, fax machines . . . What do they mean if we don't save lives, if we don't help people?"

"Amen." I said. Silence filled the room again. Pages turned while silverware clinked. Someone passed gas, though no one would admit to it.

I broke the crystalline quiet. "It smells like something died in here."

"The one who smelt it dealt it," Andre chided.

"Listen, guys," I said. My misguided attempt at humor embarrassed me, if only because Lois was here. As for the others, I wouldn't have minded, but I looked up to Lois like an adopted mother. "Back when I had my first family, before I fell from grace," I continued, "my daughter Carolyn was reading the Personal Ads in the paper one day when she shouted 'Holy crap! This one's so tender, so sweet!'

"Let me see it," I told her, but she wanted to make a game of it. Carolyn handed me the whole page full of ads for the lovelorn. "Come on, I'm your father," I demanded, but she wouldn't budge. Carolyn wouldn't point out which Personal Ad had struck her fancy. I searched those ads for the longest time, some of them depressing me with their whining and plaintive beggings for intimacy, until I came across one that I thought looked heartfelt, looked right.

"Is this it?" I demanded again, but Carolyn sat stone-faced in her purple hair and with her diamond stud through her nose. That's another story. I tried reading it aloud:

### *"Affectionate, Blind*

*Gentleman Looking for Tender Loving Woman Named Debbie. Must Be Willing To Accept Love & Understand the Needs of a Blind Person, Call 215-555-8614 9/30/'98"*

"Try asking Mom," she said coyly, then left the room. I was alone with my newspaper and with questions.

"Ellen," I yelled in my best Archie Bunker bellow. "Ellen, come here." Remember, I was king of my row home then. Before it all came crashing down.

When my bride showed up, I showed her the ad, of course.

"I don't get it," I admitted. "Why the hell does he have to find a woman named *Debbie*? Why won't any sensitive woman do? Why Debbie?"

Ellen scowled at me, all those years ago. "If you don't get it, you're hopeless," she said. "You're just like all men, can't see past the end of your damn nose. *You don't know what true love is.*"

"Come on, hun, tell me," I pleaded. I just didn't get it.

"Eddie, you're pathetic," she said. "Get help." If you don't see it, I'm certainly not going to tell." She padded off down our hallway, out of the living room where I sat in my Barkolounger, the tails of her bunny rabbit slippers bouncing, my last year's Christmas present from hell. I didn't know it then, but she was hopping right out of our lives, my life.

"For days to come, I took the Personal Ad for Debbie to work, tried in on the teachers in the Business Department at the community college, tried it on secretaries, on some of the admissions people, on the librarians..."

"So what did you find?" Andre interrupted. He stood up from out breakfast table, began to clear the food and flotsam and jetsam from our table, signaling what was for him the end of that meeting.

"It broke down by sex," I told him.

"Most things do," Margaret agreed. She rose too, began to pile used plates in her sink.

"The women, almost to a person, got it. They knew what the ad was all about. We men didn't have a clue..."

"I can tell you what it meant," Lois said. All eyes were on her then.

"Do tell," Harry growled.

Lois looked at me, saw a glimmer of recognition there, then trusted her intuition. She pretended to look to the heavens for divine inspiration, saw instead Harry and Margaret's old brown water stain spread on the kitchen ceiling from '93 like an irregular Rorschach blotter, the winter of the ice storms and ice-clogged gutters that even old New England Harry from Maine didn't dare ladder up to break free. "Well," she said, "it's like this."

"The blind guy must have had an affair with a woman named Debbie, maybe they were even married; I'm not sure," Lois said.

Margaret turned from the hot soapy water to nod and smile a knowing smile.

Lois continued. "What I do know is that the blind ad writer still burns the candle for *this* Debbie. He wants her and her alone to recognize him in his ad. He's begging for a second chance. He's publicly declaring his love for her in the hopes that Debbie will see their relationship in this Personal Ad."

"So, it's only for one Debbie, **The Debbie**," Harry repeated.

"Yes," Lois nodded wisely, looking away from the ceiling to the cloud of steam that Margaret stood by at the sink.

"Jeeze," I never would have gotten that in a million years," Andre said.

"None of the men at school, Professors and janitors alike, got it either," I remembered.

"That's the whole point," Margaret said. "That's what your daughter was trying to teach you, numskull." She took the stopper out of her drain: the dammed—up soapy water, mixed with bits of swollen bread and dark flecks of food, turned in an ever tighter, ever faster, clockwise circle down the drain until it all disappeared.

"More proof that life sucks," she said. "Especially for sentient women dealing with dipstick men."

## Chapter 25

### *The Great Wallendas, as told by Lois Kenny*

"I'm not afraid to die; I just don't want to be there when it happens."—Woody Allen

I am sorry I have talked so long. A woman my age doesn't get to share her mind so often. I've outlived my friends. You don't mind, you say? Well, there's just a little more to tell. And some of it is so terrible and grand that you can't keep your eyes off it: it's an auto accident or another's misfortune or glory. It is someone else's. It is our own. Karl's crazy dream? He couldn't talk about it any more. No circus would pay enough to put the fist back together, whole, unless the Wallendas could do The Pyramid. But how could they if most of the seven had to leave the fold and be free, just as he himself had done? They found a steady job. Things got a little better. Then Karl's non-Prodigal son fell badly in Italy. He lay on the thin blue matting, hurting, feeling pain everywhere. This was the crossing point, the moment of truth. It was clear. If he did what his mind told him to do, quit this damn act he'd never liked, support his father's nagging fear about his son's lack of heart, then it was all over. The dream. Everything. He *was* the last hope; there was no one to take his place; he was all that stood between his parents and the desperation of old age and failure. You got it. He was a *Wallenda*: he got back to his feet, climbed back up the tower to the platform, the little crowd in northern Italy going wild, and he positively *nailed* all those insane jumps his father had willed him to learn. Another maniac was born. Maybe crazier than the first. Here one of the world's finest wire walkers came to be. He could do over a thousand jump-rope leaps of the high wire, leap over his mother, his father, his sister and a hired outsider in shows, once did a jump over *seven* people in practice. This one and Jenny were Wallendas you could rebuild the craziest dream on.

The others? Of course, they joined up with other circuses, became stars shining in their own smaller constellations. Sometimes they called home to whatever mobile home that was, but Karl seldom could bring himself to the phone. Sometimes they told him how they felt, but it was never really right. Then even Jenny left. She snuck out of the rear window of their trailer, ran away at *thirty* years *old to* marry a tiger trainer. She fainted dead away when the justice of the peace read the solemn vows. Five days later, she was back in the trailer with Mom and Dad, her brother and her new husband, who, quite naturally, became part of the act. The years flowed on. There was talk of Karl's having to retire. The non-Prodigal son decided he had to leave to join some of the *others*, just to keep the bill collectors away. He cried so much on the short airplane ride that the other passengers had an attendant ask him what was wrong. What was wrong?

*Everything put together falls apart.*

We're starting to think alike, the young me who saw it all in Boston and an 87 year-old named Lois. And you. Well, you know who you are. The others pooled their savings and bought a house for their mom and dad in southern California, an American base of operations. Now that they had no need for a big place, now that the animals were long gone just like the fist had broken, Karl Wallenda and his first wife had a permanent roof over their heads. And sometimes when the palm of the fist was between engagements in Europe and America, the others came to Los Angeles to visit home. But they were visitors, and the second guessing and the old wounds were as frequent as the laughter and the hugs. Only one of Karl's step-sons ever dared to point out the kind of contradiction that all of us can see except when it involves ourselves: he flung it at Karl's astonished face . . . "How can you say I betrayed the family? ***You*** abandoned *your family,* didn't you?"

> *Watch now, see how the Wallendas keep from falling apart. One, Two, Three,* **STEP.** *More than halfway across. God is here or nowhere. How easy it would be for the Wallendas to fall apart. Karl's nephew feels his shoulders sagging from the enormous weight piled on top of him . . . The 45-pound pole begins to drag his hands lower, just a little lower . . . This is where the men on the bottom are actually walking uphill, because, even with* **16,000** *pounds of pressure pulling on the cable to keep it taught, pressure from 14 guy wires ratcheted as tightly as the steel rigging will bear, even **this** is not enough to keep the high wire from sagging just a little under the weight of half a ton of human beings and 350 pounds of poles. This is where all the practice and **suffering** will strengthen you or kill you.*

We'd better keep it down or our seatmates will shush us again. See, now. See what's happened? One of the men in the base has stepped too slow, and the base has separated just a hair. See how it makes the whole thing tremble for an eternity, ripples after ripples after water after stone's throw? Four and five a day practices on the low wire in Karl's backyard are nothing now. Nothing without God.

Without some higher power, some calling together, some unity, the Wallendas might just as well be spread across the globe, every artist for himself, fighting alone to survive, just as it was before they all came together. I agree. You're right, no doubt. But, when they came together, what an ensemble it was. Who cares why they did it? A psychologist might say for love or fear of Dad. A marine might say for honor and the family name. A businessperson could cite the mortgage payments. But we know better: it was for the fist held angrily up against the sky; for the answers from the sky that were to come, one way or the other. Sometimes it was three generations running around the Los Angeles home, homemade soup and bread between the afternoon and evening practices, Karl beaming at his legacy, and everyone splashing happily in the backyard pool at the end of the long, happy days. Other times, it was the old blood anger or mistrust that seemed to always precede failure.

Yes, I've heard that too. On one of their first practices assembling The Pyramid, before all the Wallendas were again in the fold, an *outsider* that Karl had had to recruit to make seven nearly brought them down. The family came *thisclose* to disaster when, a few feet from the end of the high wire, the *outsider* couldn't take the pressure any more, the constant feeling that he was not one of them, the fear of death always palpable in every wrong step he might take. Just those few feet from the end, he lunged wildly for the platform, for safety, to save his hide. *No net, **ever***. Not even in practice. The oldest Wallenda daughter, on top of the second crossbar set of three, took three quick steps back to compensate, to save the whole damn thing. God knows how, but the eldest Wallenda son, the stocky one, the handle of the horsewhip, somehow held on, *held on*, when his sister's last saving step backward broke out several of his teeth.

*Just the slightest trembling ripples through them all.*

They *held on*, pressed on. They went up before the crowds. I agree with you entirely, both star struck girl and old woman now. Looking back on it all. For the longest time, the standing ovations, coming night after night, the awestruck faces below, the purity of being up high, it was all enough to make it work. It wasn't just necessary; it wasn't just a job; it was fun. It was a bracing swim in the deep ocean we call living. So what happened, you're asking? The water, or the rarefied air they walked on, grew too cold. The

Pyramid brought out every weakness of character, every all too human failing, picked the scabs off every old scar, abraded the skin covering every purpling bruise. The Seven broke apart only months after they had all come together, fractured by the same, tired refrain.

*Whatever needs too badly to be together is destined to fall apart.*

That's it, you say. What needs too much to be together will fall apart. The Wallendas all quit and went to separate homes. So, this is where the story would have ended, ended without climax, without resolution. This is where it ends. Except beginnings are ends and ends beginnings. You know it already, don't you? Of course you do. You're here, here now, aren't you? The lead talent scout for the Greatest Show on Earth saw them before the break-up. This Ringling Brothers representative showed up a year later at Karl's Los Angeles house early one morning with a long simmering question. While the question had heated up, Karl's first wife, the mother of his children, had left him for the very same thing that had brought her to him: that damned willful stubbornness, that perfectionism that nearly killed them all. That same old dilemma ticked like a time bomb in their living room, that which needs too much to be together falls apart. After all those years, they argued with renewed vigor. She'd say things like, "I've done your laundry for over twenty years, and now you act like you don't know me at all!" She'd stand up to his obstinance sometimes: "I don't take nothing from nobody!" Karl Wallenda would furrow his brow, warn of their future should they split up: "Half of nothing will be less than before!" Karl would remarry shortly thereafter. She never would. You know the question. Could the Wallendas accept one of the fattest contracts in the Greatest Show's long history to do The Pyramid for two years, beginning with a triumphant return tour of most of all these United States?

*Could* they? Would they? Of course, they *couldn't*. The family was flung all over. Of course they did accept. Mrs. Wallenda herself would put past over future and rejoin the act once and for all.

Maybe we shouldn't talk about what happened next. After all, they're . . .

> so *close* to the other end of the tightrope, *so close* to the safety of the platform and to all that rich applause. If they can just hold *together for a few more steps, we can turn our attention elsewhere, maybe to salt peanuts, cold drinks or painted turtles. If they can just **hold on** . . .*

Perhaps it's not the ideal time to talk about family history clinging heavily to their backs while they're on the wire. Maybe it's a jinx to mention one of the Wallendas tumbling to earth, crushing her back, falling within a spider thread of death. But I've got to finish it out, my friend. I grow old now. My buddy Eddie says that the Buddhists are right: everything is linked. Besides, old ladies like to talk while they can still draw breath. If you look at death carefully and for long enough, if you stare at it first in those older than yourself and then in those your age, then younger, you see the ever larger face of the predator which we thought we had triumphed over long ago.

Yes, you say, that's true. What's that? Yes, war is the same way. That idea gives me the shivers too. Study war carefully enough and see the loose and ravenous circus animal we humans thought we had caged years ago. It's the same with families; the politics of the family are potentially every bit as turbulent as the politics of nations, just on a smaller scale. Think about The Seven. Think about the ones who remained true to the fist resenting those who walked away. Consider how one older brother and his wife were banished from the ones who would walk the wire for the Greatest Show on Earth's triumphant American tour. The *outsider* who panicked was traded for *another* non-family member. Spouses and nieces and nephews had to be painstakingly trained in Los Angeles before they all boarded Ringling's mile long train to do the country right.

The banished one and his family showed up right before the tour began, demanding to rejoin the fist. Some of the others wanted him to take the new outsider's place. Although each finger of the fist voted in its own way, in the end it was Karl himself who held sway like some Old Testament God. Banishment was banishment, though he would bend a little: the prodigal son could come along and be their maestro on the three-ring floor, conduct their orchestra on high. The prodigal son's wife warned Karl, just as he himself had said so many times, that outsiders were poison, not to be trusted, but sometimes our best lessons are lost on ourselves.

You know it. Karl wouldn't listen. But his eyes misted the first time they did The Pyramid to perfection. Afterward, his soon to be ex-wife cried and cried, although the family wasn't sure whether the tears were of joy or sadness. No matter. The show went on. The Pyramid assembled itself divinely out of chaos and walked and walked up above it all. It wasn't long before the pressure built up too high for the *outsider*. One night in the Deep South, just before the miracle act, he chickened out, something no Wallenda had ever done, and leaped down from the high wire onto the blue mats *during a performance*. The family canceled the performance. Later that embarrassing night, the outsider bashed his head again and again against his train car's walls, sobbing inconsolably, saying that he couldn't take the family's pressure. The Wallendas could either keep yoking themselves to a man coming unyoked, or they could surrender the money and the dream. Or, you say, they could . . .

> *The Seven was swallowing Karl as surely as skin cancers invading him piece by piece. What could he tell the Ringling management at curtain time in Virginia in two nights? His youngest daughter, **tired** of her older siblings' demands, announced she'd had enough. Karl agonized until 2 a.m., uncharacteristically drinking too much, then finally broke another of his own rules. He ran away. An hour later, he flipped his truck over an Interstate 85. He spend hours in the emergency room, bleeding internally from the crash, going more than 24 hours without sleep, when it finally was clear to him. He had to forgive. There were few things as precious in life as second and third chances. He'd let his banished, oldest son rejoin the **family** up high.*

So, you see, you were right. Trust those intuitions, instincts. Karl's younger daughter left too, but, when she heard about her father's mishap, she had a change of heart and showed up in Virginia. Family came first, after all. She was a little shaky over what had happened, but she was there. And the old man, the grand master of Zen and human will, couldn't consider the thought of postponing The Pyramid once more. The Greatest Show's management would lose all patience, if it hadn't already. Not everyone was master of the quirky event, the unpredictable. Not everyone knew that whatever you do, you pay seven times over, seven times over seven. Karl Wallenda was still bleeding inside, and he was in pain. His youngest daughter seemed distracted, unfocused, but she had come back for him, for family.

Karl Wallenda was the only man with the power to stop himself, his prodigal daughter, his prodigal son, and the rest of the family from going up. In an uneastern fog of distraction and doubt, Karl climbed gingerly up the ladder to the platform to get ready for the tricks his fist of family performed every show before The Seven.

> *He had forgotten to make his customary last inspection of the rigging just before the show. He only knew that he **loved** his first wife dearly, and, though she was here with him, he knew that they were through. He knew his abdomen hurt, that his truck was wrecked.*

Well, things do have a way of working out sometimes. Yes, you're right, although sometimes they don't. Sometimes the magic works; sometimes the magic doesn't work. Karl Wallenda, the patriarch himself, knew that he couldn't do the act much longer. The alter boy, grown grizzled, remembered his lessons well. Time and chance happeneth to us all. There would be life after the show. Life after . . .

He watched his youngest daughter run toward his stepson, approaching the middle of the high wire for the over and under stunt. She leaped, a tumbling blur of Arctic White and Imperial Blue costume in the bright lights. It was hard for him to know what, exactly, happened next. Yes, I know that you know. Maybe she missed her jump that badly, Karl thought in retrospect. Maybe the cable, not quite attached tightly enough to the opposite tower, he agonized, might have sagged as she landed, and then rebounded, throwing her off. Perhaps, he tortured himself, the rigging wires were not stretched quite tight enough. He saw her over and over again, his favorite, falling in slow motion kaleidoscope color, breaking ribs and puncturing a lung as she hit the cable on the way down, her desperate hand grabbing the wire just long enough, damn it all to hell, to swing her further outward, past the outer edge of the thin blue mats so far below. She fell and fell and fell over and over again in his mind's eye. Until, finally, she hit the ground with an arena—sickening thud, her body just off the mat, her chaotic legs jackknifing over her head, crushing vertebrae, severing her spinal cord.

> *The old man forgot his **dream** when he saw. His faced drained of blood. For **nine hours** of extremely risky surgery, he and his **family** watched the doctors' faces for the frown or shake of the head that would signal life or death, magic or no magic. **God** or no god.*

Weeks later, Jenny Wallenda's little sister, still surrounded by her family, started talking. Her mother had made her feeling clear as ice: she was through with The Seven; she would take care of her daughter for the rest of her natural life. Some of the others kept it quiet from Karl, but they were never going up again. I agree with you. I am an old lady now, have lost two children of my own. Even Karl must have had grave doubts about the dream as he stood watching his youngest daughter, tubes sticking out of her chest. She called them closer to her hospital bed to say this:

> *"Let me see the light of God in front of me again," she said between the pumping of her respirator. "You must do The **Seven** again," she managed. "Do it for me. Do it for family."*

Jenny, in tears, found herself driven to nodding yes. The others did too. Karl's eyes burned with salty tears. What would you have done? I guess it doesn't matter what we think, because The Pyramid went on. Let us not turn from the truth, whether it is ugly or sublime. As you might imagine, the Wallendas still argued. But the arguments grew tempered: one of the fingers on the fist raised to God need only mention their sister, their daughter, their niece, their sister-in-law, for all the blood anger to pass away. One mention and voices hushed; critiques of each others' artistry began to come with encouragement also. In-laws became sisters and brothers, and the family was *one* tribe. More so than ever before. The Pyramid became *fun* again, even for Karl, mastermind of it all. Just when you'd think it would have been scarier than before because of the short time the new Seven had to harmonize their steps, their very psyches, all the fear seemed to go out of them. One of the clan called home to the youngest Wallenda every day once she was out of the hospital. She welcomed the calls and loved to talk except on the days when the pins in her back ground with too much pain. Sometimes, she even traveled with the family in her wheelchair to watch the shows. Karl told her that the doctors were wrong, that she'd walk again, hell, she'd walk on earth and on the wire. He half-believed it. He'd tell her that Wallendas are made of different stuff than normal human D.N.A. But all too often the family would look up from the lunch or dinner table and see that their father and husband was gone. Sometimes they'd find him outside in the weeds beside the train tracks or practicing on a low-wire beside the great tents.

> *Karl never wanted his children to suffer, as he had done. He couldn't bear to let them go, even when they'd grown up, because he wanted to shield them from all the pain in the world. It haunted him that, although he'd planned everything, the only thing in his life that looked planned was running away to join the circus when he was a teen. Everything after that just seemed to have happened. Did he hear the faintest laugh back on earth coming from the clouds and sky as he stood, fist in the air?*

You're right. If you could ask him whether he could have ever imagined things would turn out like this, Karl Wallenda would likely laugh in your face. Who could have known that he'd get his dream but that it would be a different dream? Who or what could know that he'd put his family back together again and again, only to put his daughter in a wheelchair? I think if you or I asked him this, Karl Wallenda would just walk away and cry.

*But look! They're almost **finished**! The Seven walking only have a few more steps to take in perfect harmony, and they'll be across to the opposite platform and safety. We'll be able to **breathe** again and listen to the crowd roar. Sweet relief.*

Oh, God. Give me back my binoculars. It looks like Karl's nephew is struggling. Oh, Eddie, his hands are dropping lower and lower from all that weight. His shoulders are sagging badly from all the gravity and weight. He's Syphasus and tired of pushing stones uphill. Even the 16,000 pounds of pressure pulling the cable taut aren't enough to keep the playing field level. Karl Wallenda's nephew is tired of walking uphill. God, almighty, The Pyramid is shaking! The Seven can't **hold on**!

*It all comes **apart** before our very eyes. Bodies are falling everywhere. Falling to earth as we all must do. Women and men and children are screaming out their lives. Karl, Zen master, dangles from the high wire by his foot, his pelvis broken, his ex-wife and true love's niece clawing to his back for dear life. Dear life. Below them, a horror is emerging in front of all our retinas. We see, but we do not want to see.*

*Two fingers of the fist lie dead on the floor, blood oozing from mouths and ears, scarlet trickling on the blue matting. Karl's oldest son is moving a little bit, writhing on the mat in pain, but he will be paralyzed for life. These things I see and know but do not want to know. **Where are you God?** It's true that five survived, but why did you give them so much talent* *and frailty if you wanted them to **die**? Eight feet from the end of a 34-foot lifetime up high ... So **close** to the dream ... **Why?** They're falling.*

Falling ... As Stephen Crane put it so well, "why must we swim so far, God, only to drown?" Falling ... The act is *over*. It's Boston. It's Detroit. I get confused sometimes. I'm 87 years old now. The *family* falls and falls. There is a poem I read somewhere. It's about the Tuscany Airmen, a crack group of black pilots from Alabama who trained together, segregated from the rest of the Army Air Corp., and then flew, segregated from the rest, in some of the worst air battles in Europe during World War II. The poem is about two pilots, best friends, who bunk together and fly together, knowing that each day could be their last. The two have a friendly argument over which man gets the best air mattress, the one that doesn't leak, to sleep on. When, finally, one of the friends is shot down in battle, the other inherits his best buddy's air mattress. The surviving Tuscany Airman spends the night alone, his first time during the war. He sleeps restlessly on his *dead friend's breath* in the air mattress, tosses and turns, haunted. I slept that night, after the falling, as restlessly as the Tuscany Airman must have slept on a bag of his friend's *very breath*.

The incident with the great Wallenda family, the poem about the Tuscany Airmen have taught me something. They, and all my decades, have taught me this. I want to set it down. Set down this:

***You'd better be sure that what you're living for is worth dying for ...***

What you're living for must be worth dying for. That's because it is more than likely that you will die. That's a sign outside a little white church Charles and I used to drive by in Duxbury, Massachusetts another lifetime ago. I think it means that sometimes people pick the wrong life's work, and it kills them. I think it means that people sometimes screw up their priorities so *much*, like living for work or fame or fortune instead of wife or husband or relationship or children or *family*, that it kills them. One way or another. I think the pastor of the church so long ago meant that without faith in something, God perhaps, life is hollow. I think it means a lot of things. *You'd better be sure that what you're living for is worth dying for* . . . Most of the Wallendas were sure, and that surety gave them purity and grace beyond this earth.

Charles, *my love*, I have gone ahead without you. Our children have gone ahead and had our grandchildren, and our grandchildren have gone ahead and had our great-grandchildren. We have all moved on. Moved on to a life sometimes of ease, sometimes of disease, to a life of failure and success and faithfulness, the thorn and the softest baby's breath, of every inch of delight in warm sunshine on the body's skin. I took the road we built and started well down together. I took it the *rest of the way* without you as if, in taking our intended path after all this, I could most *love* you.

# Voices,
# Inner Chapter Seven

*Once in a Lifetime Love*

## Eddie/ Ann

## Third

We met sometimes on furtive lunch breaks outside the computer place, in a little, treed park area behind the industrial park. One of the last times I saw Ann was a time of grace when everything fell naturally into place without much conscious effort, when all was rest, peace, quiet harmony. I'd called her earlier in the day at her office cubicle, asked her to an impromptu picnic out back for lunch, using the few things I'd brought in early that morning to stuff in the little office fridge.

"Not sure," she'd said, reluctantly. "We'll talk later." She hung up, leaving me listening to a severed dial tone.

Later, there was a seductive message on my voice mail from her. I played back, "Meet me in the park by noon. Meet me as far back in the trees as you can go." I played her voice over and over in between scattered stretches of pretending to care about the temporary work on my borrowed desk.

I walked past the small grass clearing in front of the trees a little before noon, past the children's play equipment, the monkey bars and teeter totters in its center, listening to my heart beating, feeling its beat. I walked further than we'd ever ventured back into the cool of the mature hardwoods until the back of our building looked like a veiled and branch draped toy set. My heart leaped up and down in my chest, louder, stronger, as long minutes ticked away and birdsong came to me.

Finally, I watched Ann come out of the tiny back door into the full afternoon sunlight, growing larger, more real, more beautiful, as she walked past the play equipment toward the canopy of trees and toward me. I thought she smiled slightly as she drew close enough to see me standing in shade, holding my cool brown bag like some overgrown school kid.

We held hands without talking and walked a little further up the bark-covered trail that led away from the clearing deeper into the cool quiet of the tallest trees. We went as far as we could go, away from it all.

"Why did you agree?" I asked.

Ann pressed my hand tighter. "Maybe springtime sap," she said. "Maybe goodbye. Maybe."

"Maybe we should talk," I offered lamely.

"Not today, Eddie. I want to stop thinking for awhile. Just be together for now."

We didn't say anything more. We came to a small, flat spot where an vine-covered chain link fence marked the end of the common area, and, beyond that, there was only a thicket of bushes punctuated by more trees and, somewhere beyond, the sounds of cars, other lives, plying a hidden highway. We sat down, side by side, on the forest mulch. I took the two sandwiches and the bag of red grapes from the bag I'd brought.

Ann pulled a couple of paper napkins from the pocket on her dress. "Perfect atmosphere," she said quietly, "but a blanket would be nice."

I gave her a sandwich, then put the grapes between us. It was cool in our shade, and filtered sunlight danced on her hair fanning that classically structured face, those elegant cheekbones, that blue eyed woman of women. Goddess.

"Peanut butter par excellence," Ann praised me.

"Years of practice," I said. I moved closer to her, leaning on my elbow on the tree bark carpet. This time, I saw she was smiling for certain.

The scent of her hair, fragrant with something fine, mixed with the warm smell of her body, heated a little from the walk. When Ann shifted her weight, the movements of her body under the simple blue dress made me feel sharp prickles of fire beneath my skin once again.

Moments later, when Ann stood up, I stood too, surprised. Did she mean goodbye? We faced each other, just inches apart. I took her into my arms.

"Eddie," she started.

"Don't say anything."

I held her tightly to me, knowing that I could hide nothing now, that she'd feel my passion, my man's excitement, and, perhaps, allow us to love.

Ann reached up her arms behind me, pulling me to her with a power almost equal to my own. We held each other for long moments until she turned her mouth up to meet my fathomless kiss.

I felt her warm lips again, felt myself more alive than dead, felt myself falling once again into a vortex of deep emotion that I knew would batter me senseless sometime soon. I didn't care. I felt it all would be worth feeling anyway, then forgot about thinking. I moved my tongue shyly into her mouth, afraid she'd turn from me, and tasted the faint, wild taste of grapes. I drew away and held her face between my hands. I watched those blue pools of eyes that were filled with love and sadness.

The sunlight fell through the tallest trees, yellow bronze through the green all around us. Neither of us heard the cars that must have been whizzing past nearby. Looking up at me steadily, Ann said, "Yes. I . . ."

"No need for words," I answered.

I held her close again, then sank to my knees, rubbing my face across her perfect small breasts. I felt her erect nipples grow harder through the dress.

Ann sat down beside me on the forest floor, hesitated briefly, then pulled the blue dress up over her head in one quick motion. She tossed her crumpled dress aside, then lay down next to me. She was completely naked, beautiful.

"So you've planned all along," I laughed.

"No talking," it was her turn to say.

I stood again to undress, feeling her eyes on me, and I stared at her body. She lay directly in a pool of afternoon sunlight, waiting for me, her eyes closed now against the bright and a deep pink blush under the skin of her face. Her legs looked so white against the green and brown of our mulch bed.

I reached down and touched the soft pale skin of her flat belly. I worried that my hands were too cool to lay on her, but she held them against her skin for a moment. Moments are what we have. All we have. I hurried the rest of the way out of my own clothes, felt the air on those hidden parts of my skin, lay down softly beside her, pressing against Ann's warmth. I kissed her throat, running my tongue like electric fire down the center of her chest, moving to circle one hard nipple with my mouth. Ann opened her eyes wide to the muted sun and treetops. Warmth.

I still kissed her nipples as I moved my hand down across her belly and further down to the warm wetness between her legs. Her hips moved against me, arching higher and higher. Her thighs closed on my hand.

"God," she said.

"Goddess."

I gently spread her thighs wider apart and began to move my fingers, making love, making love to Ann. Moments. She moaned.

Then my head was between her warm thighs, my lips kissing and caressing the center of her sensations. She arched higher still and moaned louder, almost uncontrollably, gasping and panting as waves of tree branches swept over us again and again and the shifting treetops blurred in the light above. Strange, so very strange and fine.

I moved my body over hers, forcing her thighs still further apart with my own. I watched her face change as she welcomed me. I lay unmoving, savoring, until her hips started to move again and I felt that delicious compliance.

I began thrusting, gently at first, feeling her body alternatively tense and relax, until I could no longer be gentle.

Human love mixed with animal need. Ann with me one more time. One more moment.

She moved sharply with me, pushing her back forward on the rough floor, thrusting up hard to meet me. She clung to the back of my neck to hang on, fingers digging into the nape of my neck through hair.

I lost myself then, becoming only our mutual motion and grace, moving hard in the dancing forest light from above, moving hard toward the crest, toward the hot pool of me in her, toward the one thing together better than both of us. Better than all the nonsense that wasted our too short time together.

"Please give it to me," Ann whispered in my ear.

I exploded in her and fell softly upon her, biting at her lips, her hair, pulling her head tightly against my bare and heaving chest. My whole body hummed, bell struck, for once fully alive. I felt the pressing of her breasts under me, felt her legs warm around mine, felt her arms holding me tight.

"Thank you, love," was all Ann said. "Thank you."

We lay still for a long while without talking, then I felt her legs relax and fall away from mine. Ann moved to gather her dress.

"Maybe not so smart to make love outdoors behind work," she said.

"Shush," I said. I didn't want the moment to ever end.

"I need to finish some things."

"I understand," I said, moving to kiss her again, this woman I'd never have enough of...

We didn't say anything more. We listened to each others' hearts beating and to the birds. The fine picnic in the trees. I'd conjure it up often, I knew already while I still tasted Ann. The most perfect time in my life, best shared moment. Ann's body part of mine forever in the trees. She was the way to dancing light for me then. I will never forget.

Ann invited me deeply into her life, the greatest gift I have been offered, only to have to say goodbye.

## Chapter 26

### *Sex with a Stranger*

### Eddie

It began, as most things do, simply enough, but, as things often do, it got complicated in a hurry. Eddie Couch was shocked by how fast this problem grew from one little one to many problems that rained down on him like tickertape confetti. He first knew when Ellen told him she wanted separate vacations. That wasn't good. Then she started complaining about the house. About every damn little thing possible . . .

He was generally a positive guy, Eddie, except when he got depressed. Thankfully, that didn't happen very often or last too long. It was beyond his control anyway. He loved Ellen deeply, but sometimes it seemed they were from separate worlds. She was from the east: a city girl. He was from the west: grew up rural. As a child, he grew up in a military family, moved from station to station, base to base. She lived all her life in Philadelphia. Now, as an adult, he hated change, wanted the comfort of things staying the same. Ellen loved change.

That is why it came as a rough shock for him when he heard Ellen say the words "This summer I'm going away on my own."

Crapola, he thought. When did he lose so much control? Eddie looked across their kitchen table at his wife. She was still beautiful to him: her blue, blue eyes, the left one with a black speck distinguishing the blue iris, her tufts of light brown hair framing her elegant cheekbones and strong face. Crapola. He'd have to watch the kids alone.

"What's the point of going on a vacation without your spouse?" he remembered he asked.

"That is the point," Ellen shot back. The conversation went like that. Time passed.

As Ellen made preparations to go away, Eddie made some plans of his own. After his affair, after all the shit he'd put her through, after all the hard relationship work they'd done to even stay together this long before come what may, he wasn't going to go down without swinging.

> *Ellen made her plans, and I, on the QT, made mine, having sneaked her password on our old computer. It was a long time ago. Our marriage was falling apart then, for even more reasons than I've had time to yet explain. I had to do something, to give it all one last chance. So it was that I suffered the ignominy of flight again, not leaving a survivor's letter this time, flew all the way behind Ellen to the Bahamas, Freeport, all in secret hopes of watching the new life she wanted, seeing if it might still include me. Love can thrill, we know this, but mostly love hurts with an ache that never goes away.*

She went home with a Greek guy that first night. I watched it happen like some pathetic fool, from a distance, from an outside patio, while first he sent her a drink as she sat, alone, looking beautiful and sad, at her inside table, ringed in indoor light strands and reflections and half-light, and then as he, tall and dark, approached, talked with his hands, and she, my Ellen, invited him to sit with her. I needed no language to know the hurt, hurt that I had caused and gone on causing, my own demise. I didn't want to see, to know, but that was why I'd come all those miles, to know. It hurt like hell. Still does.

My pathetic, self-inflicted misery knew no bounds.

I followed in my rental car, tracked them to her condo, just blocks from my own. In those old days, I could afford to suffer my own self as a fool. I watched them embrace outside her door in moonlight wash like anesthesia clouds, watched her kiss Him back strong. At least I had the sickening decency to drive off after awhile, an hour or two or three, to spare myself the newer ignominy of watching Him leave her at some creepy dawn's light.

Back in my own rented place, I tossed and stormed on rented sheets all night. Was he a better lover? Clearly, better looking... Was I the most pathetic human ever to stay up all night with Gold Bond Powder commercials leaking out in muted and sad wash of flickering television light? What in Sam's hell was I doing in Freeport spying on my future ex-wife? It seemed I'd finally hit bottom. Sometime in the darkness outside it rained and stopped and rained again.

It was raining when I watched her rented car pull up by the outdoor pool parking lot at our Bahamian resort. I remember silently thanking God that she was alone that next day, that at least he wasn't with her. Ellen walked up to the cabana and spa area, her face obscured in a huge yellow umbrella I didn't recognize from home, her sandals sending fine mists of water spray behind her heels as she walked under the covered overhang. I had to get within earshot quickly.

I got out of my rented Festiva, shut the tin can door as unobtrusively as I could, then stole across asphalt, behind the outer pool fencing, all the way around the back of the pool and near the cabana area where I heard her voice. Heard my Ellen talking. Her voice sounded deeper, sexier, than I'd ever remembered.

"I'd like to sign up for a message," I heard her say, separated from me by fencing and wet, warm Freeport breeze. I couldn't see the employee she spoke with. I hoped it wasn't a man.

"Just pick your day and time right there in the binder," a second woman's voice answered. "Sign up for any open half-hour slot. We take all credit cards, cash or check. All the majors, anyway. Or you can charge to your room number."

I blessed my luck in hearing, hoped for more. I got it, for once.

"How about tomorrow at 11 am?" I heard my future ex-wife answer.

This was key. Perfect. I had time then to act, to try to remove those future and ex modifiers from my wife's name. I had some knowledge, but a little knowledge can be a dangerous thing.

I escaped undetected back to nether regions of the parking lot, watched her fold her big yellow umbrella and shake it as she tucked into her little non-descript car, caught just a glimpse of her hair blowing in the wet wind, saw the elegant profile of her face before she closed the driver's door and pulled away. Her hair, my Ellen's hair, was henna red.

She's already gone, I remember thinking.


I spent another night tossing and storming on rented sheets while the television flickered and tried to sell me things I'd never need. What I needed had escaped my grasp. What I couldn't do was let the blackness take over. What I had to do was try to get her back.

I had to get to the pool cabana early. That was in the plan, such as it was. I am not good at making things up as I go along, but the old, stumbling romantic in me was driving me on to near madness. The plan was the only thing ahead of him, that romantic fool ready to risk the last of everything, that Eddie of the tortured heart I'd let myself become.

Retracing my route from the day prior, I arrived at the same black asphalt, this time awash in brilliant reflected sunshine and birdsong from the nearby tropical trees. The sun hurt my eyes as I got out of the Festiva and walked across rainbow colored oil stains where yesterday's puddles tried to dry out like returning vacationers back home to responsibilities, bills, jobs. My flip-flops stuck satisfyingly to the soles of my feet.

When I got to the cabana house where my Ellen had stood just the previous afternoon, standing the same ground, I had no idea what to say to the attendant. The plan was gone, just as Ellen and the kids had been, suddenly, inalterably, when I confessed my sins. I felt my wallet through Khaki shorts, traced its bulge. The pretty young woman looked at me as if I had bats in my non-existent hair.

"Can I help you?"

The plan was gone. I had only willpower now. Stumbling feelings.

"This is going to sound stupid," I stammered. "But my wife is going to come in here in an hour for a message, and, well, I was wondering," I rambled, "wondering whether if I paid the resort enough, you know, enough to cover any liability and all that stuff . . ." I ran out of words for a long moment.

"Yes?" she asked, trying, I hoped, to help me spit it out.

"Just promise me you won't say no yet," I begged. "You see, my wife and I are separated. She's here alone and I came too, alone, to see if we could meet up, to try to patch things up. I can prove she's my wife, that I'm not some stalker," I offered pathetically.

The young woman surprised me. "Do you still love her?" she asked. I was glad of no line behind me, of this sudden sunshine.

"With all my heart." I said.

"And she you?" my sister confessor asked.

"That's what I've got to find out. I hoped I could give my Ellen the massage myself," I blurted out.

My wallet was out, crudely, awkwardly in the sunshine. I set it on the little window lip in front of my new almost friend. "I want to surprise her that I'm here, that I'm in love and desperate enough to follow her here and tell her the way I feel. Tell her I'm sorry for all the times I've come up short in our life together."

"Oooh," she said, looking through the open oblong window down on me, "that's about the sweetest thing I've heard since I've worked here."

"Mostly it's guys trying to buy a peep of a naked woman," she said, disgustedly. "It's a real risk," she considered.

"I'll pay anything to take the masseuse's place," I hoped. "It's the only chance. It's all I have left. After that, I've got nothing." This was not scripted.

I opened my wallet, pulled out all my $100 bills, pushed them through the opening and met her hands.

"If you're some pervert, I'll have you arrested," she said stridently. "Otherwise you're the most romantic man I think I've ever met."

*I waited in the semi-dark for Ellen. I waited, heart pounding through my chest in the shadowed recess of the cabana room behind a closed door that wouldn't open for the longest time. I stood next to a folded out message table and wondered what the hell I was doing. How low I had stooped to be spying on my wife. How elegiac I had become in my old middle age? How much the fool?*

*The door opened before I was ready. I had to disguise my voice. I had to look differently in the sudden wash of backlit light that made Ellen's shape glow and bounced suddenly off white walls. My baseball cap was down over my eyes.*

*I thanked the door silently when she shut it and took her aura away.*

*"I've never done anything like this," she said huskily.*

*Nor have I, I wanted to say, but didn't dare the words. I moved over to the light rheostat past the table. "Mind if we make the light more comfortable?" I said in what sounded to me like bad falsetto. "I can leave while you change and get your towel on," I stammered badly. The plan.*

*"I changed outside in the shower room," she reassured, sexy as hell. "All I have on is my towel and I'm feeling kind of funny about it," she said. "Do I get on the table now?"*

*I could barely see her in the muted darkness. There was a cut-out area in the table for women's breasts to suspend through. "Sure," I said with false bravado, ball cap down, "Climb on up. I can help." The plan.*

*"Don't need help," she said.*

*She fell out of her towel on the way to lying on my table. I saw that, even in the indoor twilight. I wondered whether some newfound wild hair was driving Ellen to do things like that by design of her new life. Her life without me. Her life I had fractured apart from mine. But this was my chance, and she was beautiful. I saw this beautiful grown up woman, showing all of God's plenty to a stranger, the stranger I'd become, either by design or accident, making no attempt to cover up in the dark as she climbed gracefully onto this message table. I saw shower water still faintly glistening on her bare tan skin, the whole length and breadth of her, no hint of shame on her elegant cheeks as I may have watched, had I been a player. Her breasts, firm and large, swung free for a moment as she climbed up into my baseball cap bill view of our dark little crescent cabana world. They were perfect to an old adolescent heart like mine. I saw dark brown circles at the end of each perfectly formed breast; I saw two half-erect nut brown nipples graze by, not two feet from my subterfuge face. I saw things no stranger should see. Ellen's creamy belly was still flat as it sought my table; below, the gentle strophe of womanly hips tapered to tan and muscled long legs. I couldn't keep my hat restricted vision off the thick tangle of glistening wet pubic hair that softly bearded above where her upper thighs joined. She was on my table, waiting. But for what?*

*I put my calloused hands on her gently, starting at the nape of her neck, working the tension cords out with my thumbs and forefingers pressing down lightly at first, then more firmly. I had no idea what I was doing. She was a stranger to me and me to her. All I knew was that it felt good.*

*Her shoulders were under my hands now. Neither one of us had spoken another word. My fingers traced the curve and outline of her skin, alternatively rubbing muscles below, the tense places, alternatively tracing just the soft skin of her shoulders and upper back with my fingertips alone.*

*These familiar places felt so differently to me after so long apart, yet it all felt deliciously good. I thought she moaned a little when I touched a corded back muscle. I felt my groin tighten.*

*Just the tracing of fingertips on her cool, flawless skin now, just electricity flowing familiar and strange from her into my hands, my being. Should I reveal myself? If I blow this, I thought, I will have blown it all. There was no more thinking. Just traces of fingers on cool skin, the sounds of Ellen breathing there in the draped dark warmth. My hands on her tracing, then finding the center of her spine, then my two thumbs moving pressure down each elegant lumbar of her frame until my hands were at racing curve of tailbone just above crescent pear of rear. My throat was full of feathers; my hands felt on fire. My own breath sounds merged with hers now in the restricted cabana space. Then she rolled over. "Don't say a word," she said, her voice a throaty roar in my burning ears.*

*She stood, naked and glistening, in front of me in the dark, close air. Ellen stood on her toes so she could reach up, knock off my cap, and get her hands into my neck hair. I felt her lips so softly on my cheek first, then around my jaw, soft at first then growing stronger. On my closed eyes and forehead and all the while her hands were locked behind my neck, in my hair, as she murmured, "Don't you say a damn word."*

*Did she know? I felt her breasts, nipples erect, above my stomach. How could she not? And if she didn't, what the hell had I gotten myself into realizing? No thought. Just feeling. She pressed her full mouth against my lips, softly, teasingly, then harder, me kissing her back strongly, until her mouth opened and she invaded mine with a fiery sweetness, an exotic taste beyond words.*

*She reached for my hand, lifting it to find her right breast. Ellen's tongue licked fire beneath my ear and I got hard as a baseball bat, started to stammer something. "Not* one word," she warned again, her voice as deep as mine, her hands undoing my masseuse's belt, undoing me. My pants fell down to the floor. No thinking. She lay back on the table, pulling me down on top of her, my shirt still on, excited manhood standing through the boxers I still had on. No words.

 I fell onto her then, fell into her so far and for so long that I forgot any practiced rules of lovemaking, responding only to here, now, to the glistening, warm, beautiful woman's body and blue eyes that narrowed while I filled her, eyes that never, not once I imagined in the dark, lost sight of me at all now that my eyes, too, were open. We saw and saw and touched as if we couldn't exist without the other, as if this time were all time. No future, no past. Just this.

 And it was more than enough a time of possibilities. Ellen climbed on top of me on our table, straddled me with her long legs gripping strongly, rocking to an internal rhythm and center she'd created, full of us both. No thinking. Surely, God, she must know. Our bodies moving as one in the dark.

 She stopped for a moment, breaking the building wave crest for a delicious moment, just long enough to reach down from above and rip the wide-opened slot in front of my torn boxers all the way apart, to let us move the way we needed to move. And then the waves built again.

 This is the way it is. This is what life should be. So much more alive than dead. Passion. No thoughts. Ellen was beneath me, on her side; our table was a boat sailing us away together to the center, a boat we guided, commanded to take us to where we wanted, needed, to go. I found the side of her face, tasted salty sweat, found her mouth with my tongue, tasted that exotic flavor inside. My tongue traced her neck, her left shoulder, her arm to elbow. All was motion. She was breathing heavily now, panting like some chased animal unsure it wants to get away. My heart hammered in my chest. Motion. Just here. Just now. She turned toward me, eyes that must have known, must have seen. *"I, I, I, yes,"* she said.

*"No words."* Ellen's long left leg bent. I moved and moved from behind. I ran my left hand up from below across her panting belly to cup her breasts, to trace my fingers around each puckered aureole circle, to put moist drops on each rock-hard nipple. My right hand rubbed her back as it slid up and up higher on our traveling ship. My left hand found her mouth. Ellen found one finger, then bit down. Hard. I have no words.

Hot warm wetness between us. We were storm and rage and passion. I have visions of stopping to run my tongue like electric storm down Ellen's chest to circle and kiss her breasts again and again with my speechless mouth. Visions, memory of below when my face was between her heated thighs, my mouth kissing and caressing the center of her sensations, the center. I see her arched and moaning low and throaty, almost uncontrollably, gasping air, panting as storm waves swept over our boat again and again and everything blurred to warmth and heat and light. Starting again. Stopping. No right words.

I am on her lithe body again. With her. I see it all from somewhere above, but it is all within us. Us. We two. The only humans on the face of the planet for now, this time. She opens her thighs wider still to welcome me. I am still for a moment until her hips move and all is that wonderful, perfect soft velvety compliance again. Motion and power. Need and love. Ellen and I, me losing myself and almost lost, she moving sharply with me, pushing her back on our upholstered table, our ship, thrusting up hard and just as driven to meet me. No words can describe. Can't be gentle. There is too much need in us. Can't be gentle to get where we have to go.

Ellen clings to the back of my neck to hold on, fingers in my hair once more. We lose our separate selves then, *become one for a long time, becoming only motion and power, passion in the dark message light, moving hard together toward the largest wave's crest, toward an explosive hot pool of me in her and her very center deep around me, in me, toward that something older and greater and better than either of us can ever be apart.*

*"Please," she says. "Please cum with me now."*

*I launch up toward heaven and stars in her while Ellen screams out in joy, then fall softly upon her, spent, biting at her lips, her hair, pulling her head against my chest and shredded shirt. My whole body is humming, tingling, alive. Her legs spasm together outside mine beyond control. I feel her breasts under me through tattered cloth, feel her legs hot, pressing and trembling against mine, feel her hands on my back, tracing circles. Feel it all.*

*"I, I . . ." she tries to say.*

*"Shush," I put my finger to her lips.*

*I feel her whisper against my hand, "Oh, Eddie."*

*I am saved, at least for now. And if I am not, I harbor no regrets. A man lives a lifetime in an hour, if he is lucky. No words sacred enough.*

# Voices, Inner Chapter Eight

## *Eddie*

Dear Ellen,

P lease don't trash our relationship any more. For whatever reasons, you are being very unreasonable, even cruel. It is not normal to freak out at someone for taking a five-minute shower, for whatever reasons. As to the sin of talking ... I have always loved words and the stories made up out of them. I make a living with words. If you did not want to be with a verbal person, a full-time Business teacher and a part-time writer no less, you should never have married me. That's what I am. I refuse to be psychologically beaten down for loving what I love. So I like to talk. Big deal. I always have. Plenty of people talk a lot more than I do, and you don't freak about that.

Speaking of talking, I have been trying to talk *with* you for some weeks now. You keep refusing, refusing intimacy as well, as a symbol of what you see as wrong with me. That's why I have been inviting you to lunch, movies, etc. I have been trying to tell you that I still love you. Always will: come what may. And I have been trying to re-propose. Re-propose to work on *Communicating* on loving each other... That's why I had your diamond reset some weeks back. It is a symbol of my love for you, just as it was in 1911 when my grandfather spent over a year's salary on it, gave it to my grandmother to propose, got married, had two kids and died suddenly when those kids were only seven and three years-old. Life's too short to yell and bicker. These are supposed to be good times. Times to enjoy kids, grandkids, each other. We can't enjoy each other if you don't value us. It is extremely hurtful to me when you make it clear, on a daily basis, that you do not much value me and us together. It is cruel, and I do not believe, deep down where it matters, that you are a cruel person. You are better than that too.

Anyway, there's a recent jewelry store near town, and I took the ring in for an informal appraisal, free, and, when I asked and the owner assured me that I could watch him reset the diamond in person, I made an appointment and then went for it, hoping to give it to you as a small surprise for Christmas, a symbol of the love I have for you, just as it was years ago. The ring just needed a new gold crown head. I paid for it (reasonable) nearly two months ago. With the way you are talking now, with the threats you are making about how we're over, as far as you're concerned, after Christmas, I can't wait until X-Mass to give this to you. It is just what it is, no more, no less: a symbol of my love for you.

Please accept this re-proposal, this ring, via this letter, because you won't let me tell you face-to-face. Please consider wearing it and resolving to do better at the way you treat me (and us).

Love,
Eddie C.

# Chapter 27

## *9/11/'01*

## Lois

What are the odds of finding it? Finding it the first time? Love, that is. I found it, love, that first time with Charles, all those years, children, grandchildren, great grandchildren ago. Bill Evans was experiment, daring. Charles was love. When Charles left me, passed on up to stars, I didn't think I could go on, felt half of me was severed. Married 61 years. And I was supposed to go on alone. I did go on. Went on for the kids' families. Went on to this new, mad cap family in my twilight years. Went on. Isn't love why we breathe, what we're put here for? Memories of my Charles and me, our life together, new experiences with my new friends, kept me going on.

Margaret and Harry's house had a T.V., of course, a little non-cable, color set in the living room that we ex-stowaway book people liked to ignore as first the months and then nearly two years rolled by. One clear, early morning, I woke up alone, having felt a little sick to my stomach the night before. Andre, Eddie, Margaret and Harry had already left, as planned the previous night, without me to get ready for the weekly session at the Wrightstown Library. My stomach still felt a little queasy after my oatmeal and blueberries and black tea, and I felt unaccountably restless. I turned on the

T.V., hoping for solace, not expecting to find anything like it. What passes for entertainment in the past few decades is often pandering and lowest common denominator sleaze. Charles used to say, though, there's some things you have to know. He liked Chet Huntley. I hoped for Charlie Gibson and for my stomach to settle down.

The little set flashed on with a click and popping sound. An image built, took form in my friend's room, competing with the brilliant sunshine that poured through their drapes and fell in splotches on green carpet. I saw New York City, what looked like one of the World Trade Center Towers, and thick, angry smoke poured out. My stomach fell. A voice on "Good Morning America," my Charlie perhaps, tried to make some sense of it all.

"It appears a single-engine small plane has struck the north World Trade Center Tower. We can't confirm, but we're beginning to get unconfirmed cell phone reports passed on that it may have been a twin-engine jet that's hit the building. Perhaps a commercial flight. We'll let you know just as soon as we can confirm information. It's 8:46 am, and we have some sort of catastrophe here."

*"It was a commercial plane, eyewitness accounts are reporting, a twin-engine commercial style jet that slammed into the North Tower minutes ago. These images are horrific as the Trade Center is burning. We'll let you know just as soon as we can confirm the nature of this terrible accident."* My stomach burns up to my throat. My left arm tingles. Everything grows tight. *"We're getting reports now that there's been some kind of explosion at the Pentagon in Washington, D.C., possibly a second airplane?"*

*"Oh, God, Oh, God"* a woman's voice says. Diane Sawyer, not my Charles. My arm is on fire. *"There's a second plane or explosion, Charlie. My God, the other tower's been hit by something, by a second plane!"*

*"This is stunning, folks. I hesitate to say that this is terrorism until we get confirmed reports, but we're clearly seeing an explosion in the South Tower, fire, perhaps by a*

second plane. We'll try for eyewitness or video sources, Diane, just as soon as the producers can get them. This is horrific." I see the World Trade Centers, both bold, black towers, burning on Margaret's T.V. It all seems like a perverse cartoon. My chest grows tight.

"We have confirmation of an airplane having struck the Pentagon. Confirmation from Boston Air Traffic Control through our Affiliate that at least two planes from there, an American and a United flight, having been high jacked and enroute to New York City from there. I am getting confirmation on my headset, too, Diane, of another flight possibly high jacked over Pennsylvania from Newark. Relatives are getting cell phone calls from relatives on that plane and are calling authorities." The images spill out of the T.V., but I am unable to believe. My chest pounds.

"I can't say with certainty, Diane, but all of this smacks of something more than terrible coincidences of accident as we see the Twin Towers of the World Trade Center burn." My chest hurts. I can barely breathe.

I see New York City, imagine Pennsylvania, see the Pentagon burning in Washington, D.C. The images are a sickening kaleidoscope view spun out of control. I am panting.

"Oh, my God," the woman said, "the North Tower is collapsing!" I see it fall in, an impossible horrible miracle of floors falling into floors until the flagpole spike plummets ever downward in a roil of black smoke and imploding rubble.

"God, yes, Diane, we're seeing the Tower collapse. We should go to our reporters on the street to confirm this, but, yes, there can be no doubt that the building has fallen." I cannot breathe. Everything is coming in too fast to process. My eyes see but do not see. I have lived too long.

"There seem to have been people jumping to the street, Diane. Are those helicopters at the scene? Yes. There's a news helicopter, some kind of helicopter, perhaps some rescue *effort circling the top of the other Tower of the World Trade Center. It's a clear, sunny morning in New York, and at 8:37 am we can confirm seeing the North Tower collapse. This is stunningly unbelievable."* Lived too long. Isn't love what we're put here for? Not this. Not senseless destruction. I cannot catch my breath, am fighting to breathe. I move to the phone to call for help, eyes never leaving the twisted pageant play on the television.

*"Charlie, something is happening to the other Tower. It's coming apart. God, it's coming down too."*

*"It's just surreal. I think it's safe to say that this is an act of terrorism, some kind of attack on our nation. This is just beyond belief. We're seeing the second building of the World Trade Center collapsed in just seconds. There's dust and debris obscuring our picture, the sounds of sirens, police, firefighters. 9:14 am and the South Tower is down."*

*I fall before I get to the end table where the phone sits. Even if my new family had called, I couldn't reach the phone. My family are dead. Charles, my children gone. I am coming home. I fight for breath; my chest is lead, and I am coming home to my loves. I lie on the green carpet, fighting for my very breath. This is all right with me. I have lived and lived. My eyes are on the pulsing T.V., and this is more weight than I can bear.*

*It's all O.K., Lois, it's O.K. to leave, cover all this killing up with softness. The dying is easy. It's the living on that's hard. Without love, what are we put here for? You stay here, I am going on home, am already gone on to someplace better where this pain is gone.*

# Chapter 28

*Losing You*

*The Boy Who Could Cry at Will*

### Andre/ Eddie

Two men were evicted from a sandstone cave they had lived in for 11 days after pleading guilty to using a New Jersey state forest for residential purposes.

One man, identified as Eddie Couch, and his friend, whose name has not yet been released, had makeshift beds, some books, as well as clothes arranged on hangers, along with pots and cutlery for cooking in their small cave in the Wharton State Forest near Medford Lakes, New Jersey.

The pair was arrested Friday after a Tabernacle Road resident who had been camping in the state parkland reported seeing the suspicious pair retreating into their cave opening with firewood bundles. Couch and his partner pleaded guilty in State District Court in Trenton on Monday. Couch was sentenced to one year of probation and banned from the forest. His unidentified friend's sentencing has not been determined as of press date.

\* \* \*

"Ever since I was a little boy, I had this weird gift," Eddie said, stirring the embers in the small campfire that divided him from Andre. "I could cry whenever I wanted."

"Join the club," Andre interrupted. "I just watch the news to do that." He chewed a particularly difficult piece of "Slim Jim" that the men had bought the previous week in Medford Lakes when laying in supplies to disappear for a while with.

"No, you don't get it," Eddie soldiered on. "I could make myself cry over anything. Real tears, real tears at will. Kids would bet against others on me that I couldn't do it, but I was always sure fire at forced emotion."

"Bet that came in handy in a child's life," Andre said, then spat out gristle into their fire. Fat sputtered for a second and sizzled away.

"Mature, Andre, mature. Why can't I cry now?"

The question hung between them, unanswered, in their little cave. In the dusky silence inside, only their voices resonated and disappeared. Outside, drifting through the ragged mouth opening, the men could hear faint rustlings of wind in dwarf pine trees, sometimes echoes of owl song. Margaret and Harry's house was only an hour and a half away, eight days behind them to the west across the Delaware. They would never go back to the life they left. So many things had changed about them, about the world.

"Why can't I cry now?" Eddie repeated. Small tongues of firelight reflected on the cave roof only a few feet above their heads.

"You can do it," Andre said. "Think of her, of what she meant."

*I can't believe it. I knew somehow deep down it was possible, of course, even likely, but I never expected it to happen. Not that way. I can't believe she's gone. Our Lois. Our world inside and outside, our worlds the way they were.*

*I can't stop seeing it. That goddamned video of the plane slamming into the South Tower, the over and over replaying of both Twin Towers coming down. The confusion and the wondering and the damn ugly truth. It killed her.*

*The barbarian bastards destroyed so many families. They killed something in us all, and we let them. It's been eight days since I couldn't watch it anymore, five since the little funeral for our Lois, and still it's all I see, even in the dark. There's no running away. No hiding. And all the blood anger, the lust for retaliation against the shape-shifting monster, all of it won't bring Lois back, won't give those poor people back the ones who went up in jet fuel flames or under tons of twisted concrete and metal. The goddamn video replays and replays over and over in all our heads until it's all we see. We are blind to everything else. Even a flower here, if there were a flower, we would not see. The faces of those lost ones on kiosks in New York City. The funerals in Washington, D.C., and Pennsylvania, and New York. Amazing Grace. Danny Boy. Our memorial at the Quaker Meetinghouse in Newtown, PA. It all has become one, and I am blind to the rest of the natural world. I do not see to see.*

Morning leaked into the cave in the form of muted sunlight creeping into the sandstone cavern on a little hill among the trees nearby the sandy-bottomed river. Light lit the black, char skeleton of the dead fire. Light licked Andre and Eddie's faces until first Andre and then Ed fidgeted and tossed on rock in borrowed sleeping bags. Andre opened his eyes first, then Eddie, at the sound of someone walking into their lair, at a voice.

"Get the hell up," the words said. "You've no permit to be camping with a fire here."

Eddie's back hurt. He saw edifices coming down, again and again, inside his eyelids, burning in his brain, as he opened his eyes to an angry silhouette in front of bright dawn's light.

"Get the hell up. I'm not telling you again."

# Chapter 29

## *Long Term Care*

### Margaret/ Harry/ Andre/ Eddie

Margaret and Harry sat on the second bed in the "Red Roof Inn" room they had rented for Andre and Eddie in Trenton, N.J. They had not thought twice about helping when Andre had called to say that he and Eddie were out of money and in some trouble with the law in New Jersey, that they needed a jump start on healing but that they couldn't go back to their life before. Andre and Eddie sat on the other queen bed, Andre's hands folded in his lap, Eddie's fidgeting nervously. Harry held his hands in a little teepee shape under his bellicose nose, his thumbs hooked under his jaw line, thumbs pressing against his Adam's apple.

"What if we all had terminal diseases?" Andre asked. "Would we choose to end it on our terms?" He turned his hands over on his lap, palms upward to the sterile, white roof above. "How would we choose to go out?"

Eddie shot him a look of disdain. "What a freaking cynic." Margaret looked strongly at both men, her fond companions now on the run from all that had happened. From it all. "It's a legitimate question," she said.

"Yes it is," Harry added gruffly.

"Lois was healthy," Margaret said, "but the world killed her."

"Shut the hell up, Maggie," Harry interrupted. He got up off the bed, irritated, moved toward the window.

"The last thing these guys need is a reminder of what the hell happened to our Lois, to us all." He looked out the window, saw an overlook of grey asphalt, dark oil stains in the mostly empty parking spots, an occasional car. "We're all still grieving here."

Margaret looked to Andre and Eddie for help then. "Harry, we're all still smarting, all of us, the whole country's still in pain. But what good's being nasty to each other going to do?"

"Yes, children," Eddie added, scolding, "what good is fighting among ourselves going to do?"

"You shut up too," Harry said, quietly, his back to the other three, staring out the window. He felt a tear trickle down his cheek to the side of his mouth, tasted warmth and salt. He could not turn around. "A little bit of all of us died," he said. "Some of each of us is dying now." He saw an older couple come out of the building, work their way laboriously toward one of the cars, arm in arm, supporting each other until the older man had his partner safely in the passenger side of the car, door closed, and had climbed in the driver's side. They looked to Harry like little cartoon characters as they drove away slowly in their tiny cartoon car.

> *"You may have six months," Dr. Gottlieb told me. "Maybe more. You may make a liar out of me, Harry, but eventually it's going to catch you. The chemotherapy and radiation will give you some time, but you're stage four, and you need to prepare."*
>
> *The first thing I remember thinking was how am I going to tell Maggie? Do I tell her at all? Then I got caught up in living the time left, living it well, and Lois and the boys came into our lives, the book club, and, well, I never told her at all. No point. Told nobody at all. Funny how precious the living time becomes when you've less of it to live. When the time lived is the iceberg under water and time left is all the little visible pinnacle you see. Funny. My burden to carry alone and my joy, the time left.*

"So back to the question then," Andre said. "How about it, Harry? If you were dying, how would you take things in your own hands?"

Harry wiped the drying track of moisture from his cheek with a calloused hand. He turned to face the two beds at the center of the small room, the three loved people sitting on them. "I'd blow my freaking brains out," he said.

"No you wouldn't," Margaret said. "Not if I know you."

Harry moved to her bedside, sat down next to his partner. "You're probably right, Maggie, I probably couldn't do it. More likely, I'd pull an elaborate Willy Lohman, something not too obvious, leave you and these guys some insurance money."

She turned to Harry. "Harry Dorris, don't you damn dare talk like that, like it's something you'd really plan. That's not God's way." She reached over and rubbed her hand in his hair, leaned against Harry.

"But it's a way," Eddie said. "Me, I'd accidentally fall off the Walt Whitman Bridge, maybe 'forget' how to swim if I survived the fall. Or maybe I'd remember how to swim and float all the way down to the Chesapeake Bay, crawl out on land, assume a new identity and then live for a while longer. Kill myself later with women and drink or an overdose of morphine. The key would be how to get away with it so you all could inherit my millions."

"Yea," Harry said, strangely serious and somber. "That's the key. It can't ever look like suicide, euthanasia."

"Damn it, Harry," Margaret said, moving far enough apart so she could look directly into his eyes. "You're starting to piss me off. You too Eddie. Hasn't there been enough of dying, of tragedy, these last weeks? Isn't there always too much of dying?"

"Not if you believe," Harry said, "in a higher place, Maggie, in that better place of your Quaker God." He looked back at her with the eyes of a deer frozen in night headlights. "Then the dying is easy, just a part of life that moves you on to a better place."

"You sound like you've thought about this," Andre said.

"You asked the question," Harry said.

"You know I love you, Harry," Margaret forgave.

The late afternoon light poured through the window into their little room at the "Red Roof Inn," blocked only slightly by streaks and splotches of ammonia based window cleaner on the panes of glass that made weird shapes fall on the faded brown carpet at their feet.

# Chapter 30

## *The Free Man Who Fell from the Sky*

### Harry/ Margaret

When Harry finally told her, his Maggie, she understood. She fought a great spiritual battle within herself for three days, then came to a distinct resolution. Margaret, with resolve, was a formidable woman. Love finds a way. The love of a Quaker person is a force of nature. She helped him make the arrangements. They planned together, as they had for all their mutual adult lives. The only thing to be settled was her role: how or if she would go on. Harry argued persuasively, of course, for her to go on; Maggie argued just as voraciously for them to stay a pair. For once, Harry's logic, his sheer tenacious will matched hers. Someone, after all, had to keep the family together, to look after Eddie and Andre, the Di Javons, the Tans, the Killians, Andy Ferazua, the Barts, so many others, boys with blankets, lost library souls, just as Karl Wallenda had been the glue and bailing wire that kept the great Wallendas aloft for so long. Just as Lois had gone on after her Charles and the battered little family had stumbled on without Lois herself. Just as the nation was learning, haltingly, how to go on after 9/11. She would go on.

* * *

An elderly man recently diagnosed with terminal non-Hodgkin's Lymphoma leaped to his death from a vintage airplane he rented to celebrate his 80$^{th}$ birthday, Pipersville, Bucks County officials said yesterday.

Harold Dorris took off his safety belt at 500 to 600 feet, stood up in the open cockpit of the two-seat biplane and went over the side Monday, despite the pilot's desperate efforts to wrestle Dorris back into the plane and to nose the aircraft steeply upward in an effort to force Dorris back into his seat.

"The man was determined," Pilot Fred do Cormo of 'Pipersville Nostalgia Rides' said. "He knew aircraft. There was no stopping him."

"I think it was Harry's idea, to go out in a flash of glory," said Margaret Dorris, who had helped her partner arrange the charter flight on a biplane similar to the ones Mr. Dorris had flown in World War II as a young Civil Air Patrolman.

The man landed on an apartment patio on the outskirts of nearby Quakertown, horrifying those who witnessed his fall.

"After 9/11, we didn't know what to think," a "Pheasant Run Apartments" resident said. "Everybody in this country is on edge, and, when a man falls from the sky into your neighborhood barbecue party, you don't know what to think, what to do. Your first thought is terrorism. But this poor guy was probably just looking to end his own life."

The Quakertown resident continued, "We saw him hit the power lines, and our transformer blew; we heard tree branches breaking. It was a sickening sound. Worse when he hit the concrete patio. I can't describe the sound, the feelings. I didn't really think it was real."

\* \* \*

*I am Forrest Gump's single feather floating. In his beginning, the white feather I am roils above where Forrest sits on a city park bench, riding city air currents, falling and rising as cars and buses go by and as the wind blows through the trees* in a park. Eventually, the single white feather lands on Forrest's shoe, but I am not rising and falling over a city. I am careening down toward green upper Bucks County, and it is beautiful. The wind combs my hair backward, forces tears of joy and exhilaration.

In the end of the film, after Jenny, Forrest's lifelong friend and eventual wife, dies, leaving him alone with their son, Forrest Jr., Forrest sits by a row of mailboxes at the bus stop as his son is about to go away to his first day of school. And, after Forrest Jr. boards that bus and leaves in a cloud of diesel smoke and dust, Forrest is alone again, as I am on high. There again is the single white feather, blowing off in the wake of the bus, blowing on toward some other destination. Floating. I am the feather, blown on currents of strong destiny and stronger fate and accepting, finally, the rush of the wind, the pell-mell approach of the ground below, following the wind and the stronger pull of gravity wherever they take me. I sometimes rise, sometimes dart sideways, rise and fall again. I am movement itself, a part of nature, floating mostly downward without concern. Floating. I am that feather and nothing else. I let the wind comb my hair. Let tears cleanse my eyes of the world's dirt.

We were going to talk about T.S. Elliot. His "Quartets." We were going to do "East Coker." "In my beginning is my end. In succession/ Houses rise and fall, crumble, are extended,/ Are removed Destroyed, restored, or in their place/ Is an open field, or a factory, or a by-pass./ Old stone to new building, old timber to new fires,/ Old fires to ashes, and ashes to the earth/ Which is already flesh, fur, feces,/ Bone of man and beast, cornstalk and leaf..." Maggie and I understand him know. Really understand. I see a tiny cornfield now through salty tears. I see a building next to a tiny road. I am falling to earth.

\* \* \*

"The sound of the branches breaking made us look up for a second. He looked like a big bird swimming through air. He landed right on the patio, just missed the hot grill. We heard bones braking; a lot of the women and kids and some of the guys screamed; there was blood spattered all over. He looked like a broken rag doll lying there lifeless on the cement, blood oozing everywhere, but, I swear, it looked like he died with a smile on his mouth."

\* \* \*

*I am a feather, nothing more, and nothing less. The breeze carries me, and I am light. I have learned to float and fly and fall without even trying. I am immune to all but gravity. I let the wind comb my hair on the way down to earth. I let the wind carry me.*

# Voices,
# Inner Chapter Nine

### *Ann Lauren, Eddie's Ann*

A̲nn Lauren had cemented back to her husband, Kent, emotionally, seven years prior. Physically, literally, they hadn't been apart since getting married 22 years before. They had two great kids, girls, one 17, the other 12, had waited five years after marriage for the first. Their lives were good, even when she fell for Eddie, even when he fell from his Ellen for love, for Ann. Everything had changed. Kent had been in the north Tower on a business trip. Kent was gone, buried with no one in his flag-draped casket. One of the lost ones. The three women lived alone in their silent Levittown house, Ann never thinking, never even daring to entertain the perverse thought of letting Eddie know what had happened all those years after the cement of the past had forced her, them really, to let each other go. To give up on the one best love. How could she even think of such a thing when her husband, like so many others, had been taken by darkness in the world? She was a religious woman, Catholic in the best sense, had suffered enough self-imposed guilt and recrimination for the love of her life, for the affair, that her dead husband had never know about. She had walled up that short, bittersweet time in her life, locked it away in a place so private that even her conscious mind seldom went where only wounded heart could plumb. She had taken to crying to after Eddie, crying intensely privately. She never knew when the tears to hide away would come. In these new dark months, after she had recovered as much she ever would mend from love lost, loss revisited her again. It was almost more than Ann Lauren could bear. Scars on scars. But she was a strong woman. She had her girls to think about. She had a good family for support.

Ann found herself crying one morning at her little, folding kitchen card table, in her blue terrycloth bathrobe, after the girls had gone off to school for one of the last days before Christmas break. A tear fell on the *Bucks County Courier Times* newspaper she'd been absently skimming, smearing the print. She looked down below the table to the dark violet nail polish on her toes separated by the V of her blue flip-flops. Ann's eyes refocused on the paper, searching headlines. One swam into soft focus through liquid.

\* \* \*

### *Elderly Patient Commits Ariel Euthanasia*

An elderly man recently diagnosed with terminal non-Hodgkin's Lymphoma leaped to his death from a vintage airplane he rented to celebrate his 80th birthday, Pipersville, Bucks County officials said yesterday . . . Harold Dorris took off his safety belt at 500 to 600 feet, stood up in the open cockpit of the two seat biplane and went over the side Monday, despite the pilot's desperate efforts to wrestle Dorris back into the plane and to nose the aircraft steeply upward in an effort to force Dorris back into his seat . . .

\* \* \*

*My God, it's Eddie's friend. It's one of the ones he told me about in the couple of e-mails he sent with updates of how he'd gone on without me. Messages I could never answer because I was not brave enough. It's Eddie's friend Harry. All kinds of death is dropping out of the sky.*

Ann Lauren cried for her husband, Kent. She cried for the life they'd built together, now gone. She soaked the "Life" section of the paper crying alone for our country, for her family, for her past, present and future, for old falling men in as much control of their lives as is frailly, humanly possible in a complicated world, and, most of all, she cried for Eddie, for what they had together so briefly, so purely, for the love of her life that could never, never ever be, not even now that all that had kept her from him was gone. Especially now.

There are not enough newspapers in the world to soak up all tears of pain and joy that love can cause.

# Voices,
# Inner Chapter Ten

## *Dear Ann*

It was the first letter Eddie had sent her. Ann had kept it, hidden shut away in a locked drawer, even now that there was no need to hide the gift of their past love, their present limbo, even after 9/11 had taken away that need to hide, ashamedly but with fierce dignity as well, the best of her life.

Goddess Ann,

> You should get rid of this as soon as you've read it.
> I want you wrapped up in my arms, want that as well more than anything. You know that. But we're damn married to others. Still, everything's O.K., babe. More than O.K. Our love's a gift, a blessing maybe from God. I'll wait for you if need be, hold on to future possibilities. You know I want to make love with you, show you or remind you what a man and a woman can do together when passions are high. What red-blooded male wouldn't? Especially one who's fallen for you like a 1 ½ ton horse and rider off one of those old Atlantic City steel piers. But I can wait if I have to, out of respect and honor for you, for our commitments to those others. Don't want to but can and will.

If I ever cause you more hurt or pain than joy, you just have to say so, and I'll leave you alone, watch your life unfold from a distance. Meantime, I'll take whatever affection you can give: no pressure. You are worth waiting for. I'll try to hold out until somebody's 60 or more or until lives change as they sometimes (actually often) do. Do the best I can. Just have to keep working out for another 10 to 20 years!

As to those things you said you can't tell me, you can tell me anything you feel comfortable with sharing. On your own time. Again: no pressure. I would never betray your trust. That's not me, although here I am willing to betray long ago promises I made to Ellen. Forget that. It's not me to ever betray you. I think you know that too.

Does this make any sense? So, as far as I'm concerned, everything is good. Best of times although not easy by any stretch. Out to dinner with others later, wishing it were you. Will drown any sorrows that arise with rum and Coke or Drambouie. I know, it already sounds like I've had a couple . . . Just your love making me the fool. Hope to see you fixing that damn software very soon. Have something still, still to whisper under my breath for just your ears.

Love (there I said it),<br>
Your Secret Admirer

Ann Lauren took their love and Eddie's letter to bed that night and every night to follow until her life did change again.

# Chapter 31

## *Whole Life*

### Eddie and Andre

Andre and Eddie used Margaret and Harry's loan, the one they'd promised to repay after they were on their feet, the one that Harry and Margaret had no intention of ever recalling, to travel west. They wanted to see the Lois' mountain, the one that she'd told them about, the sacred place she and Charles had visited so many years before when they were newlyweds, traveling the country all the way northwest by train and horse drawn buggies, and, once, a 1915 car. Andre and Eddie wanted more than the world could offer.

The two men flew on Margaret and Harry's money from Philly to San Francisco, landed in the big United jet at S.F.O. They rode a little shuttle bus, crowded with oriental tourists and American families on summer vacations, to an auxiliary terminal out beyond the twin main runways at S.F.O. A short while later, they were up over the Bay, climbing steeply upward in the blatting twin engine United Express turbo-prop shuttle plane, the Golden Gate on their left, the Bay Bridge on their right as sailboats on the blue bay receded to the size of seagulls and were gone.

Stepping off the plane in Redding, CA, a dry blast of heat enveloped the men as they went to collect their minimal luggage and to arrange a rental truck. It had to be a truck, Eddie and

Andre knew. Within 20 minutes, they were on their way north, up Interstate 5, to Lois' sacred place.

They spent the night in a little place called the "Edelweiss Inn" in Mount Shasta City, a little burgh literally in the shadow of the great mountain, the southernmost and some say the most beautiful of the Cascade Range. 14,000 plus feet of ice and snow draped symmetrical volcano. After they pasta loaded at a nearby Italian place, "Luigi's," the men walked back to the lodge under a vault of stars and a sliver of crescent moon that lit up the severe outline of the impossibly high peak white and ghostly. The big dipper shone so brightly above that Eddie felt as if he could reach up, snatch it from the night sky, fill it with alpine water, and drink his fill from it. Eddie and Andre checked out by 9 a.m. the next morning. The sky that morning was blue enough to reach up and scratch with fingernails. The robin's egg blue of the northern California sky was the color of the New York City sky that fateful day months before, light blue and pure and innocent.

> *We'll do it together, we two, the last of the family tribe. There are no books to tell Andre and me what to do, only inner compass. Only Margaret at Philadelphia International to say goodbye. Lois gone first. Then Harry. There are no books to tell us what to do when the world goes mad. Nothing on paper worth talking about. No formulas for giving up a love so strong that Ann and I will never feel anything like it again in five lifetimes. No passion so strong that it wouldn't have been worth it to break apart two loved families for. They have broken apart anyway. Mine by my own hand and wandering heart. Hers, she told me on the phone after years of silence, by the shape-shifting monsters that came out of the sky over America with a shrieking hatred so perverse that not only were so many lives lost but the whole meaning of life was torn asunder too. Her husband gone, taken by terror. Ellen gone on without me, forced away by my weakness. Both Ann and I alone, never likely to*

*find each other again. Only a grieving Margaret at the airport to say the final goodbye, "I will always love you guys, as long as I draw breath and longer." We are all of us grieving, and there is no solace of Lois' voice.*

The men got half way up Mount Shasta by the late morning. Eddie could drive them no higher on the steep forest service roads. The last few thousand feet of climbing had bounced the rental pickup hard, jostled their kidneys. Andre and Eddie knew that sane climbers started their ascent of the north face well before dawn, in order to climb down to a base camp and warmer safety before dark, but they had a different idea.

Eddie and Andre started hiking with small day backs on their backs. These were their only provisions. The men each had a set of rented crampons wrapped carefully in their jackets so the spikes wouldn't jab their backs, and the ice axes they'd rented in Mount Shasta hung from their belts, Eddie's along his right leg, Andre's down his left. They felt the altitude change, the thin air, even at the 7,500 foot level. The life they'd left behind in Bucks County was lived at 50 to 150 feet above sea. The north face of the peak rose at an unbelievable white angle ahead and above. Already, there were great thunderheads around the peak and just covering the summit in dark cloud. Andre's strength was not good lately. Eddie's worse. They hoped what they had left would be enough.

The sunlight on their faces felt hot, but the men saw the icy lower fingers of Hotlum and Bolum glaciers reaching down the mountain to just a few thousand feet above them. They reached the end of the caterpillar tractor-blazed road and began to pick their way upward over loose rocks and between boulders toward the stunted tree line where green ended and became grey and white. They hoped to get on the ice before the afternoon sun hit the glaciers and made the surface too soft for their crampons to grip. Eddie and Andre couldn't afford to waste any energy, not with Andre nearing 55 and Eddie close in age and both of them having lived the sedentary lives of hiding and books and talk and hiding more. Their legs were stiff from flying, driving; their joints ached as they climbed. Eddie heard himself wheeze as he took in deep droughts of breath, breathing in the cold, crisp air. They would have to turn grief into strength.

They climbed slowly over the talus and andesite, stopping every few steps to pause and begin again. The slope already hurt them, but they were stubborn men. They had made up their minds to do this: it was the right thing. Eddie and Andre had done many things in their decades, had broken things and fixed things, had worked hard, had been homeless, and they could do this for Lois, for themselves. They worked hard to reach the end of the tree line. There was nothing to save themselves for, no future, no regret, only this. Sweat ran down their temples as they stood among the last of the dwarfed and misshapen pine trees. Some of them had been broken by winter snows and summer rock falls. Most had survived the winds. Now, in July, they would have to watch for tumbling boulders and, higher up, for avalanche. Andre and Eddie did not want to die by accident.

> *We talked about the plan on the way to the airport in Margaret's car, but we did it in generalities vague enough for Margaret to ignore. Andre told me he'd do whatever I asked of him, even this sacrifice. I knew what I wanted to do, but, as the grey Philadelphia cityscape rolled by on our right on Interstate 95, as the row houses, the narrow streets, the billboards, the old church steeples ticked by, and, as we passed underneath the concrete overpasses by Penn's Landing, felt the constricted concrete walls close by and the sudden loss of light, I felt unsure of my resolve. By the time Margaret's car sped back out into the light, before we passed the construction of the new South Broad Street sports stadiums, before we prepared to hurtle through the atmosphere at 40,000 ft., I felt O.K. about it all again. I'd left my last survivor's note, left it for Ann to be delivered on exactly the right day.*

*When Margaret admonished us, "Please, please be careful guys," right before the last hugs and kisses on the cheek at the airport, both Andre and I had made promises I knew I had no intention of keeping. I didn't guess my friend did either.*

When Eddie and Andre came to the bottom of the glacier, the sun was moving toward the western mountains. The friends were tired. They sat on a large rock that had been pushed down the slope by the advance of the ice, took off their daypacks, got out their crampons and their bags of trail mix. Eddie got out his one liter water bottle and washed down the snack. Without the heat of exertion to warm him, he felt colder. A stiff wind blew up the ice. He guessed they must be nearing the 9,500 foot level. The peak above them was lost in angry grey clouds, but still they sat in sunlight.

*He and I have no terminal disease but sadness. Neither Andre or I need the Molotov Cocktail that so many have to take, the thing they suggest when it's over, the morphine, when they want a patient to slip away with less pain. Maybe I should reconsider; think about the fact that some say light follows the darkest darkness. I have a rich past life well lived, if not pretty. Have the kids, Eddie and Caroline all grow now, have grandkids I seldom see for Christ sake. My ex-wife lives in the house I bought us long ago. She has our two dogs, the boarded horse I bought Caroline long ago when I was teaching and things were good. Ellen runs our old menagerie with the kids' old cockatiel in a cage I bought and a lizard in the tank I built. Perhaps this is not wise. But to turn the momentum of the great ships we are, once set steaming upon a course of action, is not an easy thing. The momentum and force of our pasts keeps us plowing ahead unless strong currents force us to turn.*

When Eddie and Andre were through resting, they packed their water and food away, then strapped the spikes to their hiking boots. Andre took a long time with the straps, making sure not to leave any loose ends that could catch under his own bootstraps and trip him.

"Come on Kemosabe," Andre said, breaking the long, wordless beginning they had embarked on, breaking Eddie out of reverie.

"I live for the day," Eddie answered.

As he tied an extra length of crampon strapping into a tight knot, Eddie saw a splash of color in his side vision. Another floated by. Then the two friends were in a storm of orange butterflies floating and diving around him as they rode the air currents up the glacier. Eddie and Andre marveled at the bright Monarch as they flew upward just a few feet over the white ice. Some of them wobbled, gave up the petal-like dance for a second, then flitted upward just before striking the glacial ice. What were they doing so high above the tree line, as seemingly out of place as two broken hearted middle-aged men from Pennsylvania climbing for their lives on northern California's greatest mountain? Eddie wished he could ascend so easily to where he wanted, needed really, to be. Beautifully, slowly, one butterfly quivered and fell to the ice, wings opening, closing. The men watched it build its strength for a time and then launch upward into the rising cloud of orange. They set off again on stiff legs, their slow hearts pulsing the butterflies' song.

> *Perhaps this is not wise. Lois said "never cut what you can untie." I could live another 20 years, could try to forge some future life with Ann if she would ever have me.*

The slope was severe, and it would get only progressively steeper. Andre took a false step, suddenly fell to the ice on his stomach. The footing, as they had feared, was not good. There was a layer of half-melted slush on top of the hard ice, and their crampons did not get a certain bite in the ice with each step.

"Need help?" Eddie asked.

"No," Andre replied, fighting to his feet, pushing on his ice axe, stubborn. They were here too late in the day to get as high as they might otherwise, but Andre would do the best he could. He always had: he had survived poverty, homelessness, depression and had kept his soul mostly intact. He fought up off the cold glacier and kept climbing.

> *Andre heard Carrie Kirby and her lover kissing, rollicking in her bedroom down the hall. He pulled a pillow over his head to mute the sounds of lovemaking, then tossed it to the floor. It didn't matter anymore. He would move out in the morning. He would lose her. He would lose so many others, family, friends, Lois, Harry, the countrymen who were strangers in the Twin Towers. He would find out what the Shastan Indians had always known, would find out where the very stars at night were born.*

Andre and Eddie were fighting for air and lung power. The incline was beyond belief. Every few steps, they had to stop for long pauses before moving on again. Eddie's head felt light; his fingertips tingled. They were nearing 12,000 feet, a world of white and ice with the summit of the perfect side cone of Shastina off to the right of their vision, below the north peak up in angry cloud, grey clouds just sweeping off its lesser summit like an irritated old woman's hair. Above them, Eddie thought he saw great swarms of orange butterflies hugging the glacier, but then the descending wall of cloud blocked his sight. Were they real? Was anything but the end waiting patiently for everyone real?

They talked for almost the last time, playing mind and question games with whatever spare air they had.

"Best lover?" Eddie asked.

"Carrie Kirby," Andre said.

"One true love?" Andre demanded, his breath coming out in clouds.

Eddie didn't have to think. "Ann Lauren, hands down," he said. "I'm leaving the best of me with her."

Far below the men, the Shasta Valley spread out like a green and brown quilt leading to the Siskyou Mountains and the Oregon border. Ridgelines receded in neat angles for fifty miles until they could see only blur and haze at the end of the sky. Andre and Eddie felt as if they were part of the sky up here, flying in an airplane, but the plane had burst its pressure. There was not enough air. The natural world was still startlingly beautiful, but there was not enough human hope in the world anymore.

Eddie and Andre grew colder, and Eddie needed to piss. He dug his ice axe into the glacier, held fast to the handle with his left hand, and undid himself with his right. He felt something hard hit his scalp, and then the clouds were swirling all around them. Hail pelted their heads and necks and shoulders. Eddie finished urinating.

"Glad to see you don't need any help," Andre said, flatly.

"Glad to see my prostate still lets me pee," Eddie smiled. "What's your secret to holding it so long?"

"Drink less," Andre said simply.

The men heard each others' voices but couldn't see each other even though they stood only yards apart. They couldn't tell directions, couldn't even tell with certainty which way was up. Only the sensation of their feet on ice told them the ground. Everything was grey and frigid, a surreal world of falling ice pellets and cloud. Eddie held onto the axe handle, slid off his pack, and felt for his jacket. Without letting go of the ice axe, he worked his jacket over one arm, then changed hands on the handle by feel and got the other arm in its sleeve. With the jacket on, he would be all right. He could keep in body warmth and keep out most of the wet cold. He hung onto his axe and waited.

"Wimp," Andre accused.

"So you must have seen."

"I saw something," Andre said, "but I'm only guessing you put your 'Eddie Bauer' on."

Suddenly, Andre was right next to him, coalescing out of cloud vapor. Eddie hadn't heard footfalls. Strange. He had his climbing jacket on too.

Just as abruptly as the clouds had dropped, they broke apart. Jagged patches of blue sky showed through the dark clouds, and the hail quit. They climbed upward again, breathing hard, watching the clouds lifting higher up across the glacier, feeling the sun again on their faces. The angle of the mountain was awesome; they could barely hold their spikes in after pausing between each forced step, but the men were encouraged by the new-found warmth. Eddie and Andre used their ice axes with every new baby step, stabbing the sharp end of the handle into the ice and pushing off with their hands on the axes' heads to give themselves a third grip on the glacier. They climbed higher yet, climbed without speaking, conserving breath. The altitude was fierce, but they were stubborn. They had both survived without family, without normalcy, had lived through stinging losses that, individually and at different times in their lives, they thought would surely kill them.

The thunderheads were gone. Eddie saw the summit stretching endlessly up above him, a spire of rock busting up the sky from out of the impossibly white ice. The peak itself was a massive cone shrouded in white glacier, but the summit was a bare rock outcropping jutting defiantly upward. He knew they would not make the top; they were at about 13,000 feet, level with the summit of the twin, smaller peak Shastina on the right, and his wind was gone. The sun was far over in the western sky, dropping toward the raw backbone of the Trinity Alps.

Andre and Eddie had not come to Lois' mountain to conquer it, for men cannot conquer mountains; they had come for the climb and for themselves. They had come for the plan, for human volition, will. Their lives had to be more than their bodies, more than their tortured minds. They only wanted to climb as high as a man could before dark came, to find out what was left when the machine broke down, the world broke down, to find out what, if anything, mattered anymore.

Eddie limbed on heart and will now, Andre right behind him. His legs were gone; his lungs seared with each inadequate, icy breath. He was freezing: his doctors would have already judged him near death, but they did not know his spirit. The men fought upward in a glacial world, each new bite of spiked step, each push off on the ice axes' handles, costing them. As Eddie marched upward through his inner memories, shivering in the wet clothes under his jacket, he felt as if all his life climbed with him, as if the body he was pushing upward toward the summit were as long as he had climbed and longer, as if he were some 54 year-long creature stretching ever upward thousands of feet, as if he were dragging his beautiful absent wife Ellen upward with him, as if his daughter was born only where they had rested below on the mountain and had grown up so quickly until he and Andre had stopped again in the hail when she married his son-in-law and started a family of her own. Eddie felt vivid colors and sounds and tastes, and he was all ages at once now, all a fusion of past, present and future in the now, and they all were all with him. His newer family, Lois, Margaret, Harry, Andre, everyone the book group had touched. His immigrant Italian parents were somehow alive again on Mount Shasta, and he was back east in high school and elementary school and then college learning business and working with friends who came and went; his best lost friend forever, his Ellen, was 40 and 16 and 30, now she was pregnant, and he was in Vietnam, then home again to "I Dream of Jeanie" and buying a house, and he had a beautiful baby girl who was worried about him giving up just last month, and his Ellen was gone by his own hand and could all those years have passed so quickly, and Eddie was walking on an uphill world of ice and altitude and fiercely blue sky, was old sinew and bone and muscle and blood, and he was so confused about the outside that he saw everything on the inside with perfect clarity. Mostly now, he saw Ann. He heard her voice, not just in imperfect memory, but in his head, clearly, whispering "Don't give up on me. Come back to me."

Somewhere on the outside, Andre was hiking just behind Eddie, and the sun painted watercolors behind the waves of eastern ridges, in cold and pale abstract pinks. Inside, he was ringing, bell struck from within. Eddie was only here in himself, and it didn't matter if he climbed where he'd wanted to, or anywhere near where firm plans and others told him to go, for there was only love in the end anyway, and it was the only thing that couldn't be killed or maimed or broken in the world. Eddie was dying inside, fighting his inner death now more than the mountain.

The world changed again. "Shit!" Eddie shouted back to Andre. He'd taken his eyes off the way ahead. "Crevasse, Andre! Crevasse!"

He felt himself take a bad misstep, felt himself sliding down ice, losing traction in a heart pounding slip of less than a second. Eddie slammed his ice axe point into the surface down slope too late, heard its pathetic ungrounded scraping as he went over the uphill edge. His hands caught cracks in the ice edge as he went over; his ice axe fell behind him into the sudden opening, bouncing off ice wall until it settled with a hard thud somewhere far below him.

Eddie heard Andres' booted running steps. Then his friend's hands were on his, gripping.

"Tie off!" Eddie yelled. "Bury your axe if you can hold me with one arm for a second!"

Andre said nothing, but his hands circled Eddie's wrists so tightly that his nails cut Eddie's exposed inside wrists. His stomach was on a frigid vertical wall; Eddie's front boot spikes kicked into the wall but caught nothing firm, slid off again and again uselessly.

Eddie felt Andre's grip loosen ever so slightly.

"You can let me go when you've had enough, Andre," Eddie said, looking above at only their interlocked hands and arms and sky above. "It's all right. Just do it. Let me go on."

Eddie turned his head away from the ice wall to look down. His feet still tried to find grip, uselessly. He saw little flecks of disturbed snow and ice fall into the endless deep fissure he clung to, saw them disappear beyond downward vision.

*Ann and I, we are meant to be together. Meant to be. It's not too late to make it work. I've got to survive this, even this, give it a chance for love to find a way.*

"Andre," please pull me up," Eddie pleaded to his invisible friend. "Help me get the hell out of here." Then, desperately: "I want to live!" He saw Andre's face appear over the straight edge.

Eddie looked up at Andre's straining red face, saw something strange come into his friend's eyes, a look of distant separation, of world-weary resignation. What Eddie saw in Andre's eye light made his gripping hands turn cold: huge, dilated pupils and a gaze that focused far past him to the waiting yaw below. Andre was not going to allow any change of plan, no sweeping turn of ocean liner, and his eyes made Eddie's blood pump cold.

*Falling, falling. Fell.*

Andre let go. Eddie heard his friend's voice receding above, "I can't do it," until all words and sounds were gone, and he was falling, face up, back toward distant ice ground. Eddie slammed against the far side wall and lost his awareness of where, exactly, he fell. He did hear the sickening thud of his body come crashing down, finally, on rock hard ice bed. He thought he felt some ice spire sticking between his ribs. Darkness.

Then came a little light. Eddie felt his side with his right arm, felt the stabbing pain of movement of his broken arm. Sure enough, a spike of ice like a canine tooth poked up though his side, spurting blood at the base of the puncture. Not good.

"Andre?" he shouted up, regretting the exertion. Eddie heard nothing back, not even the higher sounds of Andre's muted boot steps as he began hiking somewhere, above, around the crevasse trap and upward, higher, to his own planned death.

Eddie's ice axe lay yards away, useless on the blue and waving headwalls of ice. Eddie's lungs drew in frigid blasts of still air and sent them out again, spent, in cold clouds, but he did not feel the burning. He was broken in too many places inside to feel. Eddie didn't see the last of the sun's cool abstract expressionism turn to blue and purple twilight above. The hard edges of everything real were no longer defined. Things were grey and then black, and Eddie lost his center, lost his sense of where his true being was. He felt his body's pain and weight disappear, felt himself rising somewhere.

*Let it wash over me. Don't fight it. Let the feelings wash over me.*

Eddie hovered above where he had been lying like a bright Monarch butterfly, saw his human rag doll body there below on ice, apart from where he floated now, and he knew his life was ending, that his spirit had left his body.

*Ann.*

Too many times he had not given in. Eddie had survived too much to give in so easily. He had to get lower, to keep from floating away upward, to force his battered soul back in. He saw Ann's perfect oval face, the robin's egg blue of her eyes, then remembered his baby girl Caroline, now grown and worrying for her father. Eddie Couch breathed, breathed in the frozen air again.

Eddie saw again, saw above. He saw things above through a wedge of open crevasse like the open panel of an observatory where his eyes were the telescope seeing it all through an open-shuttered ribbon of indigo open sky.

He wasn't cold anymore. Eddie wasn't aware of being anything but part of the mountain's skin. Then, above, he saw the first star at the eastern edge of his pie-shaped upper world. The high night clouds were beginning to separate, and, between the shifting blankets of high frozen water particle, a bright white point of light shimmered. The light danced on his eyes, played in his retinas, showing the way he knew to be the Shastan and Lois' path to the land of the dead, the Indians believing the stars along the way east were the spirits of their lost loved ones, their blazing fire pits, visible forever as they walked away from this life to one better.

Eddie Couch felt himself warming. He lay on his broken back in Mount Shasta, his feet splayed out unnaturally, climbing boots at severe outward angles, eyes upward, watching the star's bold light. He felt warmer still, sleepy. He could not feel his legs, felt nothing but a diffuse warmth spreading thought his being. Lights came out all over the night observatory above. Eddie's eyes closed, but the eastern star was in his head now, and the other stars were coming out all over inside his body. They had come through his eyes during the gift time his spirit had been given, and now the stars were a part of him forever. The Milky Way swept across his head, down inside him, the Big Dipper floated through the night, and the North Star stood absolutely still in him as the millions of others blurred through time into white hot streaks. There on the north face of Mount Shasta, Eddie followed the star path to where he was with his beloved Ann in the warmth of future. He's up there still, his body frozen in the crevasse, his spirit forever one of the white hot lights in the eastern sky at night.

# Chapter 32

## *Final Obligation*

Three thousand miles away, back in Bucks County, Pennsylvania, a certain Caitlyn Sheepdog and a particular yellow Labrador barked enthusiastically at a Sheltie walking its human master by on Mohawk Drive in Richboro. Out in the backyard, a groundhog, startled, crouched lower in his hole. Shiny black grackles in the leaning Willow tree stopped singing for a moment, and then, in a tick of cosmic clock, sang again.

Meanwhile, not so far away to the south, Ann Lauren checked her mailbox in front of her 9/11 widow's home in Levittown. Among the bills and junk mail, she saw something that made her heart race. Ann held the official looking Bucks County Community College notification letter in her right hand, ignoring traffic going by in front of her on the residential street, then opened the letter and began to read. The other deliveries fell away from her hands, floating to the fresh-mown grass at her sandaled feet. One piece of mail landed on her right toes, painted lavender. She did not feel it.

" . . . at the notarized request of Eddie Couch, deceased, the entire of his Bucks County Community College Metropolitan whole life insurance policy, $103,789.67, and his State Employee's Retirement System pension, either a lump sum of $209, 816 or monthly beneficiary life annuity of $998.17, shall be paid to sole beneficiary Ann Lauren, SSN 215-58-5567. Please contact the

273

college's Benefits Office at your earliest convenience via the number listed below to arrange beneficiary administration . . ."

Ann Lauren sat down on the cut grass near her mailbox, dropped her remaining mail, and cried silently. The tears rolled down her cheeks and blurred her vision, making little ants in the sand around the concrete base securing the post of her mailbox look like moving grains of black rice. Ann picked up a small round rock, held it in her folded hands, in her palms, then rubbed it unconsciously between her right thumb and forefingers, and the tears came and came. She did not see a bright orange Monarch butterfly drift by behind her and alight on one of her Azalea bushes.

28 days later, the Mohawk Drive sheepdog and yellow lab barked full-throatily again when a postman shoved a certain check in Ellen Couch's white mailbox, slammed the door shut, then accelerated hard away in his jeep before squealing to his next stop. Inside the metal box in brown manila, lay all the small assets Andre had scraped up in his mortal life, legacy for Ellen for a silent, secret dalliance he had taken to an icy, high grave. Only Ellen would remember and feel. Only she would know.

# Voices,
## Inner Chapter Last

### *Lois*

This is the end of the beginning... So many years ago, before grand mom and I came in from the reading porch and out of the chilly Christmas air, Grammy told me something else. Something I'll always remember, even now that she's long gone on and my end is coming.

"The evening star and the morning star were the same star, child," she reminded me, her voice lilting for once, not in strident command. "It took someone who stayed up all night to show people the truth.

They were one star in the same. Same way with people, Lois, same way. We're all one in the same."

I remember this about that Christmas day. Not long after our cardinal flew off, a crow came to eat Mom and Dad's suet, his eyes reddish black beads of fierce and beautiful light.

Grandma said, "Look there, child, that Christmas crow at dawn replaced our boy cardinal, just like the two stars. All the same. They're all the same. God's creatures, the stars, the snow, the trees, all the same."

"Was the morning star, the evening star, that same star also the star of Bethlehem?" I asked. "The one that brought the wise men to baby Jesus?"

Grandma looked at me, quiet for a long time, her breath coming out in clouds of white that hung for a while in the cold air, then vanished, went away. Before we went in to the warmth of family, the warmth of Christmas dinner already cooking, she pulled our blankets a little tighter around us. We stopped rocking. The book she'd been reading fell to porch with a thud. I heard her breathing, her very breath next to clouds of mine.

She looked at me hard, then spoke. "Everything is on its way somewhere. Everything. You can't stop anything from going where it has to go."

Those were the last words I ever remember that she spoke.

—Lois Kenny

# Afterward

*The Courier Times Newspaper*
Bucks County, PA
Friday November 22, 1991

by Peter Jackson
Associated Press Writer
Augusta, Maine
C. 1991 by Associated Press

## Homeless Men Create Hideaway in Library

Two homeless men set up a comfy hideaway in the crawl space of a library for two months, pilfering tuna sandwiches, a television and VCR, and leaving apologetic notes for workers. Mr. Jatho, 20, was charged with burglary and theft yesterday after security guards found the little haven in the Maine State Library. The other man had already moved out.

The two men slept on mail bags used as makeshift hammocks. Their amenities included a radio, a fan, a crock pot, an overhead projector and books by such authors as Charles Dickens, Mark Twain and James Joyce.

"Quite unbelievable," said Donald Suitter, chief of Capitol Security, whose officers arrested Jatho on Wednesday. "He had everything you could think of."

Library employees said they had been puzzled since mid-September by a series of thefts at the state library which also houses the state museum and archives. Refrigerators were emptied and video equipment disappeared along with such items as flashlights and extension cords. The thieves sometimes left written apologies.

Delores Pushard, the library's business manager, said employees were sympathetic toward their uninvited guests once security officials figured out that someone was hiding in the building.

"We were basically talking to the ceiling panels," she said. "We were saying, "if you're up there and you can hear us, if you need something, let us know."

Suitter said the men apparently entered the space through a 1 ½-foot-by-2 1/2-foot opening that gives access to bathroom pipes. The space, filled with heating ducts, has no more than 5 feet of clearance, he said.

They slept by day and roamed around at night.

Officers first suspected employees and visiting workers of the thefts.

"Everybody was on our list," said Sgt. Adelard J. La-Chance Jr.

Jatho, who gave an address in Santa Clara, CA, said he didn't venture far from the space after the other man moved out.

"I was pretty much trapped on the third floor when my assistance left," he said.

He said he left California because he believed "financial affairs in Maine were a little better."

Jatho was charged with burglary and theft and released on $1,000 bond. His lawyer, Paul Bourget, said he left him with social workers who promised to find him a place to stay for the night.